HARD FALL

SARA NEY

Hard Fall

Copyright © 2020 by Sara Ney

Editing by Caitlyn Nelson (Editing by C Marie)

Proofreading by Julia Griffis

Cover Design by Okay Creations

Formatting by Casey Formatting

All rights reserved.

Contents

Hollis

"**T**hanks for lunch, Dad." I lean over and give my father a kiss on the cheek. It's tan from time out on the golf course.

"I'm just glad I got to see you. You're too busy for your old man these days."

Old man? Hardly. My father is the epitome of youth and vitality, thanks to a few plastic surgeries, fillers, and some strategically placed Botox. He and my mother— whom he divorced ten years ago—can barely move their faces, but who am I to judge?

Dad smiles (or tries to).

"Kiddo, want to walk me to my office?"

I glance at the entrance to the baseball stadium, peering up at it through the window of my car—a college graduation gift—and inwardly groan. No, I actually don't want to walk him inside; that will take another hour *at least*. I'll have to say hello to every janitor, administrative assistant, lackey, coach, player, and staffer we walk past on the way to his office, located at the far ends of the earth, down the hall, and to the right.

Ugh! "Yeah, sure—of course I have time."

No time, actually, but I cannot say *no* to my father.

No, I do not want to risk the chance that I'll bump into Marlon Daymon, first baseman and ex-boyfriend. Boyfriend? Eh, it's a stretch to call him that, considering "dating" him was emotionally exhausting, played into all my insecurities, and made me feel like shit in the end. Conveniently always forgot his wallet. Took hours to reply to messages. Was always late. The last straw? When he "borrowed" my car and was photographed soliciting a prostitute, though who even noticed? Oh, just the tabloids and their millions and millions of readers, that's who! Luckily, no one knew it was my car, so my name wasn't dragged through the mud—but it could have been.

Fortunately, Marlon is no longer my problem, no longer my boyfriend, and I have no desire to risk seeing him inside this building yesterday, today, or tomorrow.

Shit, shit, shit.

Dad unbuckles and slides out of my white SUV, motioning for security to come over and play valet while I gather up my purse, phone, and water bottle.

Holding the skirt of my dress down as I slide out, too, trailing behind Dad. A few people are gathered outside the gates—as usual—hoping to glimpse or meet whichever players happen to come outside. Several of them have posters, one or two of them t-shirts. All of them are wearing huge grins when they see Dad coming toward them, his expensive gray suit gleaming in the sun.

He shakes a few hands. Poses for a few photographs.

Puts his hand on the small of my back to lead me through security when we're finally inside and I set my purse, water, and phone on the conveyor belt for scanning. Grabbing it at the other end, I follow Dad across the main floor.

We're at the back of the building, the exact opposite side of the concessions, making our way toward the executive offices. The concrete beneath our feet has the sound of my heels clicking, echoing because the halls are virtually empty.

It's a Friday and the Chicago Steam has a bye week. They might have been in the building to practice, but they certainly won't be here for a game, so anyone who happens to be here should be clerical, office staff only. Maybe.

Here's hoping.

I cross my fingers behind my back, and we arrive at the glass corridor that houses Dad's office. Glass, glass, and more glass. He pulls the door open and holds it for me.

"Thanks, Daddy." I call him that every so often, just to give the old man a thrill, like I'm a kid again and he's actually taking care of me, though I'm an adult now, with a real grown-up job, paying my own grown-up bills —who just *happens* to enjoy a free lunch every now and again.

Do you blame me!

We're greeted by anyone and everyone, mostly ass-kissers trying to remain on Dad's good side, but little do they know, he doesn't really have one. When his business blew up and the money followed, he became a real pompous windbag. When he worked his way through the ranks, and had pleased my grandfather enough, he was able to assume the position of general manager for the Chicago Steam, his ego inflated to epic proportions.

Lucky for me, I don't live off my father; therefore, I don't have to kiss his ass like everyone else. Like my sister, Fiona, or my brother, Lucian—both trapped under Dad's thumb, both at the mercy of his pocketbook.

Not me.

I'm not rich or wealthy by any means—not even close

—but I get by just fine; I have my own little apartment, pay my own bills, work for anyone other than my parents.

I step over the threshold and go to a plush seat opposite his desk. Plop down and glance around, then lean forward, fiddling with a metal paperweight on his desktop. Pull back one of the balls and watch it tick tick tick, back and forth like a pendulum.

Tick, tick, tick.

"Hollis, would you please stop that."

There's the Dad I know—now that we're behind closed doors, his impatience is showing.

"If you don't want anyone touching it, why do you have it on your desk?" I can't stop needling him; it is too easy.

"That art piece was very expensive."

I tilt my head and twist my mouth. "Really? Because I swear they sell this same thing at Sharper Image for like, thirty bucks."

Dad's face gets red. "Hollis Maxine."

I sigh, releasing the silver ball one more time then bringing the pendulum to a full stop as I roll my eyes. Dad is so uptight.

He sits, already shuffling paperwork. Puts on a pair of reading glasses before glancing up at me. "What are your plans for the rest of the day?"

Ah. He invited me in and already wants to get rid of me. I served my purpose—handfuls of people saw him acting like a doting father—and he has no need for me now. Excuse me for sounding bitter, but my dad is an asshole.

I hold back another eye roll and smooth down the fabric of my skirt. "Well, considering I had to take some paid time off to have lunch with you, I'll probably head back to work."

Dad glances up. "That wouldn't be an issue if you worked for the organization like your brother and sister."

Hard pass. "I'm good—but thanks." I prefer to live my own life, not have everything lorded over me and used as emotional blackmail.

He grunts. "What is it you do there, exactly?"

I feel my nostrils flare and my spine stiffen. "I'm a junior editor for a publishing house."

We have been over this no less than a million times, and I'm not prone to exaggeration. What the heck does he think I do all day? I *know* he knows he isn't paying my rent or buying the gas in my car. Yes, yes, it's the car he bought me, but what was I supposed to do, refuse it? Only a fool wouldn't take a *free* automobile—more money in the bank for moi.

"What does junior mean?"

"It means..." I pause to collect my thoughts. "I still don't have a ton of my own clients and someone has to oversee what I'm doing, the books I'm selecting, but otherwise I get a lot of freedom to choose." My answer is vague, but I know he isn't listening—why bother with an actual explanation?

He grunts again.

It might not be as glamorous a job as he desired for me, but it's respectable enough that he isn't embarrassed to brag about me to his friends and colleagues, even though he *has* tried marrying me off to a few hideous offspring of said colleagues and friends.

My mother, on the other hand? Couldn't care less what I choose to do as a job or career, as long as I'm happy— which is one of the reasons she and Dad are divorced. They have glaringly different philosophies on childrearing, commitment to family, and marriage.

She shouldn't have married him to begin with. He's the

same person he was thirty years ago, and he'll be the same until the day he dies.

What does make me happy? Reading. Discovering new talent among writers. The editing part sucks sometimes. Often authors don't want to listen to feedback—some of them get butthurt about suggestions or plot changes, or when things aren't making sense—but overall? I love it.

I watch him work for a few minutes, his head down. I gaze at his receding hairline, the thinning at the top, the wrinkles at his forehead. *Stress and a bad attitude do that to a person*, I muse, pressing my fingers to my own skin, kneading at my temples.

No worries, no wrinkles.

I smile and stand. "Well, Daddy-O, time for me to fly." Crossing to his side of the desk, I plant a quick kiss to his cheek then ruffle his hair, to his irritation. "Will you be there for dinner this weekend?"

After all, it is Father's Day, but that's no guarantee that the father in this family will be there, not if he has plans to work instead. No rest for the weary, he always used to say. Although, how weary can the man be when people wait on him hand and foot and he sits in an office making phone calls all day?

Dad nods. "I should be."

Yeah, you should be, but you probably won't.

I zip my lips shut. Give him a little wave, whistling as I breeze out the doorway, exhaling when I hit the hallway.

Hang a left. Find the elevator. Punch at a button and stare up at the wall, watching the numbers get smaller and smaller. Nine.

Five.

Two.

Seconds later, I hear the ding, the telltale sign I've

reached my destination, and step out onto a concrete floor without looking.

Glance around.

"Shit." Wrong floor. Must have punched the incorrect button when I hopped in. No big deal.

I give the up arrow a poke then stand back, staring at the metal doors to an elevator car that's probably on its way back to the top floor, and I wait with a sigh.

Tap my foot.

Pull out my phone and—

"You lost, sweetheart?"

Sweetheart?

Gag.

I pivot on my heel and spin around.

It's a player, of that I'm certain. Tall, broad shoulders. Cocky, arrogant. A smug tilt to his perfect mouth.

Something Wilson? Walters? They call him…

Let's put it this way: I know this guy, *kind of.*

I know *of* him—vaguely. I know every player on the team to some degree, by default. See, as the general manager, my father is essentially everyone's boss. But before he took over, the GM was my *grandfather*, Thomas Westbrooke, Sr., who now owns the team.

Ah, nothing like good old-fashioned nepotism.

"Did you just call me sweetheart?" Man, I sure do wish I could remember this douchebag's name so I could chew his ass out for that sexist, antiquated endearment.

I'm definitely not sweet and I'm definitely not his sweetheart.

TRACE

H er dress is prim. Proper.
But when I saw her standing by the elevator, she was tugging uncomfortably at the straps and wiggling around in her shoes, so I bet a cool hundo she's good and ready to get out of them.

I could help her with both those problems.

"Did you just call me sweetheart?" she asks again.

"You look sweet to me, darlin'."

"Oh my god—gross." She jabs at the up button, desperate to get away from me. Well too bad—I'm going up, too.

"Calling someone sweetheart isn't a crime."

"No, but you don't know me, and I find it offensive and condescending."

"Let me take you out and make it up to you."

"No thanks."

"Lame." I cough into my hand, stifling the word, but not well enough because she whips around and glares at me.

"*What* did you just say to me?"

"Nothing." I snicker. Jesus, how easy is it to trigger this chick? Does she not like hearing nice things?

The young woman rolls her blue eyes. "Honestly, when I was in grade school, the boys used to do that. They'd cough to cover up whatever idiotic thing they were saying, to pretend they hadn't just said it. But that was back in sixth grade—although..." She gives me a once-over, starting at my feet and working her way up. "I'm not surprised to hear it coming from you."

"Ouch, I think." Was that an insult? It's hard to tell. She's no longer looking at me—she's staring at the elevator door, likely willing it to open and swallow her whole.

The elevator arrives, doors open, and we both step in.

"Looks like we're both headed the same direction." I move to the opposite side of the car, wanting to give her space; this woman definitely looks as if she wants to tap me in the nutsac and send me to the ground.

"Hooray." Her pink-tipped fingernail whirls through the air near her head, sarcastically.

Wow. *Okay, maybe not so sweet after all.*

"Hey…sorry I called you sweetheart. I didn't realize you're actually super salty."

This comment causes her brows to shoot up. "Just stop talking."

But I can't. She's too cute and I'm an attention whore; she's ignoring me now which makes my verbal diarrhea worse.

"I was kidding about the date."

"Well I wasn't going on a date with you, so…" She shrugs, still not looking at me.

"You're not my type," I blurt out.

Her low chuckle says she doesn't believe me.

But she is my type—just because I don't date women who look wholesome, doesn't mean I don't appreciate women who are. Just so happens I can never get decent, respectable women to go out with me for long.

Party girls, yes. Club goers, yes. Gold diggers, yes.

Classy working girls? Yeah, not so much.

Tripp says it's because I have a shitty reputation, and none of those women want to end up splashed across the tabloids, potentially having their careers ruined after being photographed with me. Which sucks, because at some point, I'd like to make my parents proud by producing Buzz Wallace, Jr., heir to the baseball legacy, fruit of my loins.

My mother would fucking kill me if I brought home a career bottle girl from the club. One time, I dated a girl whose job it was to sell shots, and she spent her evenings with her tits out and glow sticks hanging around her neck —which is all fine and good, but not the type my mother wants popping out her grandbabies.

This petite sadist screams good girl and respectability, although I'd bet the farm she has one helluva potty mouth.

"I'm sorry, I didn't catch your name," I try again, laying on the charm.

Another eye roll. "I didn't throw it."

Cheeky.

I like it.

"What's your name?" There. Try evading that.

"I'm not telling you."

The elevator rises to its destination a short few moments later, dinging as the doors slide open, and we both step out on the parking level.

She glares at me as I trail along. "Stop following me."

Pfft. "I'm not. I have to grab something from my car." The lie would be more plausible if I had a set of keys in my hand or pocket, which I do not.

"Whatever." The wind kicks up, lifting the hem of her pretty, floral dress, tan legs exposed. Smooth. Lean. Great legs. "Stop checking me out, creep."

Creep? What the…

We both walk past the security booth, and I nod to Karl, the guard, slowing my gait on the way to my car since I can't actually get into it. I need her to get to her car first and drive off so she doesn't know I'm a liar.

Her gait is confident, her gaze trained on the horizon, not on her phone, as she scans the parking lot, key fob for a luxury SUV in hand. Nice wheels. Nice legs. Smart mouth.

With a glance over her shoulder, she meets my eyes before she grasps a pair of sunglasses and slides them on, opening her door and climbing inside. She spares me no second glances after that—not a single damn one.

Rude!

Shuffling my feet like a loser, I meander my way back from pretending to get something from my car, nodding again at Karl, who has his head sticking out the side of the guard booth.

"You sweet on Ms. Westbrooke?"

"Who?"

"The young lady you were just with—that's Thomas Westbrooke's youngest. Don't see her around here too often, but Ms. Hollis sure is a nice young woman."

My eyes stray to the departing vehicle, its blinker on to take a right-hand turn out of the parking lot, apparently carrying the general manager's daughter. Which makes her the team owner's granddaughter which makes me look like a giant asshole.

Jesus H. Christ, I just hit on the GM's daughter.

Thank god she doesn't know who I am or I'd be a dead man...

2

Hollis

"**Y**ou sure the guy hitting on you at the stadium was Buzz Wallace?" My best friend Madison reaches across the counter and nabs a French fry, digs around in the brown paper bag, and stuffs three in her mouth at once.

She was scrolling through her phone on my front porch when I got home, waiting for me to feed her dinner like a stray cat, wanting to have a quick chat—mostly to mooch off me, since she always seems to be broke—utterly bored. As usual. I've known Madison since college and she's always been the girl who has to be entertained, has to be busy. Never settling, forever restless.

She's restless now, leaning over my kitchen counter, stealing the food I was too lazy to make. I grab a fry too and chew. Suck the salt off my fingers and crook an eyebrow.

"Yup, I'm sure it was Buzz Wallace." *Trace* Wallace, his biography online said. "I got curious, so I looked up the roster online. He's such a douche."

"But he's so hot," she argues, filching my cheeseburger to take a bite, the melted cheese oozing out the side. I scowl, grabbing it back out of her hand.

"Get your own! If I knew you were going to be here when I got home, I would have gotten you one." The burger isn't big enough to share when I'm this hungry. "Go make a frozen pizza," I snip.

"I don't like the loaded pizzas you buy." She sniffs, sneaking more of my dinner. Madison isn't a meat lovers, all the veggies, and extra cheese kind of girl like I am; she's more of a Margherita type. Thing is, if I make a frozen pizza, she'll eat that too—regardless of her protests.

"So, back to this guy—he was hitting on you?"

"Probably not on purpose. I feel like a guy like that cannot help himself. It's like word vomit to him. He would have hit on me if I had a paper bag over my head, was hunched over, and walked sideways."

Madison rolls her brown eyes. "Don't be so dramatic. Why wouldn't he have hit on you? You're gorgeous, happy —practically *oozing* with charisma."

Oozing? "That's the cheese from this burger."

"I'm being serious."

"So am I. He didn't even know my name, and here he is asking me on a date." So there.

My bestie isn't buying that argument. "Um, hello—if some guy hits on you in a club, the chances that he knows your name beforehand are slim to none. Cut the guy some slack."

I rest a hand on the counter. "Madison, you know what I went through with Marlon—I am not dating a player. *Or* a player." Ha!

I hate calling Marlon Daymon my ex "boyfriend". We dated for scarcely three months last spring, but I had thought he was fantastic. Tall. Athletic. *Funny.* So, so funny he charmed the pants off of me the minute I was introduced after a Chicago Steam game I attended. He came up to the stadium suite to schmooze with my father and I believed every word he spoke when he opened those pouty lips of his.

My mistake. Marlon Daymon is a conceited. Spoiled. *Liar.*

"Not all men are like that. It's not your fault he turned out to be a total fucker."

"Thanks, that's really sweet of you to say, but I should have known better. Most of those guys are playboys."

"Okay, but some of them aren't."

"Um…" I disagree. "Maybe not, but Buzz Wallace is. Hello, he dates supermodels and actresses—not girls who work at publishing houses and read books for a living." Nerd alert! "A professional baseball player is not my speed, Madison. You know this about me."

But they are her speed and that's why she's so desperate for me to date one. I hear about it nonstop, and I wish I were into men who are into themselves, but I'm not.

I had that desire sucked right out of me when my last love interest wanted nothing more than his golden ticket to the owner's suite. I was simply a pawn to him.

My phone rings, vibrating on the counter, and I flip it over.

"Oh, it's the silver fox!" Madison enthuses, hopping up and down like a hyper toddler.

"Stop."

I hate when she calls my dad a silver fox; it's gross and weird.

I set the phone back down. Dad can wait.

"See what he wants!" she pushes, nudging it toward

me. Poking the green talk button, forcing the video call on me.

"Hi Dad."

My best friend leans in to see the screen. "Hi Mr. West-brooke!" She says it in a slightly smarmy way that has me swatting at her to quit it.

Shut up! I mouth with an eye roll, strategically shifting the camera away for a moment. "Sorry about that, Madison is here."

Dad clears his throat, unsure about how to reply. He's not great with young adults, and he certainly has no idea how to act around my best friend—not when she hits on him every chance she gets.

His throat clears again, all business. "Earlier when you were here, I forgot to mention the commission-sponsored fundraiser this upcoming weekend. All proceeds go to fight human trafficking, and I have a ticket for you."

I groan. That is one of the world's worthiest causes, but I'd rather go to an actual meeting to learn more about it than spend an afternoon in a room full of fake people at a fundra—

An elbow hits my gut. "She'd love to go, Mr. West-brooke. Will *you* be there?"

Jeez Louise, she's full-on flirting with my father.

"Er, no. I'll be out of town, but I can have my secretary send over the ticket."

"Can you send over *two* tickets?" Madison's eyes are wide and hopeful. "Then she can take a date." *Me,* she mouths with a wink.

Dad hesitates, not one to be strong-armed by an inter-loper who isn't even part of the family, and he's never been overly fond of Madison. "I don't know—can you guar-antee you'll get Hollis to attend?"

No! I mouth, stepping away from the phone and crisscrossing my hands frantically in the stop-no-no-no signal. *I do not want to attend!*

My whining and gesture do not work.

"Of course I can, Thomas. You leave it to *me*." Judging by the look on his face, it hasn't escaped his notice that she's just used his actual name and not called him Mr. Westbrooke, a breach in etiquette he won't forget any time soon. Old fashioned. Stuffy. Stuck up—just a few words that describe my father.

"Dad, it's kind of you to offer, but really, I—"

Madison pulls me into her, covering the phone with her right hand. "You are going—*we* are going. Do not ruin this for me. I am single, dammit! You are single, and there will be single guys there."

Is she nuts? Going to a fundraiser for a serious human rights organization to pick up dudes? I cannot with her.

I resist, though I know it's pointless—she will win this argument, like she always does, because I have nothing going on this weekend and she knows it, and she's going to drag me there whether I want to go or not.

"Right, exactly—you know who is going to be there? Marlon. He's at all those freaking things because he is an ASS kisser," I hiss. "I don't want to risk running into him."

"Don't be such a pussy," she hisses back. "Suck it up. At some point you're going to have to see that piece of shit, and wouldn't you rather have me by your side when you do it?"

"No! God no, you'll make it worse. I don't need you stabbing his eyes out with a fork in public."

"At least I wouldn't stab his dick."

The sound of a throat clearing has us both looking down at my phone—down at my father's bright red face.

"Oh shit." Madison laughs.

Oh shit is right.

"I'm still here," Dad somberly intones. Unamused. Unimpressed.

Your dad is so hot, Madison mouths.

I could kill her.

"Send over the tickets, sir. We're going to that fundraiser."

I hate my best friend sometimes.

3

Trace

There's a lot to be said for being attractive.

I would know, because I'm handsome.

I can't control what my face looks like—it's not my fault I'm so damn good-looking. At least, that's what my mom always told me when I was growing up. Then again, she told my brother the same thing, and he's not even half as gorgeous as I am.

I swing my car around and put it in park so my asshole brother can climb in; he loves riding together to visit our parents. No idea why. I suppose it's because he's one cheap son of a bitch and loves saving the gas money.

Tripp earns more than I do by almost double; he can afford the quarter tank of fuel it takes to get to Mom's, but does he ever volunteer to drive? Fuck no.

"Get in, bitch, we're going shopping," I tell him as he squeezes his large body into my luxury sports car. It was my first stupid purchase after I signed my contract with the Chicago Steam, but it wasn't my last. Car. House. The diamond watch glittering on my wrist, casting prisms throughout the interior of my car.

"Shopping? I thought we were going to Mom and Dad's," Tripp says, buckling himself in, not trusting my driving. The guy is one of the worst backseat drivers on the planet. Such a nag.

"We are going to Mom and Dad's. Stop being so literal —I was making a joke."

Not nearly as good-looking, and not nearly as clever— my brother doesn't think anything I say is funny, and I'm hilarious, just ask me.

"Is True going to be there?" Tripp's referring to our younger sister as he shifts in the seat of a car that realistically doesn't fit either of us in it comfortably. Too tall, too broad, too big for this boxy, compact sports car.

"No, Mom said she's got something going on. Packing to go out of town or something like that."

Our sister works in athletics, too, as a junior agent for a management company, and she spends a lot of time going on recruiting trips with scouts. It's baseball season at the university level and we haven't seen True in weeks.

"Maybe we should FaceTime her later—make sure she's alive." For all the grumbling and bitching he does about us, Tripp sure has to know what we're doing all the damn time. He's not even that much older than we are, the three of us each only a year apart. Boom, boom, boom, our parents banging us out within a four-year period.

Literally banging.

"I wouldn't worry about True. She can take care of herself."

Tripp grumbles. Crosses his arms in a huff because I'm disagreeing with him. Stares out the window. "Can you make sure you come to a full stop at all the intersections? You almost gave me a damn heart attack last time."

We go to our parents' place almost every week if we're

around and not playing ball. In fact, each of us just got done with work.

I play baseball, Tripp plays football, and we bought our parents' house together. That fucker over there in the passenger seat tried paying for *all* of it, but I found out and wedged my way in—no way was I going to let him lord that shit over me the rest of my life. Oh, and I bought them each new cars. Then dipshit over there bought them a cute little lake cottage, but then I went and got them a Jeep for the cottage.

The list goes on and on—not that we're competitive.

It's just that I'm better. He simply won't admit it.

I give my reflection a once-over in the rearview mirror and adjust it at the same time.

Approaching the intersection he's suddenly *sooo* concerned about, I rev my engine, listening to it hum and purr—like my last date did when I made her come.

That thought makes me chuckle as I roll through the stop sign to piss my brother off, and it does, just as I knew it would.

"What the fuck did I tell you, man! One of these days you're going to get pulled over, and your popularity isn't going to get you off."

"Ha!" I laugh. "You said 'Get me off.'"

He glares, clutching the brace bar above the window. "You're an idiot."

"*You* are."

"You are."

"I just said that—you can't say it."

"Make me," he mutters, glaring out the window, grasping the bar tighter.

Yeah, we argue like we're twelve. So what?

I give him a sidelong glance, slowing my speed to appease him. "You're not actually worried I'm going to get us killed, are you?" The truth is, I've never been pulled over for speeding, or breaking any laws. Have I broken them? Yes, but they were only minor infractions. Anyway, I would never do anything illegal. Not on purpose. And the truth is, I am a conscientious driver—just not when Tripp is in the car. He is way too easy to needle.

"Just watch where you're going." He doesn't look over at me.

"How about not telling me how to drive if you're not going to do it yourself."

"I'm your guest," he pops off, still staring out the window.

"You're a pain in the ass, that's what you are."

In the reflection of the glass, I catch him rolling his eyes and do a brake check, causing Tripp to lurch forward.

I snicker.

Ha!

Too easy.

"Knock it off!" His irritation is palpable.

"Then quit ignoring me and I won't have to beg for your attention." My eyes are glued to the road in front of me, even though I like to pretend I'm hardly paying attention.

"You're so annoying."

I mean…he's *not* wrong.

～

"Can I get you boys anything while I'm up?" Mom worries around the kitchen, hovering like a hummingbird, fussing over her babies.

Me. I'm the baby.

"Ma, sit—you don't have to fetch us everything. Tripp will get it." I kick my brother's shin beneath the table and he flinches but doesn't rat me out. She'd yell at us both, no matter who did the kicking. "Go help Mom."

Tripp levels me with a hard stare then rises, retrieving the tray of glasses our mother has set out, and the pitcher of iced tea. Bashes me in the back of the skull with the platter and smirks. "Whoops, sorry bro."

Sorry my ass.

I glare, jostling him with my elbow, digging it into his ribs when he leans to set the whole thing down. "Knock it off, asshole," he mutters out of the corner of his mouth.

"Make me."

"Boys." Our mother shakes her head, still not ready to rest, or be idle—this is how she is whenever we come by, excited to have us home. Wanting to feel wanted by the two sons who want for nothing. Need for nothing.

Nothing but an orgasm with no strings attached and a beefy taco afterward.

Mmm-mmm delicious.

I lick my chops, mouth watering, reaching for a glass. Grab the pitcher away from my brother as he goes to reach for it. "Loser."

"Boys!" Mom scolds again, a secret smile tipping her lips.

We might be monsters, but we're hers and she loves having us home. Granted, we take up all the free space with our giant bodies, but we kind of always have, hitting our growth spurts early on and filling out by the time we were juniors in high school.

Man-children she'd call us because even though we looked like grown-ass adults, we still acted like kids.

Still do.

"So, what have you two been up to besides work?" Dad asks, coming from the office off the kitchen. His thick mustache twitching, he pulls a chair out and plops down next to us.

Dad's not nearly as big, not nearly as tall—we get our height from Mom's side of the family, Tripp and I each measuring in at over six foot three and over two hundred sixty pounds.

"Practicing. Hanging out with Harding."

Noah Harding is one of my teammates, the shortstop on the Chicago Steam, and my best friend. He has a sweet house with a huge pool and—more importantly—a fully stocked kitchen. I don't know where all the food comes from because I doubt he does the grocery shopping, but I'm not complaining.

"Just hanging out with Noah Harding?" Dad's brows go up.

"Working on one of the properties I just bought. Would be going quicker if this shithead would help me." Over the past few months, I've been flipping houses, investing some of my income in properties that are run-down. Fixing them up, selling them for a profit. I'm on my third one. "It sure would be nice if I had a *partner*."

I glare toward my brother and resentfully stab at the potato salad on my plate.

Tripp rolls his eyes. "Bet you're still doing that match-making thing. You could get paid to do that, like that woman on television who matchmakes for millionaires."

The fuck, Tripp! Does he have to blab everything?

Apparently so.

"What matchmaking thing?" Mom begins setting a casserole on the table and I take it from her; the ceramic pan must weigh ten pounds.

She kisses the top of my head and I sit up straighter.

Tripp scowls, shooting up out of his chair to fetch the rest of lunch, carrying it back to the table like a server at a restaurant, plates balanced on both arms like a fucking circus performer. "He meddles in people's love lives without them knowing it."

"What is he talking about, sweetie?"

"Nothing. He doesn't know what he's talking about." I kick him again, this time grazing his calf muscle.

But Tripp won't let it go now that he has me cornered and knows Mom is interested, too. *Fuck!*

"Your youngest here likes setting people up—on dates and stuff."

"I think that sounds nice!" Mom gushes, clearly pleased to discover I'm a romantic at heart, even though I'm no romantic. I just love knowing someone is getting laid because of my matchmaking efforts.

Besides, it's only been like, four couples total. I'm no expert; ain't got no time for that.

"Mom, I don't." *But I do.*

"Then what do you call Noah Harding and Miranda?"

I don't know her last name, but I know they're a great match, one I helped facilitate because Noah—bless his soul—fucking sucks when it comes to putting the moves on a woman and following through.

"Okay, first of all—he needed my help, okay? He probably wouldn't be with his girlfriend right now if it weren't for me." *Duh.* "Secondly, he knew I was trying to help him out." *Maybe.* "Thirdly, I am not a matchmaker. I'm a guy—guys don't do that."

"Right. Keep telling yourself that."

"Who are Noah and Miranda?" Mom wants to know. Dad grunts in his chair, reaching for a plate, helping himself to casserole. It's cheesy, with pasta and red sauce, and baked to a crisp. As an avid sports fan, Dad would know who Noah Harding is. Mom? Not so much.

There are only two athletes in the majors she cares about and that is me and Tripp.

"Noah is a guy on my team and Miranda is his girlfriend. They've been together a few months, I think."

"No thanks to Trace running nonstop interference," my brother grumbles, always pissing on my bonfire.

Mom sighs, ever a romantic. "Aww, I think it's nice that you're trying to help your friends, sweetheart." She ruffles my hair and I shoot Tripp a look of victory.

Suck it, asshole. "See?" I gloat. "*Mom* thinks it's nice that I help my friends."

"Alright," our dad interrupts, irritated. "Enough talk about other people—we want to hear about you."

Tripp flashes me his wide eyes—the ones that aren't nearly as stunning as mine. They're a little jaded, too. I don't know what bug crawled up his ass and died, but he's Captain Bitter-man today and it's killing my buzz.

Buzz. Get it?

Ha!

"No girlfriends?" Mom always has to ask, always hoping one day our relationship status will change from bachelor to engaged to married. Our mother wants grandkids like a nun loves to pray.

I hate when she starts up about our lack of relationships because I hate letting her down. The truth is the kind of girl she wants me to bring home? They want nothing to do with me.

Like the girl today—the GM's daughter, whatever her name is.

"I met someone today, as a matter of fact," I boldly lie. No harm in bending the truth when she can't verify it. Give the old girl something to get excited about.

Mom perks up like I knew she would—but instead of feeling gratified, I immediately regret lying. "Oh?"

"Yeah, I bumped into her at work. She seems like a really nice girl."

"What's her name?" Tripp wants to know.

"Um."

"Her name is Um?" My brother stabs potato salad onto his fork and shoots me a smirk.

I kick him again. Dickhead.

"Her name is…it's…" I look at my mom, drawing a blank. "Genevieve."

"Genevieve!" If it was possible for my mother, Genevieve, to perk up more, she does it. "Imagine if we had two named Genevieve in the family!" She gets up and flutters to the counter, opening the cabinet and grabbing a tea bag. Sets about brewing herself a cup, though it's gorgeous outside and not even a bit chilly. "Genevieve and Genevieve Wallace!" she croons, smiling to herself with delight.

Genevieve? Tripp mouths. *You're an idiot.*

Shut the fuck up, I mouth back.

"What are the odds?" Mom asks.

"Yeah, dipshit, what are the odds," comes from my brother. "And don't fucking kick me under the goddamn table."

My mother gasps. "Boys! Watch your mouths!"

"He started it," Tripp pouts, lips curled into a sardonic smile. "And his girlfriends name isn't Genevieve. He made that up."

Mom looks toward me, bewildered. "Why would you make that up?"

"He's a dope, that's why."

I earn another concerned look from my mother while she prepares her tea at the counter. "Is there actually a girl, dear?"

My nod is slow. "Yes."

26

"Well. Are you going to tell us her name—her actual one?"

"Her name is Hollis," I finally supply, glaring at my brother.

Tripp sucks and he's dumb.

"Hollis. That's a beautiful name, tell us more about her." Mom sits back down with her mug of tea, steam rising as she blows on the surface.

"Yeah, tell us more." This from the jackass to my right.

"She's younger than I am, but not by much…" I think. At least, she looked younger, but with women it's hard to tell. "Feminine. Um…to be honest, I don't know a ton about her."

"Where did you meet her?"

"Uh…work." At least that part is true.

Dad's brows go up and he lowers his paper to stare at me. "Work?"

"I mean, she obviously doesn't *work* there—she's not like a ballplayer or anything. She was there doing something."

My brother laughs, cocking his head to the side. "Really, Trace? She's not a baseball player?"

Shut your face, my glare tells him.

You shut your *face*, his says back.

I hate you, mine says.

But I don't. I just hate being put on the spot and don't want to disappoint our mother, which seems to be a common theme with me. Well, Tripp too—between the pair of us, the chances of my parents having grandbabies is looking slimmer and slimmer by the day.

Tripp is a moody asshole who scares women off with his bad attitude and me? Well. Smart women don't take me seriously, because I'm not serious enough.

So, I get stuck "dating" women I would never bring

SARA NEY

home to Mom, and Tripp doesn't date at all. I wonder when was the last time the fucker got laid. Maybe that's his problem—sperm retention.

The truth is, I'm trying.

I'm just not sure how to change—I've been at this single game so long. Never had a long-term girlfriend; never had time. I busted my ass to get myself into the major leagues. I may have gotten a scholarship to play baseball in college, but I never got any offers during the MLB draft. Instead, I got an offer afterward, as a free agent, and spent a few years in the farm leagues, busting my ass in the heat some more to prove myself.

Then, I was called up, by the grace of God, and I haven't looked back—nor have I invested a single minute into my personal life. My team keeps me plenty occupied; my friends keep me sane. If I want sex, that's easy enough —all I have to do is chat someone up at a bar or on an app.

Lately though, no strings attached is beginning to feel hella lonely.

And there's that part about disappointing my parents. Sure, I may be an ass kisser and I may try to show my brother up every damn day of my life, but part of me wants a family of my own too, despite myself and my life-style. Sooner than later.

Before my balls shrivel up.

"Trace, sweetie?"

"Huh?" I realize I was zoning out based on the curious stares around the table. "Sorry."

Mom gives me an affectionate smile—which is more than I can say for Dad and the dickhead—letting the topic of girls go so we can move on with our lunch without the endless arguing.

I sigh, not looking forward to the ride home.

28

4

Hollis

"How do you talk me into these things?" I snatch sushi off a passing tray from a wandering server and stuff it in my mouth whole. Scan the area for the server with the alcohol, knowing I'll probably need to be buzzed to get through the next hour or two.

That's the max amount of time I told Madison I'd be willing to spend in this godforsaken room, with these stuffy people, for yet another hoity-toity fundraiser.

"It's for a great cause. Stop whining or you'll sound ungrateful."

"Ungrate—" I stop. Am I? God I hate when she's right. I *do* sound ungrateful, but she has no idea what it's like having to go to so many fundraisers your whole life.

Shit. *That* sounded ungrateful, too.

"Can you try smiling?" My best friend pokes me in the rib cage with her bony elbow. "You look terrifying."

I smile, gritting my teeth. "Better?"

"Now you look like you're trying not to shit your pants."

Jeez. She is the worst. "Remind me again why I brought you tonight?"

"Correction." She lifts a finger in the air then snatches a glass of champagne off another wandering tray. "*I* brought *you*—you did not want to come."

"I don't know why my presence here was required. You seem to be doing just fine on your own."

And she is; she hardly needs me to stand here bringing down her mood. Madison has spoken to more men in the short time we've been here than I have in an entire week! She's not messing around; she wants to date an athlete and she's probably going to leave here with her talons sunk into one.

"They're all married," she pouts. "And the few who aren't won't break away from the herd. What is it with men and huddles?"

"How do you know they're all married? Half of them aren't." I know this for a fact; the organization keeps statistics on its players, and I've seen the data.

"Because I keep getting rejected. Duh."

While it's true that my best friend is stunning, her overt confidence occasionally does keep men from biting. An alpha with sharp wit and no filter, it takes a special person to "handle" Madison's special brand of outgoing.

I tiptoe around her daily, and we've been friends for years.

"Maybe...lay off the charm, okay? Try to enjoy yourself." She's the one who wanted to come, so I don't understand why she's so irritated. "Which reminds me, how long are you going to force me to stand here?"

"No one is forcing you to stand there. You're free to move about the space." She nibbles on a small shortbread cookie she got off the dessert table. "Give me a few more minutes to eat lunch then we can go. I don't want to have to go grocery shopping later." Her eyes roam the crowd lazily, interested. Taking in this man and that. His WAG. The spouses of executives and community members. A few players from other teams, not just the Steam. Pretty sure some members of the football team are here, too, and I think Dad will regret missing out on this crowd.

It's right up his alley.

"Oh shit." Madison's gaze turns from lazy to wide-eyed and mystified. "Incoming."

"Huh?"

The crowd parts like the Red Sea at Moses's command —or in this case, Marlon Daymon's, with his tan skin and black hair and blaring white teeth, which now look absolutely *ridiculous*. The people step aside, as if he were a god or a prophet—I found out the hard way that he is not.

"Why is he coming over here?" We broke up. I mean— I broke up with him, but it's not like he wanted me back. No, that would mean he'd have to give up hitting on other women and being an asshole.

"I could just punch that stupid smile right off his stupid face," Madison announces, the classy dress she had to borrow from me providing the demure backdrop she needs to make such a statement. She only looks sweet and reserved. "Look at that arrogant fuck."

I need her to lower her voice. "Would you please zip it and be cool? This will all be over in five seconds. He's probably not even coming over to me. I bet he's—"

"Hey beautiful." Marlon leans down and kisses the side of my cheek, a show for everyone watching, none of whom know we even went on one date, let alone a dozen, or that he stomped on my heart and completely humiliated me.

I wish he wouldn't call me beautiful when we both know I'm not. I'm not his typical girlfriend, not someone he'd choose to date.

He was using me, like he's using me now.

I pull away, stepping back, putting a few feet between us.

Beside me, Madison tosses her hair. "Look what the trash man dropped off," she sneers impolitely.

See, the thing is, I wasn't brought up to be confrontational like this, and certainly not in public, even though Marlon deserves it. Especially not in a crowd of people, particularly when I'm here representing my family.

It looks bad. No matter how much I hate him, the last thing I need is my best friend talking shit to an ex in front of people who are here tonight to donate to a cause.

I nervously smooth a hand down the front of my pressed slacks but still have nothing to say to him.

"What do *you* want?" Madison asks for me, reading my mind, saying it like a person would say, *This garbage smells like rotten eggs and congealed seafood—where do you want this leaky bag tossed out?*

"What do you mean, what do I want? I haven't seen Hollis in months and wanted to say hello." He knows she hates him and he doesn't care.

Marlon Daymon does not *need* to care.

Perhaps I should let Madison sink her talons into him.

"How you been doing, sweetie?" He reaches out to touch my arm, but Madison slaps it away.

"Don't call her that."

He gives her a long look, beginning at her feet, slowly dragging his gaze up before meeting her eyes. "Still a raging bitch, I see."

My best friend's mouth gapes. Closes. "I guess I'd be slinging insults too if I had a tiny dick."

Oh god.

Marlon glances at me. "*Really?*"

I mean...for someone arrogant and cocky, his dick

really isn't that great. Average at best. Unexpected considering how he struts around like a prize stallion, waiting to impregnate anyone within a three-foot radius.

I raise an eyebrow. Shrug.

It's pissing him off that I haven't spoken two words to him, and he makes one last attempt to raise my ire.

"I might have a small dick, but you're still a frigid bitch."

Now it's my mouth that opens and closes, and I can actually feel my eyes physically widen in shock, heat rushing to my face—I don't blush often, but I am on fire now.

"Hold me back," my bestie says, taking one step forward toward a man who doesn't have the common sense, or the decency, to leave. "Why are you such an asshole?"

The brows I once thought were the most attractive part of his face rise. "Because I *can* be."

Gross. Just so *gross*. I cannot believe I wasted a single second on this scumbag.

Movement catches my eye.

A bright red shirt, stuck like a second skin to a toned, athletic body. A tall, tan god strutting toward us, appearing out of nowhere.

Fuck. It's that douche from the elevator shaft, and I bet you a hundred dollars if I said shaft out loud within earshot of him, the idiot would giggle like a twelve-year-old.

"What's going on?" He plants a kiss to the top of my forehead, but I don't bristle the way I did when Marlon kissed me. "Babe."

Babe?

What the hell is this guy doing? Is he nuts?

Is he...is he trying to *rescue* me?

"I...I..." don't have any idea what to say.

"Aww, did you miss me? You're speechless." He kisses the top of my head again, and this time, I swear he takes a long whiff. Exchanges a weird handshake-slash-fist-bump with his teammate, sizing him up the way Marlon sized Madison up before insulting her. "What's up, Daymon? You behaving yourself or hardly behaving?"

"I didn't know the two of you were..." Marlon's voice trails off, his finger pointing back and forth between Trace Wallace and me as Trace slips a protective arm around my shoulders and squeezes. "A thing."

"A thing? Oh, I don't know about that—lovebirds, perhaps? And from the looks of it, you're upsetting my poopsy-whoopsy here."

Oh Jesus. Somebody make him stop. Where is he getting these endearments from, the *Cliché Guy's Guide to Horrible Nicknames*, circa 1950?

I swallow back the saccharine vomit creeping up my throat.

Madison laughs. "The three of us could be a thruple," she jokes, only half joking, poking Trace Wallace's muscle with a fingernail, once. Twice. Three times.

It's as if I'm not even standing here.

He promptly removes it, plucking it off and returning it to her like it's rancid. "Uh...yeah, no—let's not get carried away. No one is thruppling anything, ever. I don't share."

Dear God, make it stop, Lord hear my prayer.

"Since when?" Marlon blurts out.

"Since none-yo-business."

Marlon stares. Glares? Turns red.

In all this time, I haven't managed—or needed—to utter a single word, Madison and Trace Wallace coming to my rescue from a man I didn't want to see. Dreaded seeing.

Now that I have, I'm enjoying his humiliation at the hands of his peer. His teammate.

Why did Wallace come over here to bail me out?

"So," Marlon finally says. "I assume you're bringing her to the barbeque at Harding's house tomorrow?"

"Say what now?" Madison interjects. I elbow her as best I can, hindered from jabbing her good by the weight of the massive arm still draped around me. "Did someone say party? What's this about a team barbeque?"

"I wasn't planning on going," Trace tells Marlon, shifting on the balls of his feet.

"Oh, you're going—and you're taking your girlfriend." My best friend bumps Wallace with her hip, causing our bodies to press closer together still and I catch a whiff of his aftershave. Body wash? Masculine cologne—something. Whatever it is, it smells sensational.

I almost sniff the air like he sniffed my hair.

"Babe, do you want to go to a team BBQ?"

He says barbeque like B-B-Q, pronouncing each of the letters individually, and Lord help me, I smile. What a moron, this big goof. I don't even like the guy, but for some reason, I'm grinning up at him like a damn fool. "Not really. *Babe.*" I throw that in for good measure, pleased by the surprise crossing his expression. It's there and gone in a flash.

"You know what?" He ups the ante. "I think you'd actually have a good time, so we should go. You would love Noah Harding's girlfriend. Remember, I've been telling you about her?" He presses his lips to my forehead. "We're definitely going."

"Um." I rack my brain for something intelligent to say. "I can't."

"Sure you can, my little cactus flower." He boops me

35

SARA NEY

on the tip of my nose. "Mmm, you smell like honey, little sugar bee."

"*Oh my god.*" Madison busts out laughing. "Stop it! Now you're making me want to throw up—get a room you two." She glances at my ex-boyfriend. "They're always hanging all over each other. She is sooo into him."

"You never let me call you babe," Marlon pouts—actually pouts, crossing his meaty arms and scowling.

"Oh yeah, Daymon?" Trace is grinning from ear to ear. "It's probably because you have a small dick, so…"

"Shut the fuck up, Wallace. You've seen my dick—you know it's not small."

Trace rolls his eyes, squeezing my upper arm conspiratorially. Winks at Marlon. "Sure. Whatever you say."

"I do not have a small dick!" My ex-boyfriend's voice booms at the same time the band stops playing, the deafening silence in the room followed by a snicker from my best friend.

"I hate you," he hisses at me, the glare so odious I shrink into Trace Wallace's big, warm body.

"See you tomorrow!" Trace calls to him as he stalks off toward the exit, his large, brooding body crashing through the doors. Trace wiggles his fingers in my ex's direction, even though he doesn't look over his shoulder.

Madison bounces up and down, boobs bouncing too, and I will her to stop with my laser-like glower. Shrug Trace Wallace's heavy arm off from my body, easing out from under him, slinking to stand next to my friend—who is not helping these matters at all.

"What time are you picking her up?" She wastes no time getting down to business, as if she's my manager making a deal on my behalf—once again acting as if I'm not here.

"I'll grab you at noon, if that's cool? We can be casu-

36

ally late—unless you want to be casually early? That's usually my thing. Harding loves when I drop in on him unexpectedly."

Somehow, I doubt that. "Seriously, I appreciate the sentiment and I appreciate you getting him off my back, but it's not necessary to entertain me tomorrow."

"Noon is so late in the day," Madison informs him. "Hollis is an early riser—why don't y'all do coffee then make your way to Harding's? That will give you time to get to know each other before you get there."

How about *not*. "I have a hair appointment."

She squints at me. "You just had it done two weeks ago."

"It's a blowout."

"You have nothing going on tomorrow." She continues thwarting my arguments against a faux date with this Neanderthal. "You have to get out of the house and start meeting men." She glances at Trace, who is still standing there. "No offense, but you're not her type."

"I'm everyone's type," he says confidently.

"Not mine," I shoot back stubbornly. "Besides, the last thing anyone wants is the general manager's daughter showing up to ruin their fun."

"That apparently didn't stop you from going out with dipshit over there, did it?" He has a very good point. "You look like you could use a little fun and wouldn't it be a blast rubbing a relationship with me in his face? The dude fucking despises me."

"Why?"

"'Cause he's a child."

That explains absolutely nothing. "Well. I'm not going with you tomorrow."

Trace Wallace, the Chicago Steam's giant closer, levels me with a stare I'm sure is intended to make men cower.

"Suit yourself, but I'm going to that barbecue and when I see your ex *play*thing there, I'll be forced to tell him the truth because I hate lying."

I throw my hands up. "You just straight-up lied to his face not five minutes ago."

"I'm a changed man."

"Oh my god." He did *not* just say that.

"You take the Lord's name in vain a lot," he tells me, grabbing a small cup of vegetables and dip from a nearby tray, stuffing a stick of celery in his mouth.

I take the Lord's name in vain? "What, you never swear?"

"Oh, half the words that leave my mouth are curses." He chews, crunching noisily, and changes the subject. "Anyway. It was nice officially making your acquaintance. Wish me luck tomorrow. I'll be forced to come up with a backstory all on my own, and who knows how that will end."

Whoa, whoa whoa—not so fast. "Wait just one damn minute. You can't go telling him we aren't dating."

"But we're not. I'm not your type."

"That's not the point."

"Yes it is." He gnaws on more celery, dips it into the tiny container of dressing, and bites. "Although, it wouldn't be lying to say we're dating if you came with me to the barbeque as my date."

"Right, but then I'd be stuck with you for who knows how long."

"Ouch. That one hurt my feelings."

Madison's head whips side to side as we volley shots back and forth.

"I'm not going to some party with you because you're trying to manipulate me."

"I wouldn't want you to."

38

"But I also don't know what you're capable of when left to your own devices."

Chomp, chomp. "So true."

"What do you plan on saying to Marlon?"

Trace shrugs. "Don't know. Probably the truth—I saw him hassling you and came over, thinking if I pretended to be your boyfriend, he would leave you alone."

Hmm. I don't like the way that sounds either, even though it's the truth.

"Or I'll tell him you have morning sickness and didn't feel well enough to come along, because the sight of Sweet Baby Ray's makes you want to puke and it's not good for the baby."

I blink.

Madison snickers.

Trace chews.

"You wouldn't dare."

His head cocks to one side. "Mmm, wouldn't I?" Another stick of celery gets dipped in dressing. "I'm bored. This amuses me. I'd like to continue amusing myself with Daymon tomorrow and if no one is there to stop me..." He shrugs a pair of wide, toned shoulders. Every muscle flexing with the simple, single motion. "I should go mingle. Ladies." He tips his head by way of salutation, and I watch him go, stunned.

Silently, my best friend and I stand there, observing his departure.

"Wow. He is really something, isn't he?" Her tone is as dreamy as her adoring gaze.

I hold up a hand to silence her. "Do not start with that. He is a *scum*bag—did you not hear him try to blackmail me?"

"Blackmail you with *what?* No, he's teasing you. He wouldn't do that."

Wouldn't he? "Teasing me?"

"Flirting then. Hollis, give the guy a break—he came to your rescue. What would be the harm in going with him to one measly gathering tomorrow? It's not like you have anything else going on."

I hate when she points out the obvious. "Gee, thanks."

"You don't. Plus, you'd get to stick it to Marlon."

"I don't want to stick anything to Marlon, let alone it." My attempt at a joke falls flat as my best girlfriend stares at one of my father's players.

Player.

That's what Trace "Buzz" Wallace is and I'd do well to remember that.

Still. He did try being my knight in shining armor—too bad he was wrapped in tin foil.

"I can't do it. I cannot go to Noah Harding's house and fake a smile for multiple hours. My lips will fall off."

"I know, I know. Your motto is, 'If I have to fake a smile, I'm not going.' You say it all the time, but Hollis—he's so cute."

"So? There are tons of men in here who are cute, and most of them are lying, cheating, assholes."

"But some of them aren't."

I wish she would stop defending Trace. "But he is."

"You don't know that."

"He's in all the papers and gets into so much trouble."

"Seriously, Hollis? You're the one who is always telling me not to believe anything I read in the papers or online, saying the media makes up information to sell stories—so how bad could he be?"

I laugh, tipping my head back, and when my eyes find their way across the room, locking with a set of dark brown ones, I swallow. "Bad enough."

"Fine. You win." She sips from the glass she'd been

holding this entire time, which I'm sure is piss warm. Oops
—I mean lukewarm. "I won't mention it again."

I stare at her, knowing she's going to mention it again
in five, four, three, two—

"All I'm saying is, you cannot let that man go to that
party and tell people you're knocked up."

I roll my eyes. "He won't."

"No, probably not. By tomorrow he'll invent something
even more mortifying because *look* at him. His brain is
probably the size of a walnut, all loose inside his head,
knocking around in there."

"Hey, don't be mean. I'm sure he's intelligent." I study
him now, as he stands in a cluster of players and their
wives, the group of them laughing so loud I can hear them
from here. Cheerful, carefree laughter. Like they're having
fun. Like I should be.

Those people will most likely all be there tomorrow.

One of them looks over his shoulder, directly at me.
Raises his brows then turns back to the group.

Shit.

My forehead begins to sweat.

Surely he hasn't already…

Surely he wouldn't…

Again, our eyes meet. Someone else follows his gaze
and I see an elbow bump.

A knot forms in my stomach.

That asshole!

Why is he doing this?!

The last thing I need is some pampered, spoiled,
professional athlete who never gets told no using me as
some sick form of entertainment. I am not a joke! I am his
boss's daughter, for God's sa—

Shit, sorry God. I throw a prayer up, apologizing for
using his name in vain. "What the hell am I doing?"

Shit. Sorry again.

"Talking to yourself, apparently."

"I'm internalizing."

"Clearly." Madison holds up her glass, out of wine. "Can we take this little snooze-fest to the bar? I need a refill."

I nod absentmindedly as I trail aimlessly behind her, a bit shook from this entire day—and it's not nearly over yet. Tickets being forced on me. Marlon approaching. Trace ambushing us. The fake date idea.

It's too much for my brain. This is not my style. I like plans and structure—spontaneous and impromptu invites make me twitchy, so in that regard, I'm a lot like my dad.

I groan.

Stare at the back of Madison's head and start counting down the minutes until we can get out of this place.

~

Unknown Number: *What time am I picking you up?*

Me: *Who is this?*

Unknown Number: *You're adorable when you do this. It's so cute.*

Me: *No for real—who is this?*

Unknown Number: *Your date for tomorrow. I'm going to come grab you and then we can get coffee, or tea, or whatever you want before heading to Harding's. His house isn't far from mine, but I can get you, nbd.*

Nbd? What does that mean?

I google it, unsure. No big deal.

Right.

Me: *Trace I am not going to that party with you. And how did you even get my number?*

Trace: *I called your dad's secretary and told her I wrote it* *down instead of putting it in my phone and she gave it to me. The party is a backyard BBQ, so we're good. Less pressure, wear shorts.*

Me: *Look I'm sure you're a nice guy and all, but the last thing in the world I want to do is go to a party and be anywhere near Marlon Daymon.*

Trace: *Fine. But you should know he told someone else on the team that you're full of shit and still in love with him.*

Me: *STILL IN LOVE WITH HIM! I WAS NEVER IN LOVE WITH HIM TO BEGIN WITH! WE WENT OUT FOR FIVE MINUTES.*

Trace: *Why are you yelling?*

Oh my god, I'm going to kill this guy, for real for real.

Me: *Please tell me you're lying.*

Trace: *Loverboy told Jose Rodriguez you're not going to show tomorrow because you're still pining for him.*

Me: *Pining? Who even says that anymore?*

Trace: *I mean—he used different words, but you're a lady so I used my filter. Shocking, I know. My mama would be so proud.*

I cannot for the life of me imagine the actual sentence he would have said. If there's one positive thing about Marlon Daymon, it's that he might be a jackass, but he was never lewd or disrespectful. I mean…if you don't count the cheating, ha ha.

Me: *And you think me showing up today will make him stop talking about me? I never wanted anyone to know we went out in the first place. I don't date players for this EXACT REASON.*

Trace: *First rule of baseball: Nothing is sacred. Guy code. We tell each other everything—you're fooling yourself if you thought he was going to keep that shit on lockdown.*

Me: *And now everyone thinks I'm dating YOU??? That's the LAST THING I WANT PEOPLE THINKING. WHAT IF MY DAD FINDS OUT?*

Trace: *Your dad's an asshole, no offense.*

Me: *None taken **eye roll***

43

Trace: *Don't get salty, I'm just being honest. Your dad doesn't like anyone, so there is no one you could bring home that he'd approve of, player or not.*

Ugh. He has a point.

I concede.

Me: *True.*

Trace: *Just come to the party. I promise I'll behave.*

Me: *LOL*

Trace: *I'm being serious. We can even have a safe word, so if you feel uncomfortable while we're there, just say it and we'll go. No questions asked.*

I stare at that declaration, a bit surprised, chewing on my bottom lip, debating. As much as I hate to admit it, I'm warming up to him. Warming up to the idea of going to the dumb housewarming or whatever it is.

Glance down at my pajamas. They're the same ones I wear a few times a week, swapping them out for my other boring pair here and there. My "single girl pajamas," as I call them both, because they're old and worn and comfortable and I would die if any man saw me in them.

Me: *What kind of word?*

Trace: *You choose.*

Me: *Literally any word? And I say it and we leave?*

Trace: *Yup—any word or phrase. Say, for example, you were talking and wanted to go and said wiener. I would know it was time to leave.*

Me: *As if I'd be able to use the word wiener in a sentence casually in front of all those people.*

Trace: *It wouldn't have to be in front of anyone—you could whisper wiener in my ear.*

This has got to be the strangest conversation I've ever had with a man, in my entire life.

Me: *Um, yeah, no.*

Trace: *What about smegma. Or moist. Ointment.*

Me: *LOL*

I laugh, imagining the look on a baseball player's face —or a wife's, or a girlfriend's—if I used any of those words in a sentence.

Trace: *Wanker. Phlegm. Plunker. Flaps.*

Me: *No! Where are you coming up with these?*

Trace: *It has to be a word that is distinct so there is no mistaking it's the escape word!*

Me: *I get that, but does it have to be gross?*

Trace: *What's gross about the word plunker?*

Me: *LOL*

Trace: *Fine. How about…Daddy.*

Me: *LOL*

Me: *Nice try—I am NOT calling you Daddy in public.*

Trace: *So what you're saying is, you'll call me Daddy in private?*

Me: *LOL NO!*

I laugh again. Honestly, he's making me laugh and I cannot stop now that I've started snorting.

Trace: *Do you have any better suggestions?*

Me: *Literally any of my suggestions are better than those.*

Trace: *Fine, let me hear them.*

I sit back, leaning against my headboard, and tilt my chin up to stare at the ceiling. Hmmm, what are some good safe words?

Me: *What about if I said something like, "I think I forgot to close my bedroom window."*

Trace: *Ummmmmmm it's not supposed to rain.*

Me: *Oh. Duh.*

Trace: *Let's just go with 'gizzards' and be done with it.*

Me: *LOL*

Trace: *Are you actually laughing out loud or just trying to make me feel good?*

Me: *I'm laughing out loud.*

Trace: *Good, I don't want your pity LOLs.*

I laugh again but don't tell him that. He's making it damn difficult to be irritated with him.

Me: *Trust me, I use them sparingly.*

Trace: *I'll come grab you at noon and we can figure it out on the way there. What's your address?*

Before I can think twice about it, I type it out and hit send.

Shit. Shit! I hit send? I hit send. Ugh!

Trace: *Noon. Dress casual, swimsuit optional. It'll be fun.*

No way in hell am I bringing a swimsuit.

Me: *I already regret this.*

Trace: *LOL*

Trace: *We'll have fun, don't worry about it—leave it to me.*

It's not the fun I'm worried about—it's the 'leave it to me' part, and the fact that I feel too comfortable with a man who is clearly not the kind to settle down and have a family.

I might not be that old, but I know I want kids sooner rather than later, and a home, and a life that's far different than the one I grew up with—a life filled with parents who fought constantly, because Dad is a workaholic and made Mom miserable, and probably cheated on her every chance he got.

Our life might have been privileged, but it was a gilded cage I want no part of living in.

Trace: *Noon?*

Me: *Whatever you say, Buzz...*

5

Trace

To say I'm shocked at the sight of Hollis Westbrooke's apartment complex is an understatement. I was expecting a high-rise on the waterfront or a brownstone in the cool part of the city. Perhaps even a shiny little condo in a pricier area.

Instead, the address Thomas Westbrooke's youngest daughter texted leads me to what can only be described as the shady part of town, or at least the *opposite* of where I was expecting her to live.

Dang, doesn't her family help her out?

I swallow as I pull my sports car up to the curb adjusting my rearview mirror so I can check out the terrain behind me. As I grab my phone to shoot her a note, maybe this is the wrong place.

I text her to make sure, noting a woman pushing a stroller coming my direction from down the block and two kids playing catch on the other side of the street.

Head down, I double-check the address.

Me: *Hey, I'm outside, but I'm not sure I'm at the right place.*

Hollis: *Are you looking at a black door with a pineapple door knocker on it?*

Me: *Yes?*

Hollis: *Then you're in the right place. Give me a second, I'll be right down.*

I set my phone in the cup holder and wait, watching the neighbors and cars creeping slowly down the street, clock counting away the seconds it takes Hollis to bound through the front door.

"Shit. Maybe I should get out," I mumble.

I should get out, right? And wait for her? Stand next to the passenger side door or something to be polite since I didn't go up to her place? Not that I know which one is hers—I'm assuming this is an apartment with multiple units.

Yeah, I should get out.

I walk around, leaning against the black, lacquered paint job of my car, which I had washed to a high shine this morning. Cross my arms and legs like Jake Ryan in the cult teen classic *Sixteen Candles* so when my date comes out of the house, she'll see me and be like, *Who me?* and I'll be like, *Yeah, you!* The heartthrob Jake to her Molly Ringwald or whatever her name is in the movie.

The theme song plays in my head, and I imagine us eating birthday cake in the middle of my kitchen table later—but then again, I don't actually have candles, and it's not my birthday. Maybe if I'm lucky she'll make out with me anyway.

Sweet love with her mouth.

I grin, imagining the whole thing, then the front door opens and Hollis steps out, giving me a little wave before turning to lock up.

When she faces me? Goddamn is she adorable in a

bright orange and pink skirt, flip-flops, and a tucked-in tank top.

Uh-dorable.

Her hair is down, and she's carrying a gift bag I can only assume is a hostess gift, *not a gift for me.* My excitement dims a bit, because I love presents.

"Hey there."

"Hey," she says by way of greeting, and I step aside to pull her door open, letting her slide inside and get comfortable before shutting the door. I watch as she buckles her seat belt, walking around the front, a knot forming in my stomach.

Relax, I tell myself. *You're hot shit—what are you so nervous about? Everyone in America wants a piece of you.*

Not her, I remind myself. Which *could* be the point and why I'm working this so hard, when really, I should leave her alone and let the whole thing go. Unfortunately for her, she laughed one too many times at one of my stupid jokes, and because I'm thirsty for compliments, I'm not willing to walk away without a fight.

Or until I see the look on Marlon Daymon's face when I show up at the party with Hollis Westbrooke on my arm.

If she'll touch me, that is.

Er, probably not. Hollis doesn't strike me as the overly affectionate type, and certainly not with me.

But she thinks you're funny…

"Which apartment is yours?" I glance up through the window at the three stories, guessing she's either the second floor or the top—in my opinion, no single girl should live on the ground level, for safety's sake.

"Actually, I own the building."

I cringe. The place is ugly as fuck. "Oh, that's…nice."

Hollis's laughter fills the cab of my sports car, harmonizing with the rev of my engine. "It's more of an investment property. I'm slowly renovating it and will eventually sell. I'm hoping next year."

"So you're into flipping properties?"

I'm into flipping properties, too.

"Yes, I love it. This is my second place—the last one didn't take as long, but I really love this neighborhood. The outside might not look like much, but the inside has tons of charm."

Charm.

A word only a chick would use.

"Nice car," she says when I put it into drive, her nosey eyes scanning the front seat and then the back. Luckily, I tossed all the trash this morning before leaving to grab her.

"Thanks."

"Is this your Sunday ride?"

"Mostly. I have a truck, too, for when I want to feel manly and do manly things."

Hollis laughs, and my chest puffs out. "Manly things? Like what?"

"Chopping wood and stuff."

My car is filled with more laughter, and I can't tell if she's laughing because she thinks I'm cute, or because she thinks I'm an idiot.

"That sounds oddly specific. Where do you find wood to chop?"

"My parents' place—my brother and I usually have dinner there on the weekends we're home."

"Oh that's right, you have a brother. He's an athlete too, yeah?"

"Yes. He plays around with the old pigskin." That's one way of saying he plays football.

"Is he married?"

I give her a sidelong glance, only taking my eyes off the

road for a split second. "No, he's not married." Is she feeling me out to find out if he's single?

"Your poor mother, two bachelor athletes. I bet you were a real handful growing up."

That's putting it mildly. "I'm shocked she doesn't have gray hair."

"I can only imagine."

"I'm my mom's favorite," I brag.

Hollis's brows go up. "How do you know?"

"She told me."

She rolls her eyes. "She probably told both of you that and I bet she did it so you'd behave."

"No for real, I'm her favorite. She always sneaks me the last piece of dessert." Though come to think of it, Tripp always leaves their house with leftovers and I don't.

The last time we were there, he had two plastic containers in his hands on the way home.

Fuck!

"What's that look for?" Hollis wants to know, but I suspect she already does.

"Nothin."

"Oh, come on—mothers can't have favorites. That's the law."

"She gave him leftovers!" I blurt out.

My fake date looks over at me like I've gone and lost my damn mind. "What on earth are you going on about?"

"Mom—she gave Tripp leftovers last time and all I got was the last stupid piece of fruit tart!"

More laughing. "Well maybe you should pass on dessert and she'll give that to him. Then you can have take-home containers."

"I don't want leftovers. I want *cake*."

"Then why are you complaining?"

"It's the principle of the thing. Also, one year, they

bought Tripp a football-tossing machine for Christmas and they never bought me a pitching machine, even though I wanted one, and I'm a better athlete."

"How old were you?"

"Thirteen."

"My god, are you seriously complaining about something that happened over a decade ago?"

I grumble, "No."

But I am.

I clamp my lips shut.

"Thanks for picking me up. It wasn't necessary."

I glance over. "If I hadn't picked you up, you wouldn't have come."

That makes her chuckle. "True."

"What do you have against me anyway?"

"Against you? I don't even know you—I bumped into you once before you railroaded me at the fundraiser yesterday. You haven't given me a chance to have anything against you."

Valid points. Still, "So you're saying, had we gotten to know each other better, you might have organically wanted to go on a date with me."

"First of all—this isn't a date. Secondly, did you seriously just say 'organically'?"

"First of all, this is a date. Even a pretend date is a date, in my opinion. If two people are out doing something? Date. If two people are going to eat food together? Date. If two people are—"

"I get it, I get it. Fine. To clarify, I mean it's not a romantic date. Better?"

No. "Sure."

"You don't sound sure."

Because I'm not. "You have terrible taste in men."

Hollis turns toward me, surprised. "What on earth

would make you say that? You don't even know me."

"*A* of all, you dated Marlon Daymon." I pull a face. "*B* of all, you won't date me. Ergo, terrible taste in men."

She studies me from her spot in the passenger seat, wide-eyed. "Are you always like this?"

"Like what?"

"So...persistent and argumentative."

My mouth opens to argue, but I clamp it shut. Open it. Clamp it shut. Damn her, why'd she have to go and call me argumentative—who can argue against *that*? "Am I? How so?"

Hollis laughs as if I'm a stand-up comedian who has just told the world's funniest joke, tears actually running out the sides of her eyes. "Oh my god, you're hilarious. I can't." She waves a hand, fanning it in front of her face to dry it. "Ugh, for real. You kill me."

I don't get the joke, so I stare out the windshield, concentrating on the road and the journey to Noah Harding's house, which is a twenty-mile drive that takes thirty-five minutes. He lives outside the city—we both do—away from the hustle and bustle in a gated community.

For a bit, we drive in silence, the gift bag on the floor in front of Hollis drawing my curiosity, and I wonder what's inside. Probably booze. Isn't that what everyone brings?

"What's in the bag?" I ask, letting the interest get the best of me.

"Um. Let's see..." She pulls it onto her lap. "Foaming antibacterial hand soap, and..." She roots around. "Hand lotion, chocolate-covered almonds, and a candle for the kitchen."

That's really nice of her. "Where's my goody bag?"

Hollis rolls her eyes. "It's not your party."

"Yeah, but I invited you."

"You did *not* invite me! You manipulated me into

coming! *Ergo*"—she stretches the word out—"you do not get a gift bag. Stop being a beggar, jeez."

Well that was rude. "I was just asking."

"Why. Are. You. Like. This?"

I shrug. "Probably because I had to live in my brother's shadow my whole life."

"You literally just got done telling me you're your mother's favorite."

Hmm. She's right, I did.

We arrive at Harding's gate and I lean out the door to punch in the code since the gatekeeper isn't in his tiny hut. House. Whatever you call the spot where he sits so he's not bacon in the sun.

"You have the code?"

I won't lie, my chest puffs out in pride at my own importance. "Pfft, heck yeah. Harding is my best friend."

Hollis smiles out the window.

I get to show off *again* when we get to the second set of gates—Noah's actual house—and I punch those numbers into that keypad, too.

"This is so pretty."

That's an understatement; the house is a McMansion —although, by Hollis Westbrooke's standards, having grown up with a silver spoon in her mouth, she's probably *used* to giant homes like this.

Me? I was raised in your average neighborhood with starter homes, two point five kids, parents who both worked long hours, and we never took vacations. Tripp and I only saw homes like this in the movies—I don't think there were any even remotely this grand within a fifty-mile radius of where I grew up.

And here I am, best buddies with a guy who owns one.

Not to say my house isn't as nice, though it isn't. I've been doing what Hollis has been doing: buying up shitholes, renovating in the offseason, then selling them for a profit. I haven't told her that yet, mostly because for all the talking I do, I'm actually a private person, and right now, she doesn't seem interested in getting to know much personal information about me.

Damn shame.

The garage door is open, and there is an empty spot, so I pull inside, much to Hollis's horror.

"What are you doing! You can't park here!"

"Why not?" I put the car in park, cut the engine, unbuckle my seat belt. "I always pull in if the space is open."

"Oh my god." Hollis burrows down in her seat, and it's not bright enough in here to tell, but I'm certain she's blushing.

"It's no big deal—I told you, Harding is my best friend. He won't care."

Actually, he does care, because he bitches about me parking in his garage every time I park in his garage. But in my defense, it has plenty of room that he's not even using, and if I can get my sweet ride out of the sun and into the shade, I'm gonna.

I leave the keys in the ignition.

Climb out, scuttling to the passenger side.

Hollis has unbuckled, too, and is pushing the door open when I make my way over, attempting to get out of the low bucket seat of my sports car. I offer her a hand.

"I've got it."

But she doesn't got it, can barely get out, the seat she's in determined to keep her ass in it. *Smart seat.*

"Here, just let me help you."

Hollis hands me the gift bag then attempts to heave herself up. "This is ridiculous. What a dumb car."

"Tell me how you really feel."

She gives me another eye roll as she smooths out the fabric of her skirt, then a nervous smile.

But that can't be right—what does she have to be nervous about? She's the general manager's daughter, for fuck's sake. Everyone inside works for her old man.

That doesn't mean I won't try to keep making her laugh.

I let us both into the house, bypassing the side gate outside so I can set some things down in the kitchen— Hollis wasn't the only one to bring a gift. I come armed with new grilling tools and a small cooler full of hamburger patties, a roast, and several pounds of lean chicken breasts, because I'm thoughtful like that.

And let's not forget I spend half my time at Harding's house, crashing the party of two out of sheer boredom and loneliness. There, I said it—I'm lonely.

"You brought them a housewarming gift, too?" Hollis looks on curiously as I punch in the code, hip-bump the front door open without knocking or ringing the doorbell, and help myself to Harding's foyer.

"My mom taught me some manners." We're both all the way inside, so I close the door behind Hollis until it clicks shut.

"That was really nice of you. Very thoughtful."

Yeah, it is, considering I practically live here and eat most of my friend's food. Come to think of it, maybe I should actually move in. It isn't the *worst* idea since I'm never at my own place, always wielding a hammer when I'm flipping a house, spending my down time on Noah's couch flat on my back with a remote in my hand.

Things will probably have to change now that his girlfriend has moved in, but I choose to ignore the fact that he doesn't want me around anymore.

Anymore? Did he ever?

Potato, potahto. Semantics has never been my forte.

I set the cooler on the floor and the grilling tools on the counter, along with the card I bought that reads *When my roommate said he was going to kill whoever was taking all of his stuff, I nearly shit his pants* and set the red envelope on the counter.

Beyond, in the yard, it looks like everyone has arrived, and I glance over at Hollis, whose eyes are glued to the pool area—and Marlon, his arm around what could only be a jock chaser.

Real classy, bringing a groupie to your teammate's house to make someone else jealous.

Hollis shakes her head to clear it then shoots me a forced smile. "Wait! We can't go out there yet."

"Why?"

"We never settled on a safe word."

Shit, we didn't—the one thing we didn't discuss in the car on the way over is the word we're going to use if she wants to bail on this party.

"Marvin Gaye," I suggest.

"That's two words."

"Right, but then everyone will just assume you want to go get it on, and no questions asked—boom, we slip out the back door."

Hollis stares blankly. "How about something simple, like spaghetti?"

I feign a yawn.

"What? I can just say, 'Oh, I'm making sauce from scratch tonight for my spaghetti,' and then no one will think I'm being rude."

"What's rude is talking about food when I'm hungry." Which reminds me... "I like tacos—what about something having to do with that?"

"Hmm," she muses. "That would make more sense if it were Tuesday."

I disagree. "Taco kitty."

"I refuse to say taco kitty in public."

"How about 'These are na-cho tacos'?" I pause. "Get it?"

"No to tacos."

"Would you care to revisit my earlier suggestion of wieners?" I pronounce it *vee*ner, a good old-fashioned German pronunciation, though if I recall from my languages class in high school, it's a schnitzel auf Deutsch. "I notice there are no hot dogs on the grill."

We can see through the glass, and I suspect everyone can see us too, but if they're anxious for us to come outside or want to meet the girl I brought to the barbeque, no one is showing it.

"I wonder if he's told them anything about me," Hollis murmurs, gazing through the patio doors at Marlon, who has wandered and is posted up near the pool's elaborate grotto, surrounded by women—as usual. Where they came from is beyond me; no one else would have the balls to bring randoms to a teammate's house. This isn't a fucking party at a club—this is someone's private home.

Daymon is a jackass.

Hollis stares out at him, so I jar her with a gentle nudge. "That safe word?"

Without averting her eyes, she opens her pretty little mouth and sighs. "What happens if you're the one who wants to leave?"

"It could happen, I suppose." Not likely, but possible. "How about this: if one of us has the sudden desire to leave, you have to say, 'I forgot something in the car—do you want to help me find it?'"

It's a bit weak as far as exit strategies go and could lead

to questions from anyone within earshot, but at least it's not a ridiculous word like *phallic* or *wanker*. Bummer, that.

She nods.

I glance down at the top of her head, her glossy hair hanging prettily, and I want to touch it, sniff it to see if it's as delicious as it was the other day at the benefit thingy.

"You're cool if I touch you, right? For show."

Another nod. "Yes, I'm cool if you touch me, but don't get handsy—someone might get the wrong idea."

Don't get handsy? What kind of pervert does she take me for? Pulling the sliding glass door open so we can step through, I wave my hand out in front of me so she goes first. "The same wrong idea they'll get when you tell everyone you forgot something in the car and you need my help getting it?"

"Huh?" She looks confused, so I explain.

"As soon as you need me to follow you to the car, they're going to assume you want to go outside and *bang*."

Hollis's face turns red in a flash. Apparently, she hadn't thought of that scenario. "You jerk! They are not!"

I laugh again.

She shivers.

"Yes they will." I give her a light tap on the ass and usher her onto the patio.

Hollis turns shy, self-conscious when everyone seems to turn toward us, greeting me with waves and her with curious stares, this mystery girl I brought along. All eyes are on us—on Hollis—especially those of the women present, and beside me, Hollis raises her chin a fraction higher, straightening her back. These women don't know her, but the mood is particularly WAGgy and I know they're judging her.

WAG: wives and girlfriends of professional athletes. From what I've gleaned and seen over the course of my short professional baseball career, they're not known to be the friendliest bunch. Catty. Petty. Competitive.

And Hollis certainly doesn't fit the description of one, so I'm sure they're wondering what the hell a man like Trace Wallace is doing with a girl like her. Today, the girl I'm shepherding into the lion's den looks wholesome. Sweet. Respectable.

Exactly the kind of girl I would take home to my mother, but also exactly the kind of woman who would never let me.

I doubt she recognizes any of them, so there's no way they know she's Thomas Westbrooke's daughter; some of them wouldn't even know who Thomas Westbrooke is, despite him being the boss of every man out here.

I feel her go rigid at their perusal, clutching the gift bag in her manicured hand, allowing me to steer her straight toward Noah and Miranda, our host and hostess.

"Hollis, this is Harding and his new roomie Miranda. Guys, this is Hollis Wallace."

Noah's brows shoot straight into his hairline—it's shaggy, unkempt, and I should tell him he needs a haircut, but that's his girlfriend's job now, not mine. "This is your sister?"

"No, babe." Miranda nudges him with an elbow. "This must be…your wife?" Her tone is perplexed, expression priceless.

"You're married?" Noah's eyes couldn't be any wider. "When did you get *married?*"

6

Hollis

I am going to kill Buzz Wallace.

Literally. With my bare hands wrapped around his puny neck. Okay, so fine—maybe it's not puny, and maybe I won't be able to fit my hands around it, but I sure am going to try because *what the actual fuck does he think he's doing?*

He slides his big hand around my waist and gives it a gentle squeeze. "I'm kidding. This is Hollis, but she's not my wife. She was having a weak moment and agreed to come along with me today."

He kisses my temple, but my face is still frozen into a stunned smile and I'm having one helluva time trying to relax.

"But wouldn't it be funny if we were married?"

No! "I could never marry you because I could *never* live the rest of my life as Hollis Wallace." Never, ever.

No.

Everyone is laughing now except for Buzz, who is pouting beside me, hand still settled at my waist. I want to shrug it off, but I don't want to do it in front of his friends, not when we just arrived. Besides, I can feel Marlon's eyes watching us from his spot by the pool, and I feel a wave of intense satisfaction move through me.

Drink it in, asshole—drink. It. In.

"Well Hollis, it's so nice to meet you," Miranda says with a smile, and I remember the gift bag in my hand, offer it up to her—to them.

"Oh! I almost forgot, this is for you."

She takes it and peeks her nose inside the bag with a delighted smile. "Oh! I love foaming hand soap!" Removes the lid from the candle and sniffs it. "Ugh, this smells so good! Thank you!" Miranda digs through the rest, and when she lifts her head, "Hollis, want to come inside with me so I can put this in the kitchen?"

"Of course."

She's going to grill me for details as soon as we are out of earshot, I can't help thinking as Buzz leans in and smooshes his lips to my cheek.

"Don't be gone too long, sugar bottom. I already miss you!"

"Could you not?" He's laying it on *way* too thick. It's vomit-inducing, looks ridiculous, and is embarrassing me.

I wonder what his friends are thinking but can't bring myself to look at Noah, and I certainly can't bring myself to glance over at Marlon.

What a mess Buzz is making—they're supposed to think we're on a date, not in a full-blown *relationship*.

Miranda leads me back into the house, resting the hand soap at the sink, placing the candle in the middle of the counter, and removing the rest of the bag's contents. Squirts some lotion on her palms and happily locates a container for the chocolate-covered almonds.

"This was so kind of you. Thank you." Now she's resting her palms on the counter and smiling directly at me. "So. Now that we're alone...how long have you and Buzz been...you know. Seeing each other."

Why is she saying it like that? "Um. It's very new." So new this is our first date and we've only met once, one other time, for a total of maybe ten minutes, tops. *But isn't that how most people meet? Briefly, and then they go out on a first date?*

Yes, but not to a party with all the guy's friends.

Oh my god, are you seriously arguing with yourself? *Get it together.*

I wish Madison were here—she'd do all the talking for me.

My palms sweat.

"Are you alright?" my hostess asks, going to the fridge and putting some ice in a cup. "You want an ice water? You look like you could use an actual drink. Maybe some alcohol?"

"No! No, I mean—no thank you, I'm good—but yes to the water. Thank you." *Shut up, Hollis. Stop talking.*

Luckily, Miranda laughs. "I totally get it, you know. Not only is Buzz a handful, the entire group out there can be a bit much. But give it a bit of time and you'll find Buzz is actually a softie, and the group is very loyal once they get to know you."

"Buzz is a softie?" That's not exactly the word I'd use to describe him. Then again, she's known him longer than I have.

"Yes. If it weren't for Trace, Noah and I wouldn't be together, and we wouldn't be here today celebrating the cohabitation with pulled pork and potato salad."

"What do you mean, 'if it weren't for Trace'?"

"He was our matchmaker." She laughs, pushing a glass of ice water across the counter toward me, popping a yellow and white striped straw into the center.

Did she say matchmaker?

"Yep." We both look through the glass, out onto the patio, to catch Buzz Wallace doing a weird TikTok dance, arms in the air, ass shaking. "Um…so yeah, Noah didn't want anything to do with me after we had this horrible public relations nightmare and Buzz was the one who brought us back together by tricking him into seeing me."

"Buzz?"

"Yes. He's actually really romantic. I'm almost positive we're not the only couple he's tried to match up." She cocks her head to the side and thinks. "Come to think of it, I'm pretty sure the security officer at the park—Karl is his name—and one of the administrative assistants are dating because of Buzz, but you'd have to ask him for sure. It could just be a rumor."

What? I point out the window. "That guy? The one smacking his own ass right now?"

He is, smacking his own ass, doing a weird 'back that ass up' motion, hopping in reverse while everyone laughs.

I blush. "Oh god."

Miranda laughs. "He really is a good guy. I don't think he's made good choices in the past as far as his own dating life is concerned, but honestly, not many of these guys have."

I know what she means, but I want to hear her version of it. "What do you mean?"

"Well. I mean…okay, so, not to be mean, but see the guy next to the pool grotto? His name is Marlon, and no offense, but those girls with him are groupies and only after one thing: his money. Maybe his fame too, and they never get brought around more than once—twice if they're lucky. More like cling-ons, and I don't know where they come from, but they're not long-term material. Inevitably, these guys all end up with them at some point, and Buzz has gone through his fair share, too." She takes a sip of the water she's already poured for herself. "Like I said, I'm not knocking those girls—they could be very nice people. All I'm saying is these guys get used, and Buzz has been no exception."

"So you're saying Buzz has brought groupies around?"

"Just a few." She pauses. "To be honest, I've only ever seen him with one other person, and it wasn't at a private party—it was at a nightclub. I think everyone was pretty shocked to see him show up with you today."

Oh, I just bet they were.

"Where did y'all meet?"

I decide to be honest since she's going to find out who my father is one way or another, and since I never plan on seeing Buzz again after today, there's no harm in it. Anyway, Miranda seems like a really great person, and I hate lying.

"I met him at the stadium this week. He...hit on me when I was there visiting my dad, after I got off the elevator on the wrong floor." I chug my water. "Then I bumped into him yesterday at the fundraiser, and he... Okay, real talk? I sort of briefly kind of dated Marlon Daymon last year by accident." Miranda's brows shoot up at that fun fact. "Marlon wouldn't leave me alone yesterday, and Buzz must have seen him giving me a hard time, so he came over and rescued me. Pretended to be dating me so Marlon would buzz off." Jesus, listen to me, now I'm using his name as a pun. "To do that, he invited me here—in front of Marlon—and now here we are."

Miranda says nothing, and I squirm. Shit. Did I reveal too much? What would Buzz say?

I open my mouth to apologize, but,

"I have sooo many questions."

"Okay."

"First of all—does your dad work at the stadium?"

"Yes. He's the general manager."

The brows shoot up farther. "Does Buzz know that?"

"Yes."

She nods. "So you're not actually dating him?"

"No."

Her face drops, disappointed. "But you dated Marlon?"

"Sadly, yes."

"I'm sorry." We both laugh, and Miranda looks outside again. "You're sure you don't want to date him for real? He's a really good guy."

"I'm sure. I've had my fair share of athletes for the decade. I've filled my quota."

"But Buzz isn't anything like Marlon. I would hate for you to compare the two—not that it's any of my business, just saying."

I appreciate that. "I know, but…"

"Okay, okay, I won't harp on it. Just think about it." She comes around the counter to my side. "Meanwhile, we should probably…" Her head tips toward the backyard and the party outside.

I follow her back out, water in hand, returning to the group we left not ten short minutes ago. Buzz automatically flocks to my side, and if this were an actual date with actual potential, my heart and stomach would be doing flip-flops at how attentive he is. My stomach would tighten into a knot at the sight of his toned arms and wide shoulders, and the way the sunlight makes his hair look a bit brighter.

His teeth are blinding when he smiles down at me.

Nope.

My stomach isn't tightening from nerves. It must be something else—that's the only way to explain it.

I rest a hand there, on my abs, pressing down.

He notices.

"Is the baby kicking?"

A laugh bursts out of me—I cannot help it—and I smack him out of sheer panic and mortification. "Oh my god would you shut up!" I nervously laugh again and tell the group, "I am not pregnant." Turn to Buzz. "Please stop telling people I'm pregnant."

"Guys, don't say anything. It upsets her," he tells his friends. "It's not good for the baby."

I smack him again with an eye roll. "Knock it off."

No one knows what to say.

Except Buzz, of course. "Just kidding. She's not pregnant." Pause. "Yet."

I can't do anything but shake my head, and if anyone knows what to say or do, they're not saying or doing it, which is making this entire scene uncomfortable.

So awkward it's awful, and I'm not sure if I should laugh nervously or throw myself into the deep end of the pool.

"Hollis, is it?" our host asks. "Where did the two of you meet?"

I open my mouth to reply, but Buzz beats me to it. "We bumped into each other a few times, and I conned her into coming with me today."

I wonder why he isn't telling the truth. Considering these are his friends and not mine, I don't add to his story, just corroborate it with a nod.

"Yup. He definitely had to bribe me into going out with him." Ugh, I just made it sound like we've been out before.

"Have you seen him throw back tacos yet?"

I look at Buzz. "Tacos?"

"Taco Tuesday is my favorite."

A giggle escapes my lips. "What does that mean?

You're one of those people who actually pounds back tacos once a week?"

"Basically. And that's a deal breaker. Answer this question: hard shell or soft?"

I mull over my answer. "It depends. If the meat is nice and greasy, I love a hard shell. I love it when the bottom gets soft and the outside is crunchy. Otherwise, I love soft shells—if it's stuffed full and has beans and lots of sour cream."

Yum.

"I present to you: my dream girl!" Buzz obnoxiously announces to the entire backyard. I glance at the pool, calculating how many steps it would take to get to the edge and dive in versus scaling the back wall and fleeing.

The thing is, while it sounds like he's making a joke, he looks dead serious. But that can't be right, can it? From what I can see, this is a guy who doesn't take anything seriously, so I can't imagine being in a relationship with him. Can't imagine him being faithful, or attentive, or—

"…not like a *vertical* taco or anything. Legit, with beef."

I snap out of my daze and try to focus on what they're saying. Vertical tacos? What on earth is he going on about?

I mean—these people think I'm *with him* with him, so even though this is all fake, I still want to strangle him for talking stupid! I still look bad for being here with him!

One of the wives—girlfriends?—takes pity on me and changes the subject, but it's back to me, and I squirm.

"What do you do, Hollis?" Curious, she tips her head and waits for my reply, her blonde hair glistening in the sun, parted down the middle and curled within an inch of its life, probably extensions.

"I'm an editor."

"Like, for a newspaper?"

"No   one   reads   the   newspaper."   Her

husband/boyfriend rolls his eyes at her, which I think is rude. I recognize him as one of the outfielders on the Steam, Kevin something-or-other. Clearly he's a self-absorbed prick if he's going to belittle his significant other in public.

"Actually they do read the paper, but no—I'm not an editor for a newspaper. I'm in publishing. So, books."

I wait for the questions to come.

"What kind of books?"

I shrug. "Fiction, mostly. Contemporary fiction."

"Have I read anything you've edited?"

I think for a few seconds. "I edited *As I Die Slowly* which was on the *New York Times* best seller list for two weeks last year." The author just sold the film rights to a production company.

"Never heard of it," Kevin drawls, and I want to wipe that smug expression off his face by telling him who I am, but I haven't name-dropped my father in years and am not about to start now.

Still. It's chapping my ass that he's being such a...such a...

"Don't be a dick, Louis," Buzz tells him, coming to my side and bringing his arm around my waist. Pulls me in and gives me the usual sniff before loudly whispering, "He reads at a fourth grade level, that's why he hasn't heard of it."

"Shut the fuck up, Wallace."

"Please—everyone has read *As I Die Slowly*, even my brother."

I gaze up at him. "Okay, that's a bit much."

"It's true." He sips on the beer in his hand. "We're in a book club with our mom and that was the selection in November."

"A book club? Stop it."

SARA NEY

He holds the beer can and raises a few fingers in the air. "Swear to god. It's called…" He racks his brain. "Something lame like the Bellmont Readers and it's mostly grandmas and shit, plus me and my brother. Google them —they're on Facebook. Bet you find my picture."

Noah Harding pulls his phone from his back pocket and swipes the screen open, tapping away. Laughs and holds it out only a few moments later. "He's not kidding."

I lean in as Harding holds the phone in front of my face, my eyes taking in the sight of Trace Wallace, six feet something of prime man, a head or two above a room full of old ladies, his brother Tripp off to the side holding a copy of *Love's Addiction*. The caption below the picture says, *February edition of books about love ends with* Love's Addiction, *unanimously chosen by the Bellmont Retirement Home Readers for our Valentine's Day meeting. Karen brought artichoke dip, the Wallace brothers brought salad fixings, and Doreen and Blanche delighted with their famous peanut butter brittle and lemon bars, respectively. The March selection will be an old favorite,* The Thorn Birds, *with special guest Sister Lyra Mitchell from the Franciscan Convent of Maryville.*

Buzz points to his brother with the tip of his finger before Noah retracts his phone. "Dipshit there only read half the book."

"Half of *Love's Addiction*, you mean?" I laugh.

"Yes. He claims the author was pandering, there were too many plot devices, and the first kissing scene was blah. His words, not mine. I for one thought it was just romantic enough to be believable, but with enough twists to leave me guessing."

Buzz takes a casual sip of his beer, as if he didn't just summarize a romance novel, and not a very good one, according to the critics. I've seen this book—haven't read it —but hear it's atrocious.

Who is this person?

Matchmaking? One of the only male members of a book club?

Correction: a book club whose members are primarily old women?

"Why are you in a book club with the Golden Girls?" another guy wants to know after the phone is passed around.

"Because my mom volunteers at the retirement home. They have a book club, she likes us to go and it gives us something to do together." Sip, sip. "Duh."

He goes to a book club full of old ladies because his mom wants him to?

My girl parts begin that familiar tingling sensation, now on high alert. Drool!

No. No, no, no, Hollis—you are not going to let this one little tidbit of information sway you to the dark side! This man is no good for you! This man is a player—women fall all over him!

"It doesn't surprise me in the least—you're a romantic." Miranda is grinning in my direction. "Have you set any of those women up with dates at all?"

Buzz quietly sips his beverage, eyes averted.

"Oh come on, admit it!" The blonde nudges him. "Tell us who you set up."

"Fine." He sighs loudly, as if we're burdening him by asking for info. "Yes. When Harriet's husband died, she was really lonely, so I introduced her to Walt in accounting at headquarters."

Noah's face scrunches up. "How the hell do you know a guy named Walt in accounting?"

Another shrug. "He came down to the field once when we were practicing and I went over to say hello." The 'duh' is implied by his tone. Everyone stares as if seeing him for

71

the first time. "Don't you ever go say hello to the people coming to watch us? Rude."

"How did I not know this?" Noah wants to know. "You're always up my ass—when do you have time to do all this matchmaking and reading and shit?"

"You find time for the shit you care about." *Duh.*

For real—who is this guy?

The entire day, my mind reels as I watch him laugh and joke around with his friends at the party. Our host and hostess seem to love him—er, Miranda does; I'm still not sure about Noah. He seems to tolerate Buzz more than he likes him. I'm trying to figure that relationship out.

In the end, I never use the safe word. In the end, we stay as late as everyone else. In the end, he walks us to the car around nine o'clock at night, and we're both a bit buzzed from booze and barbeque—though I can't actually recall Trace drinking after the few beers he had at the beginning of the party.

Trace.

Why on earth am I calling him that now? When did he go from Buzz to Trace?

Brain addled by the sun—and the cute man helping me into his ridiculously flashy sports car—I accidentally smile up at him as he closes the passenger side door for me.

Whoops.

The engine roars to life.

We ride quietly to the front of the property then to the exit in companionable silence; he doesn't say anything and I don't feel the need, rolling the window down and letting the breeze whip through my hair.

Head back against the headrest, I tilt it so I can watch his profile as he drives, face illuminated by oncoming traffic and the occasional streetlight.

"Today was fun." Oddly enough, I had a wonderful time.

"It was." He glances over. "Thanks for coming."

This gives me pause. Did he manipulate me into coming? Because it felt like a date, although we both know it wasn't, but it wasn't blackmail either? I mean, let's be honest, I could have stayed home. He didn't have to bring me, and I would have gone months and months, if not years, without seeing Marlon Daymon again. Bumping into him at the fundraiser was a fluke.

So did I actually want to stay home? Not really.

Was I curious about this person enough to join him for the day? Absolutely.

And I proved myself right; there is more to Trace "Buzz" Wallace than meets the eye—probably more to him than anyone gives him credit for. He is not just a pretty face with a talented body.

He is funny—so ridiculously funny—and handsome and nice.

I was not expecting him to be nice...

I was expecting a sarcastic, entitled asshole, and now that I know for a fact he's not, I wish I didn't. I want to go back to the place where I put him in a box, on the shelf, to sit, stereotyped and safely away from my heart.

I do *not* need a crush on America's Favorite Pastime Playboy.

That's what the press calls him.

But...playboy he is not.

If he senses the random dialogue looping through my head, he doesn't comment on it. Rather, he watches the road and lets me sit and stew. Radio off. Window down. Two hands on the wheel.

Big, strong, tan hands...

Rawr.

No. No, Hollis, no!

Except.

The tendons in his hands are straining, his forearms gorgeous. Giant. Tan. Hands.

Do not imagine them on your body, do not imagine them on your body, do not—

God, I bet those would feel amazing on my boobs and…other places.

I squirm, rubbing my thighs together, adjusting myself on the seat, and pretend to be interested in the landscape out the window.

Ten more minutes and I can be home, in bed, doing all the thinking of Buzz Wallace I want to in the privacy of my bedroom, with my hand dipped desperately between my legs.

Do not imagine his hands on your body, do not imagine his hands on your body, do not—

Not only do I imagine them on my body, I imagine other parts of him too, not *on* my body, but *in* it and I know then that I'm in deep, deep trouble.

"You got quiet all of a sudden," he remarks, nearing my place.

"Sorry. It's such a nice night out I'm enjoying the drive." Enjoying the drive? Seriously Hollis? Gag.

His chuckle is low, as if he knows I'm full of shit.

"We should do this more often." His comment is offhanded and nonchalant.

"Random backyard parties? Where do we find more of those?"

He looks embarrassed. "Good point. I just meant we could hang out more if you wanted."

If *I* want to or because *he* wants to? "Are you saying you want to spend more time with me?"

His shoulders shrug. His big, sexy shoulders—they take

me back to that place where I'm daydreaming again. Nothing gets me hotter than a strong upper torso. The back of a man's head especially when it's clean-cut and freshly shorn.

I can see the tendons every time a car passes by, spotlight illuminating the cab of his car.

Rawr.

I can't stop staring at his profile, he's so handsome.

"Are you crushing on me, Westbrooke?" His voice teases me, out of the blue.

"What?" I scoff. "Me? God no. And the last time someone called me by my last name, I was in middle school."

"Have you ever had a nickname?"

"Not really. My brother and sister used to call me Number Two when I was younger because I'm the middle child, but no, none of my friends ever had nicknames for me. Last names don't count." I glance over at him. "What about you? Besides Buzz."

He grins. "My mom called me Butter Bean when I was growing up and I have a few buddies that call me Dick Weed."

That makes me laugh, and we keep laughing until he's pulling up to my curb and we're awkwardly saying goodbye in the dark.

He waits while I get out, walk up the stairs. Waits while I turn the key in my front door and turn to wave at him.

I wait until his taillights are out of sight before stepping inside.

I cannot get him out of my head.

I try, but toss and turn in the dark. Check my horoscope, scroll social media, eventually shimmying my sleep shorts down my hips and run my hand over my abdomen, down to my—

My phone buzzes on my nightstand, interrupting my anticipated self-love session. Irritated, I reach for it.

Marlon: *I can't believe you actually showed up with Wallace. You've proved your point—you can stop pretending now and come to Daddy.*

Daddy? I gag in my mouth a little, in no mood for texts from the ex—especially not one calling himself Daddy who tries to hit on me because he's in a jealous pissing contest with his teammate. It's shady that he's messaging me to begin with when he knows I'm with someone new.

Creep.

Light in my room off, I glare at the text with one eye squeezed shut, half blinded by the cell phone light.

Me: *What do you care? We broke up, but then again—were we even dating?*

Marlon: *Yes.*

Marlon: *Let me take you for drinks and make it up to you.*

Is he out of his damn mind?

Me: *You couldn't pay me to sit and have a drink with you. Also, Buzz wouldn't like it. We're not seeing other people.*

Marlon: *I won't say anything if you don't say anything.*

Yeah right. If I went out with him, even for an innocent drink, he would blab to the entire locker room so Buzz heard him. If there is one thing I learned about Marlon in the brief time we were together, it's that he is a one-upper. A showman. Braggart.

How did I not know that when I agreed to the first date?

Because I am a damn fool, and I was seduced by his pretty face and easy lies.

Me: *That was always part of the problem—you are shady as fuck.*

Marlon: *Pfft, whatever. You're probably not even dating him. I bet it was all for show.*

Me: *What the hell would make you say that?*

Marlon: *Because I ruined you for other ballplayers.*

Me: *Um, true, but not because you're so amazing—you're an asshole and I would never go out with you again. So, please stop texting me. I'm finally happy.*

Marlon: *Wallace isn't going to make you happy, give me a fucking break.*

Me: *Leave me alone, Marlon.*

Marlon: *Whatever you say, mama.*

Me: *Don't call me mama. And don't ever text me again.*

7

Trace

It's Taco Tuesday.

It's Taco Tuesday and I'm hungry.

Normally this wouldn't be a problem. Normally, I'd drive my ass to the Taco Warehouse, buy a dozen—both soft and hard shells—sit at a picnic table, and scarf them down like a slob.

Normally.

Today, however, is not a normal day.

Today I woke up thinking about Hollis Westbrooke. Thought about her on my commute to work, on my way to the stadium to practice for the game on Thursday. Thought about her in the batting cage, on the pitching mound. While washing my hair in the locker room shower. Pulling on a clean pair of shorts.

Fuck.

Distracting is what this is, which is why it's not a smart idea to date someone during the season. Not only can you not give them the time they deserve, it's shit like this that can fuck up a career, having your mind somewhere else. On someone else.

Instead of focused on the ball.

And in professional sports, it's always about the ball.

I scratch my nuts, adjusting myself, the hammer in my hand suspended over a two-by-four I've been pounding at the fixer-upper I'm renovating. I've pulled down all the drywall in the main living room to make it an open floor plan and am staring at the studs—starving.

I should eat.

I could go by Noah and Miranda's with a box of tacos, but...Noah would probably hate that. Not that I typically care. I do what I want where he's concerned, which could be the reason he gets so pissed off at me...?

Whatever.

Not my problem.

Against my better judgment, I fiddle with my phone and text the one person I shouldn't send a message to.

Me: *What are you doing?*

There. Straight to the point.

Hollis: *Who is this?*

She knows damn well it's me—we've texted before.

Me: *It's Buzz. Stop pretending you lost my number.*

Hollis: *Fine. But why are you texting me?*

Me: *It's Taco Tuesday.*

Hollis: *Ummmmm...so?*

Me: *I'm starving, that's why. And I want company.*

Hollis: *That sounds like a YOU problem, not a ME problem.*

Me: *That's a little harsh, don't you think? Who says shit like that?*

Hollis: *My friend Natasha?*

Me: *She sounds mean.*

Hollis: *She is. And if you don't behave, I'm going to tell her you're bothering me.*

Me: *Does Natasha also hate food?*

Hollis: **narrows eyes**

Me: *Does she? Does she hate tacos?*

Hollis: *Taco Tuesday is HIGHLY overrated.*

Me: *What the hell are you, some kind of monster?*

Hollis: *LOL*

Me: *Don't patronize me with your LOL. **crosses arms and turns to the wall***

Hollis: *Oh, you're going to be sassy now? Fine. No tacos for you.*

Me: ***runs back** Wait! I spoke in haste.*

Hollis: *LOL I'm sorry but you're killing me. Why are you like this?*

Me: *Soft shell or hard shell. You have to choose. Go.*

Hollis: *Hard shell.*

Me: *Good. When can I pick you up?*

Hollis: *UH!*

Me: *Going once…*

Me: *TWICE…*

Hollis: *Fine! FINE! Come get me. I can always eat.*

Satisfied that I've won our little back and forth, I shoot her another text, giving her a half hour to get ready. Go to the kitchen, which hasn't been completely demoed yet, and wash my face in the sink. Hands and arms too—I'm covered in sawdust and grime. Super manly, but kind of gross. No helping my shirt since I don't have anything clean to throw on, but I find a baseball cap to cover my mop.

I do a walk-through of the house, a mid-century colonial in an up-and-coming neighborhood I bought at an auction last month, doing a sweep to make sure no power tools are plugged in or left on.

Damn if I'm not whistling, totally in the mood for Hollis and tacos.

Tacos and Hollis Tuesday.

Nice ring to it, though she would probably disagree. I'll have to run it by her...

I have my truck today, the sports car an impractical mode of transportation for a construction site, and pull it out of the short driveway, feeling all sorts of masculine as I navigate my way toward Hollis's place.

It's not as far as I'd have to drive if I were coming from my house, so I'll be a few minutes earlier than what I told her, but I'll just sit in the truck and wait it out so I don't rush her.

I know how pissed my sister would get when we used to rush her while she was getting ready, and the last thing I need is a riled Hollis refusing to come outside because I've pissed her off.

Dude, I remember this one time when we were all going to a holiday play at the community center. True had to have been 17 or 18 and was the last person to get ready. Tripp and I thought it would be funny to stand in the doorway of the bathroom and remind her of the time, every 60 seconds. "It's six oh five, Trudie—hurry up." Then, "It's six oh six, True. Better finish up—Dad has the car going."

I will never forget the wild look in her eyes as she told us to shut our mouths and go away then screamed for our mother to get us to leave her alone, veins popping out of her porcelain skin.

Guess girls don't like to be rushed.

I'm early, but not unforgivably so, so I shoot her a text to let her know I'm here, in case she's ready to go.

Me: *Downstairs, take your time.*

A few seconds later: *Coming!*

I can almost see the little cutie bounding down the stairs, and then I do see her. The door to the building opens and she steps out, all sunshine and happiness and blonde hair on what was an okay day.

Ripped-up jean shorts. Yellow tank top. White sneakers.

Little ray of brightness is what she is, and I hop out of my side to greet her at hers, pull open the door for her with a smile.

She gazes at me skeptically as she hefts herself up into the passenger side with a, "No funny business. This is just about food."

"Sure thing," I tell her. Shut the door. "*Not.*"

She should stop being so goddamn adorable if she doesn't want me to harbor any illusions about changing her mind, because that's my plan.

I need a girl I can bring home to my mother, and Hollis Westbrooke is perfect in every way.

Other than the fact that she hates me…

…but let's be honest, opinions are meant to be changed, and I'm an eternal optimist, something few people know about me.

"Hope you brought your appetite," I quip when I climb in and buckle up. "How many tacos can you eat?"

Hollis considers the question. "I don't know, four?"

"Four!" I shout out an evil laugh, as if four is the funniest, most deranged number I've ever heard. "Amateur hour."

"Um…are you *trash*-talking right now?"

Yes. "No, it's just that four tacos, or four of anything, barely whets my appetite."

She scoffs at my boasting. "Well you're huge and I'm not, so." Her chin tilts up and she ignores me to look out the window.

I'm huge? Huge in a good way or in a bad way? *Tell me, tell me.*

I'm afraid to ask for clarification, so I'll just assume she means awesome and buff and move along.

"Are you pouting because I can eat more tacos than you?" It's killing me, so I have to ask.

She turns and stares like I'm mental. "Are you being serious right now?" Laughs. Laughs and laughs. "Dare I ask, how many you can eat at one time?" She throws a hand up. "Don't tell me, let me guess—an entire dozen."

Well shit. "Thanks for taking the wind out of my sails." I frown, deflated that she nailed it on the first guess.

"You are so ridiculous I don't even know what to do with you." Her chuckle is good-humored as she watches the houses turn into city blocks with shops and eateries, and finally—Taco Warehouse, aka heaven on earth.

It's not easy to find a parking spot—this place is jam-packed every night of the week, and especially on Tuesday —but I manage to find one two blocks away, in a paid spot. It's twenty-six bucks for a few hours, but worth it.

I fist-pump in the air for the sweet victory.

"Oh jeez."

Hollis is watching me, but she's smiling, amused.

Happily, I bound over to her side of the truck, reaching it before she gets the door open. Ever the gentleman, I help her get out, though she needs absolutely zero assistance.

"My lady." I present her to the concrete sidewalk with a flourish, slamming the door behind her, zip in my step as we approach beans and rice and the delicious smell of corn and flour tortillas. Some people mock this sacred day of the week; I treasure it.

"Hola, Señor Wallace!" The owners are here, and Miguel greets us, his twinkling eyes trained on Hollis. I've never brought a woman here, if you don't count Miranda, so I can see that he's curious.

I wave and smile, scan the room; there are no tables

available that I can see and no real places to sit in the entryway while we wait, but I manage to strong-arm my way in between two families against the wall, so at least we can lean while we wait.

"Sit tight, I'm going to put our names in for a table."

Hollis nods.

It doesn't take long to get us on the list, but we have quite a wait. The hostess, Rebecca, offers to create a table for us so we don't have to stand around, which I politely decline before solemnly making my way back to Hollis.

By the look on my face, she knows the news is grim.

"It's a 45 minute wait," I announce when I slouch along the wall next to her. "We. Are. Going. To. Starve."

Hollis rolls her pretty blue eyes sarcastically, but I like it. "Trace, were they going to bump you up on the waitlist?"

I shrug. Did she not hear me declare our impending starvation? Why is she changing the subject?

"And you wouldn't let them?"

"No." I sigh hungrily. "It's not fair for me—us—to just walk in here and take someone else's table when they've been waiting." I pause. "Also, how did you know my real name is Trace?"

She shrugs and pretends to inspect her nails. "I might have looked you up."

"Whatttttttt! Hollis Westbrooke, you did not!" I'll admit it, I sound like a Southern teenage girl. "You googled me! What did you find?"

God this is great news.

"Would you keep your voice down?" she murmurs.

People are starting to stare, not that I give a shit. A few of them seem to recognize me, but so far, none of them have approached us.

"I googled you after we ran into each other at the

stadium, because you looked familiar but I couldn't remember your name. So I looked you up—it's not a crime, jeez."

No, but it means she was curious enough to go searching for my name.

We stand and goof around for a few more minutes before Rebecca comes over. It sure as shit hasn't been the forty-five we were told we'd be waiting, but I don't want to cause a scene by insisting we wait longer, so we let her lead us to the far corner.

Chips and salsa are placed on the table almost immediately. Guac, too, and water. I don't bother picking up the menu, because I always order the same thing, but Hollis has never been here, so she peruses the list of options like a skilled restaurateur.

"What are you having? And please don't say a chimichanga."

She laughs. "I'm getting two soft shells and two hard shells, thank you very much."

"Beef, chicken, or pork?" I ask as I collect her menu.

"Um, beef."

"Sides? Rice, beans, or both?"

She cocks her head at me. "Rice?"

I nod. "Would you like to add a quesadilla for a dollar?"

"Sure."

"Anything to drink?"

"Um, this water is fine—wait, *what* is going on? Do you work here now?"

Now we're both laughing, laughing until the actual server comes to take our order, and I repeat everything Hollis just told me, plus my order, and soon we're alone again, laughing.

"You are so strange," she says quietly.

"Is that a good thing or a bad thing?"

She's quiet, and it's loud in this place from all the people—plus the sound of myself eating chips certainly does not help—so I concentrate on what she's about to say. What was it my mom calls it? Active listening?

"It's a…it's…" She seems hesitant to answer, and a knot forms in the pit of my stomach. I thought we were making headway here. I thought— "It's a good thing."

I slouch in my chair, tortilla chip dangling from my lips like a limp cigarette. "Thank fucking Christ."

"Pardon me?"

Pretty sure I mumbled that under my breath, but apparently not. "I said, *Thank god.*" I'm going to hell for lying. "I'm glad you think it's a good thing that I'm strange." Wait… "How is that a good thing, exactly?"

I pound a few more chips down my gullet while she deliberates.

"It's good because it's unexpected. Not to fuel your ego, but you're not what I was expecting. At all." She takes a chip, dips it in salsa, and pops it in her mouth. I wish she'd stop eating because I want to hear what she has to say.

About me, ha ha.

"What were you expecting?"

"You to be more of a douchebag."

You and every other decent female on the planet. "No, tell me how you really feel, Hollis."

Am I imagining it, or did she just shiver when I said her name? She can't be cold; she's wearing jeans.

"Hollis." I say her name again and—there's the shiver. "Hollis."

"Stop it!" She laughs, throwing a chip across the table. It hits me in the chest, and I pick it off my shirt and stick it in my mouth.

Chew.

"Crunchy and delicious," I tell her with a full mouth, and I almost do say something douchey—something like, *Crunchy and delicious like I imagine you'd be*, but that's the most idiotic thing to say and makes zero sense, and I have the wherewithal to keep my big mouth shut for once.

"Soooo…" she starts, holding another chip in her hand, breaking it into two pieces and setting them on her tongue, one at a time. "What else is going on? Besides work?"

I stuff three chips in my mouth at once, wash them down with water, and wipe my hands on a napkin before responding. "Other than seeing my parents and hanging out at Harding's house, I don't know. Reading and shit."

Reading and shit? Real fucking eloquent, you tool.

But Hollis's brows shoot up, and I see that I've managed to surprise her, yet again. "That's right. You said you're in a book club, but do you actually do the reading?"

More chips go in my mouth. I like the idea of making her wait for my answers, especially when she seems so intent on hearing them.

"Yeah. Of course I do the reading."

"Because you like books."

Why is she saying *books* like that? As if the sound of the word is turning her on—it's so weird. And why is she leaning forward, with her boobs smushed into the edge of the table? Is she doing that on purpose?

"Yes?"

"What kind of books do you read when you're not reading romance?" I hear her low chuckle over the sound of the mariachi band and the chatter of the people surrounding us.

Brat.

I rack my brain for the last book I've read that wasn't a book club selection. "It was a World War II biography written by a fighter pilot whose plane went down. He lived in the jungle for a few months without any supplies, food, or weapons to keep him safe."

"Was it a thick book?"

"Um. Yes?"

She nods. Nods again, watching me as she takes a few more chips and breaks them into pieces. "Uh huh. Tell me more."

Okay, what the hell is going on right now? It looks like she's turned on, but I know she can't stand me, so is she having a hot flash? Or a seizure? Is she so hangry she's hallucinating she likes me?

I'm so fucking confused.

The server appears as if by magic, bringing sustenance for this hungry woman sitting across from me, and I'm spared from her leering, glazed-over eyes as our tacos are laid out in front of us. Still, this doesn't seem to excite her as much as the mention of *books* did. Or the sound of her name on my lips.

I test the theory again. "So, what genre are you most into reading for pleasure when you're not working?"

Genre—nice one, Buzz.

I give myself a mental pat on the back.

Hollis raises her head, fork full of rice poised halfway to her mouth. "Romance."

"Really. You read romance novels?" I bite into my first hard shell taco and moan. "What trope?"

Trope.

Another mental pat and I smile to myself when her eyes get soft.

"Um." She brushes a strand of hair behind her ear. "Mostly the usual stuff. Uh, cowboy romance and...sports romance."

What's this now? Sports romance?

I sit up straighter in my chair. "That's a thing?"

"Yes."

"What kind of sports are you reading about?"

She ignores me for a couple beats, choosing that moment to bite into her taco—on purpose, probably!—chewing thoughtfully and not answering the question. Swallows. Takes another bite.

I swear to god she's doing that to torture me.

"Baseball."

"Like, baseball baseball? College or what?"

"No, professional baseball."

"You're reading a romance about baseball players?"

"I mean—the guy is a baseball player. The girl works as the nanny."

The nanny? What the hell kind of book is this? "He hooks up with the nanny?! Is he married? Where's the wife?"

Hollis laughs, covering her mouth with the palm of her hand. "No, he's a widower—that's why he needs the nanny."

"Oh." I think this concept through. "So his wife died, and now he's banging the nanny. That seems fucked up and shady."

She laughs. "It's not like he just put the moves on her and took advantage. They fell in love—or are going to fall in love. He needed someone to watch his six kids."

"Six kids! What the fuck?"

"It's two sets of triplets."

"That makes no sense."

"Well the first set was IVF and they didn't think they'd get pregnant again, but she did, and it was another set of triplets, and then she died in a car accident on their first birthday."

That just sounds absurd. "And you're into this shit?"

"Very."

"Um…whatever floats your boat." I can't talk about this anymore without my brain exploding from sheer boredom and bewilderment. "In my opinion, that's way too many plot devices and completely unnecessary."

"Genre. Trope. Plot devices. Who are you?"

I smirk, knowing I've just wet her panties a little with my knowledge of literary terms. "I love reading—what can I say? Just a big old book nerd. Hashtag book lover." I stuff more food in my mouth, chewing slowly, so as to drive her wild with suspense.

She doesn't look desperate for me to say more, but she is smiling.

"I got banned from a library last year." My declaration is matter-of-fact—and true—and between mouthfuls.

This gets her interested, and she seems to perk up. "I'm listening."

I set my napkin on the table, push my chair back a few inches, ready to dig deep into the dramatic story. Cross my arms and consider my first few words. The *hook*, if you will.

"It was a dark and stormy night…"

Hollis laughs and rolls her eyes.

"Kidding. It was cold and snowy. Off-season. And I like to hit the library near my house—they have an amazing audiobook selection." Her eyes do that glistening thing. "I love listening to them on my way to the stadium, or while I'm pounding nails at one of the properties." I flex and kiss my bicep—kind of douchey, but she doesn't seem to care. "Anyway, I see this woman at one of the tables who looks familiar, and I'm convinced she's the author of one of my favorite series. She had her laptop out and was pounding away at the keys. I swore I'd met her before because I've gone to a book signing or two." Pause for effect. "Signed books are my kryptonite."

Hollis is hanging on my every word, and if she were wearing a bib, she'd be drooling.

Or so I tell myself.

"I don't want to bother her, right? She's busy, and I can only imagine being interrupted while I'm perfecting greatness would piss me the fuck off. So I go to the circulation desk, grab a piece of paper, and write, *I like your books.* Then I slip it to her as I walk by, which, in hindsight, was creepy as fuck and a terrible error in judgment."

"Why?"

"Because I have abysmal penmanship." I grab a paper napkin and ask Hollis if she has a pen—she does—then write *I like your books.* Hand it to her.

"I like your boobs?"

"It says books."

"It says boobs."

"See? Do you see now where this all went wrong? Do you see now where this story is headed?"

"Don't say another word or I'm going to choke on this taco." Her skin is bright red and she's about to burst out laughing; I can see her holding it in. She is about to freakin' explode.

Obviously I say more words. "So she thinks I'm telling her I like her tits—er, boobs—which were probably sagging down to the ground, mind you." I shiver at the memory. "Instead of confronting me about it, the lady goes and tells the librarian there is a pervy sexual harasser on the premises. *She* goes and tells the security guard, and *he* yanks my audiobook selections out of my viselike grip and escorts me out. God, I was so humiliated—Betty from nonfiction and I made eye contact, and I've never felt so ashamed."

"Stop it." Tears are welling up in her eyes.

"No. She told her friend Ethel, who is a member of the Bellmont Readers, who told my mother."

"This is too much." She's swatting at the air between us. "You're making this up."

"They took my card away, Hollis! You don't joke about this shit. I'm no longer welcome at any library within the tri-state area, thanks to my shoddy handwriting."

"Oh my god Buzz, you deserved it!"

I act like the innocent party here. "It's not like I was looking at porn on one of the free computers! I gave her a note. I was *complimenting* her!"

"On her BOOBS!"

"No, on her books!" I push some shredded lettuce around on my plate. "It wasn't her, by the way."

"Stop."

"Nope. Wasn't her. Just some random lady listing all her weekly coupons in a spreadsheet."

"How do you know?"

"I could see it when I walked past the window."

"Sooo...you were creeping on her through the window?"

"I was walking past the window! What was I supposed to do, not look?"

"Yes! You could have simply not looked." Hollis is shaking her head like she's disappointed in me. "Were you trying to get another glimpse at her tatas?"

"Dear god. No. Don't even suggest such a thing—I'm lonely, but not desperate."

Shit, did those words just come out of my mouth? I can't take them back, but I can pray she doesn't latch onto them beca—

"Lonely?"

Ugh, she would mention that. Why is she like this? Why does she have to be so nosey?

"So you're an editor?" I do my best to deflect.

"Don't change the subject." She pins me with a pointed stare, biting into a taco and crunching at the same time. Her eyes narrow.

"Did I say lonely? I meant busy."

"You said lonely—what did you mean by that?"

8

Hollis

This entire dinner has been so fun. His sharing, his goofy stories, his sense of humor, even when it's self-deprecating.

He pokes fun at himself easily.

He loves reading.

I mean—he mentioned as much at the barbeque over the weekend, but to hear him talk about it with such passion seriously gets me turned on.

I'm folding like a greeting card and hate myself for it.

"You said lonely—what did you mean by that?"

I'm lonely too, but I would never admit it to anyone other than Madison, or any of my other friends. Buzz does not seem to have that problem, except when he's called out on it.

"Are you talking about the fact that you're single?"

He lifts one of his broad shoulders in reply, which answers the question for me: Buzz Wallace is lonely. Does that mean he hates being single or is just lonely because of it? Is he looking? Does he want a serious relationship, or only to fuck around?

"When was your last serious relationship?"

Another shrug. "I've never had one."

Red flag, red flag! "Why?"

I know, I know—it's so rude to ask. In fact, I read a magazine article online once that put it in the top five things not to ask on a first date, and here I am, blurting it out. Correction: this is not a date, so it doesn't count as being rude.

"Are you serious?" He sets down the fork he's been plowing through the refried beans with. "What self-respecting, nice, honest, wholesome girl would want to date me?" He holds a hand up to halt any reply I'm about to give him. "Trust me, I've tried. I took a kindergarten teacher out once—she couldn't deal with the fans."

I glance around; people are watching us, but no one has come over to ask for autographs or photos, which has been really nice.

"So she dumped me after three dates, even though I thought things were great. And let's not forget the fact that it took me years to make it to the pros—I wasn't drafted out of college like most of the guys on the team. I redshirted in college, busted my balls in the farm teams. Practiced nonstop—and when I say nonstop, I mean I don't even know how many hours a week. I was piss-ass broke, had no contract and no money, and almost had to move back home and live with my parents." He shudders.

My mouth almost falls open at this admission, but I clamp it shut.

He's on a roll now, verbal diarrhea spewing out of him like some confessional at church. "And now? I can't seem to get away from gold diggers—they're at every club, hanging out at the stadium, every bar we try to escape to just for a relaxing drink. Fake tits and Botox and injected lips and why can't I just find someone decent to like me for who I am?"

I stare.

No, I'm actually gaping at him. Wide-eyed, slack-jawed disbelief. *What is he saying?* That he wants someone normal? Not a trophy wife with giant boobs and extensions? Not that there is anything wrong with that—those women are beautiful. It just sounds more to me like he wants wholesome and...sweet.

"Hollis?"

"Mm?" I mutter, barely able to compose a sentence.

"I have something to ask you."

I manage a joke. "No I will not marry you. We've been over how I don't want to be Hollis Wallace."

"Ha ha, funny." He stirs the straw around his glass of ice water. "After the games this week, I was going to head down to see my parents, and I told my mom I was seeing someone because I thought it would make her happy, and now she wants to meet my girlfriend."

"Is your mom okay?" I clutch my chest. That poor woman must be suffering!

"What do you mean?"

"Is this her...dying wish? To see you married off before she takes her last breath?" Oh gosh, what if it *is*? How can I say no?

Buzz's handsome face contorts, puzzled. "No—my mom is fine, she just harps on us a lot to settle down. What would make you think she was dying?"

"You asked in a very dramatic manner."

"Um, actually, no I didn't."

Fine. Maybe not so dramatic, but it did catch me off guard. "Are you asking me to lie to your mother's face?"

He nods, unabashedly. "And my dad's face."

"Your mother will live if you are single for another weekend."

"But I already told her about you."

This gives me pause. "About me, specifically?"

"Yes."

"Why would you do that?!" Is he insane? Clearly he is, since he creeps on unsuspecting women in libraries and blackmails others to have tacos with them. The shell in my mouth tastes like sandpaper, and I'd spit it out if it wasn't considered impolite.

I want to strangle him!

"I just want my mom to be happy."

"But she's not dying! She will live. It is not a big deal! My parents want me to settle down, but do you see me pretending to have a boyfriend? No."

"I beg to differ." His brows shoot up. "That is exactly what you're doing."

"Oh my god! No—this is your fault! You're the one who wanted to pretend to help me. It's not like I hunted you down!" This man is exasperating.

"Semantics. The point is, you're doing it." He puts the napkin—the one that says *I like your boobs*—back on his lap. "As we speak."

"You're twisting the situation around so it suits you and we both know it."

Buzz pulls out his cell phone, taps on it a few times, scrolls—then holds it out in my direction. "This is my mom. Do you want to disappoint this face?"

Dear lord, his mother is adorable.

Sandwiched in between Buzz and a man who looks almost identical—his brother—she's beaming and tiny compared to the two of them.

"Is it just you and your brother?"

"No, we have a sister, True. She's one year younger."

He's still holding the phone practically in my face; there is no denying his mother looks delightful and not like someone you'd want to disappoint.

Still.

"This is not my problem."

"It would be an even trade."

Is he serious?

"No." I haven't lost my appetite, so I keep eating.

"Please?"

That has me looking back up at him.

Shit. Do not beg me, Buzz Wallace. This won't end well for me.

I swallow the lump of meat in my throat and shake my head firmly. No.

"Please, Hollis. Please, I'm willing to do anything." He wiggles his eyebrows suggestively.

"Gross. Don't ever do that."

The smile gets wiped off his face. "Sorry."

The thing about athletes is—the ones with the winning, can-do attitudes? They never give up. So I said no, but Buzz isn't ready to accept it, and I have a feeling it only has a tiny bit to do with his mother and a whole lot to do with the fact that he likes me.

There, I said it—Buzz Wallace likes me.

I can see it in the way he looks at me and the way he's trying to spend time with me, though it's mostly extortion and blackmail and manipulation.

Not the bad kind, but...

He's trying too hard.

Be real, Hollis—you wouldn't give him the time of day if he wasn't chasing after you like a lovesick puppy.

I study him across the table, the tacos on his plate nearly gone, basket of chips nearly empty, water totally empty, stomach definitely full. He's watching me in earnest, barely blinking.

"Fine. I'll do it."

Buzz throws down his napkin, shoves his chair back away from the table, and pumps his fist in the air. "Yeah buddy!"

Jesus H.

This man is so over the top.

But come on—what's the worst thing that could happen if I do this?

9

Trace

"**M**om, this is Hollis."

I repeat this in the mirror a few times, practicing the introduction as I pull a bright blue polo over my head. I don't typically dress up to see my folks, but since I'm taking a date, I class myself up a bit and throw on a nice shirt.

Shorts.

Deck shoes instead of sneakers.

"Mom, meet your future daughter-in-law."

If I said that, Hollis would kill me with her bare hands, probably in front of my parents.

I grab the candle I bought my mom and head to grab Hollis. She doesn't know the drive is a bit of a hike, but it's scenic so I doubt she'll mind.

She doesn't because this time when I pick her up, she's got her laptop along.

The entire ride, she contents herself with whatever book she's editing, computer glasses perched on the bridge of her nose, fingers tapping away or lightly running over the computer screen in a straight line, as if she's tracing the sentence in front of her and committing it to memory. Hollis also bites her bottom lip a lot when she's concentrating; if I've glanced over at her once to mentally imprint the image of her in those tortoiseshell glasses, I've glanced at her three dozen times.

She's just that pretty.

She's busy until, nearly two hours later, we pull into my parents' driveway, the blacktop lined with trees my dad planted the year Tripp and I bought the place, flanked by a meticulously manicured lawn.

Roger Wallace likes his grass green, trimmed, and pristine.

Hollis removes her glasses. "This place is so cute."

Cute?

"We didn't grow up here. They moved in a few years ago when Tripp and I both went pro. It's closer to Chicago than they were before by three hours."

She turns to me. "So they can come watch you play, but still out in the country where it's private?"

I nod. "Exactly. They wanted to be closer so they could see us, but don't like the city."

"That makes sense—the city isn't for everyone."

It's really not for me, either, but for now, there's nothing I can do about it.

"Tripp, True and I are here a lot. Lots of family dinners. Family first." I shrug it off, though inside, my heart leapt out of my chest at the tender expression on her cute face. A little.

I said it leapt a little—everyone relax!

Her eyes soften. "I love that."

Whoa.

What is that look? Is she...making doe eyes at me, or is she feverish?

Before either of us can say another word or even

unbuckle our seat belts, my mother comes busting out of the front door, kitchen hand towel thrown over her shoulder, smile on her face.

When I told her I was bringing the girl home I'd been talking about for Sunday dinner, she thought I was joking. Tripp was sitting next to me, rolling his beady, mistrusting eyes, snorting and grunting the whole time—which only fueled my mother's disbelief.

"You wouldn't joke about something like that, would you, Trace?" she asked me three different times.

"Mom—have I ever lied to you?"

"Only a few hundred times."

Good point. "Well I'm not lying this time—and please don't go overboard on food or anything. Hollis won't want you to make a fuss."

"Hollis," she'd said breathlessly. "I just love that name. So unusual."

Unique, like the girl herself, who's now sitting in my car, staring at the house.

"Oh my god your mother is adorable," Hollis is saying. "Jesus, I hate lying and I hate you right now. Look how excited she is, you asshole." She pushes her car door open and steps out. "Mrs. Wallace, hiiiiii!"

Women. I'll never understand them.

How can she be hissing obscenities at me one second then going at my mother like they're long-lost sisters?

I climb out at a leisurely pace, giving them time to greet each other without my interference, and then amble over, hands in my pockets.

"Mom, this is—"

"Hollis, come inside. Trace Robert, can you get the grill going out back? Your father is dragging his feet."

Then she ushers my date into the house, leaving me

standing there, the entire speech I prepared a complete waste of time.

"Mom, this is Hollis," I mumble to myself, locking the car with the remote and heading into the garage. "No, no, go on in. I'll just start the grill. No, I insist," I pout, deserted and alone.

No one comes to help me.

Not my dad. Not Hollis.

I look up at the sky as I walk through the grass, to the side yard, up onto the wooden deck Dad, Tripp, and I built last summer. Hit the igniter on the gas grill. Stand there while it warms up, scraping the char off the grates.

"This is what I love doing, being outside by myself while my date is inside being hoarded by my mother," I grumble some more.

"Are you talking to yourself, dill hole?"

Shit.

My fucking brother.

Just what I do not need right now.

How did he even get here, anyway? "Who invited *you*, *asswipe*?" I accuse, turning to face him.

"It's Sunday, asshat."

Asshat? Real original. I just called him asswipe—that's like stealing. Or copying.

"So what if it's Sunday. Did Mom tell you I brought someone or is this a coincidence?"

"Yup, she sure did. Told True, too."

"You drove all this way, by yourself, just so you could be here to spy on me." He hates driving alone and hates having to pay for the gas it takes to get here.

"Yup." He pops the P then pops a can of beer, sipping the foam off the top with an annoying slurp.

"Stop doing that."

"No can do." He slurps again.

I ignore him, walking toward the patio door, and give it a yank.

It's locked.

I press my face to the glass, eyes roaming the inside of the house where the kitchen is.

"They're in the front room. Mom is showing Hollis your baby books."

Fuck. That means he's already been in the house.

My brother gives his eyes a big roll. "This is why we don't bring people home, idiot. She's going to get attached and when this Hollis chick wises up and dumps you, it's going to break Mom's heart."

He's right, Mom *would* get attached if Hollis and I were actually an item.

"Hollis isn't going to dump me." *Because we're not even dating. I guilted her into coming along, but no one knows this but her and me, and no one is going to find out.*

Obviously I don't say that out loud.

"She's not your type," he informs me, taking another swig from the beer can.

"What the fuck, Tripp—yes she is."

"No she's not. Your type is 'thirsty' and 'clingy', and this girl is neither of those things. I bet she even has an actual job. Where did you say you found her?"

"Work."

"She works for the Steam? Don't shit where you eat, bro."

"No, she was at the stadium last week for a meeting and I bumped into her."

"What was she doing at the stadium? Is she a reporter?"

"No, she's in publishing. Books."

"That doesn't explain what she was doing there." He won't let it go.

"Having lunch."

"With who?"

Why is he like this?

"God, why are you asking so many damn questions? What is this, the Spanish Inquisition?"

"I'm looking out for you! You don't know this girl. For all you know, she's a gold—"

"Hollis is not a gold digger." I laugh and laugh, as if he's just said the funniest thing.

"How the hell do you know? You've known her all of, what, five days? Seven? For all you know, she's—"

"Her dad is my boss."

That shuts him up for all of three seconds. He opens his mouth, takes a deep breath, and begins bitching at me all over again.

"Hollis is Thomas Westbrooke's daughter? Dude, are you insane? I just told you not to shit where you eat! Dating your boss's daughter is like shitting on your entire meal, plus your salary and your car and all the coats you own."

"How about you let me worry about it?" I begin the walk back to the front of the house. "Better yet, how about you worry about yourself?" He's such a goddamn commitment-phobe. The dude doesn't even do casual sex with strangers.

"How about you take my advice and lis—"

Our dad rounds the corner, a scowl on his face, stopping us both in our tracks.

Hot on my heels and still lecturing, Tripp smashes into my back.

"You two at it again?" our old man asks. "Jesus Christ, you're loud enough that the neighbors can probably hear you in the next county over. Tripp, leave your goddamn brother alone."

Goddamn brother? What the hell, Dad? That's just rude.

"And Trace, go save your girlfriend from your mother. She's about to guilt-trip the girl into taking a wreathmaking class at the rec center with Fran and Linda."

Guilt-tripping—a Wallace family tradition.

"Fine." I stomp off like an adolescent, my dad and my brother making me feel like I'm twelve, breathing down my neck and telling me what to do.

I find Hollis in the front living room, and as soon as I walk in—

"Shoes off young man!" Mom scolds, narrowing her eyes at my feet and beaming over at Hollis simultaneously.

What kind of monster has my mother become?

"Did you start the grill like I asked you to?"

Oh my god. "Yes, Mom."

"I'm going to need you and your brother to start setting the table."

Speaking of which... "Why did you invite him, anyway? He's already picking fights with me." Do I sound like I'm pouting? Sure. Do I care? No.

Our mother is having none of my nonsense. "Stop arguing and go set the table."

"Thanks, babe." Hollis winks at me, the word babe catching me off guard. Makes both my mother and I grin like fools.

The smile my mother is beaming at us could launch a thousand ships and I.

Am.

In.

Hell.

10

Hollis

Dinner was hilarious.

I would relive it again and again just to see the horrified look on Buzz's face any time his mother said something about him even remotely embarrassing. Or the times his brother told a story from their childhood.

Or when his dad scolded him like he was a sullen teenager.

I don't blame him for acting like one; his entire family has been up his ass the entire time we've been here, as if he's never brought a woman home before and no one knows how to act with me sitting here.

Genevieve Wallace won't let me lift a finger.

The boys, on the other hand, have become the lackeys. Even Tripp is taking a beating this late in the game.

I watched as the two brothers cleared the table while their father was sent to the backyard to start a bonfire, where we're all sitting around now, chatting. There's a blanket in my lap and a goofy smile on my face.

This family feels like home.

"No one is driving home tonight—you're all drunk." Mrs. Wallace announces, cleaning up the graham crackers and chocolate from the s'mores we'd roasted earlier.

"Mom, I had one beer," Tripp insists, holding up two fingers and rising from his spot by the fire. "One."

Genevieve nods her dismissal. "Fine Tripp, you can go." She lets him off the hook, but not her other son. "Trace, I insist the two of you stay over.."

"Mom, it's okay. I didn't drink that much either."

It's true. Like his brother, he's had only two beers, tops, in the course of the entire evening. Plus, I can drive if I have to.

"You shouldn't be drinking at all and driving Hollis home. I raised you better than that."

He stares in disbelief, and I'll admit, her trying to get us to stay is farfetched. A ploy we can all see straight through.

Trace tries again to talk some sense into her. "Hollis has to work tomorrow."

"Do you, dear?"

I rack my brain for an excuse, but the truth is, I don't have to go into the office tomorrow—not if I don't want to. And since I have my laptop in the car, I could technically work on the way home. Plus, I hate lying, and we've been doing it all night.

"I…" I stare into the fire, the blazing orange flames calming and hypnotic. "I mean…"

"I'm fine, Mom. I'm fine."

"Trace Edward, what did I just say?"

"That's not my middle name." He politely reminds her. "That's Tripp's middle name."

"Stop arguing with your mother," says his father.

Bonfire snacks in hand, she walks off, and I can barely stifle the laughter I've been holding in during the bickering

—gazing off into the yard, toward the tree line illuminated by the bright moon, I finally laugh out loud.

"What's so damn funny?" Buzz snaps at me from his Adirondack chair.

"You."

He makes a sound in his chest, but has nothing more to say.

"She plays all of y'all like a fiddle. It's hilarious."

"What do you mean?"

"She's trying to trap us here, so we spend more time together."

"That makes no sense—she thinks we're dating."

I snort. "Oh please, she's not an idiot. Mothers weren't born yesterday. She must have sensed that we're not that close and she's trying to make us close by forcing us together. Here."

"My mother is a saint—she would never do that."

"Um—do you honestly believe that lie coming out of your mouth? Your mom is no saint. She is the puppet master, and the three of you men dance like marionettes."

"I'm a grown damn man—my mother cannot tell me what to do."

"Okay."

"She can't."

"I said, okay."

"Right, but you don't believe me. You're mocking me on the inside. I can feel it."

I nod, because he's correct. "Then go in there and tell her we're *not* staying, you big baby."

Silence.

More silence.

The sound of a car driving down a gravel road in the distance.

An owl hooting.

More silence.

"Welp. Looks like we're spending the night."

I'm dying—can barely contain my laughter.

"I hate you so much right now," he whispers.

"No you don't," I whisper back, because he doesn't.

Not even a little…

11

Trace

"This bed is tiny." Hollis is standing at the foot of my childhood bed—a full-slash-queen, sort of, the length of which I just barely fit on. The width? Just comfortable enough that I could spread out any way I wanted to.

My bedroom wasn't big enough for anything larger growing up. This was the bed we had, and this is what my parents put in their new guest room when they moved, both of them too frugal to upgrade the furniture along with their new house. Some of my trophies are even on the wall in this room, for decoration, and I suspect if I went into the other guest bedroom, I would find Tripp's bed and Tripp's trophies lining the bookshelf, just like mine are.

Kind of weird. Kind of cute.

I love my mom. She's adorable.

"Are you a size-ist, Hollis? Bigger is not always better."

"When it comes to beds, it is." She sits on the mattress, bouncing up and down a few times, testing the springs, hands running over the light gray fabric of a quilt I don't recognize—definitely new. "Do you even fit in this thing?"

"Barely. We'll both have to squeeze—it will be like playing Twister." Which I've been known to dominate.

She sharply glances up, unamused. "Oh no—no. No way we are sharing a bed this small. I don't trust you. No."

"Say no one more time." I throw my hands up innocently. "I won't touch you with these, I promise."

"I don't want you touching me with anything *else*, either."

Huh. She must be talking about my penis. "No funny business. Besides, I don't trust my mom not to be listening for any baby-making sounds. That woman is seriously desperate for grandkids."

"One of us will have to sleep somewhere else." Her eyes stray to the ground, to the beige carpet. It's new and clean, but it's...carpet, and I'm not sleeping on it. No fucking way.

"Are you suggesting I sleep on the floor in my own home?" The mere idea has me scandalized.

"No, I'm suggesting you sleep on the floor in your parents' home."

Um, I bought half of it—that makes half of it mine, doesn't it?

Obviously I don't say that out loud—she'd probably judge me for bragging about my generosity—but it's on the tip of my tongue because I have very few actual legitimate arguments against not sleeping in the same bed.

"We'll only take our bottoms off, how's that?" As far as compromises go, this one sounds pretty darn reasonable.

"I'm very fertile," Hollis informs me, flipping her hair back. "You should stay as far away from these ovaries as you can unless you want me showing up on your doorstep in nine months." She rubs her belly in slow circles and I feel myself hardening.

I'll fucking put a baby in that sexy stomach.

"Is that supposed to be a turn-off? Because I just came in my pants twice." Pause. "Congratulations, you're having twins."

Her nose and mouth contort. "You are so gross."

"Why are you acting like I'm happy about this arrangement? Do you honestly think I want to spend the night at my mom's, in a dinky bed, when I have a California King at home and four-billion-thread-count sheets?"

"Yes."

Fine. I admit it. "I couldn't have orchestrated this any better if I'd planned it myself. There, are you happy? I'm not even a little mad about it."

"What if we wait for them to go to bed, then you sneak out and go to the other bedroom?"

Shit. That makes perfect sense, except I don't want to sneak out and go to the other bedroom. I want to get handsy with Hollis and make out like teenagers in my old bed. Is that too much to ask?

"My mom stays up late. Roger bought her an iPad a few years ago, and she'll spend half the night scouring the buy-sell posts on the internet." Genevieve Wallace loves a good deal.

"So?"

"So. If she so much as hears a peep, you're going to have to make up an excuse for why you're sneaking out."

"You're the one who will be sneaking out."

Might I remind her, "This is my room."

"Fine. I'll go to the other room once she's asleep." For a few moments, she's silent. "Or, you could sleep in the bathtub."

"Um, have you seen me? I haven't fit in a regular bathtub since before my balls dropped."

Hollis stares. "I don't even know what that means."

"Puberty. It means puberty."

"You could have just said 'since I was young'."

Yeah, but where's the fun in that? I walk to the dresser on the far side of the room and pull open the top drawer.

Empty.

Pull open the second one and am relieved to find a few old t-shirts, several from high school and another few from college. Pull one out to hold up for her inspection. "This should work for pajamas, yeah?"

"Is that for me or for you?"

"You. I'll just sleep in boxers."

Her eyes drop to my waist, face turning a pretty shade of pink, lips pressing together. She's biting her tongue, and I wonder what she wants to say but won't.

I root around in the drawer and unearth a pair of mesh basketball shorts. "Do you want these, too?"

She takes the offering from my hands. "Thanks. I'll just get changed in the bathroom."

While Hollis takes her sweet time, I strip down to my boxer shorts, folding my clothes and laying them on the chair in the corner, and decide maybe I should wear a t-shirt, after all. Level the playing field, so she's not intimidated by my abs of steel and rock-hard pecs.

What is taking her so long? "What are you doing in there? Did you fall in the toilet?"

A muffled voice comes back at me through the door. "I'm not coming out. I look stupid."

Stupid? Not possible. "Just get out here—who cares what you look like? We're just going to sleep."

I hear a frustrated *ugh* followed by another silence, followed by the sound of the lock unclicking.

Then. Hollis is standing in the doorway, framed by the woodwork, light shining behind her, glowing like a goddamn angel. The clothes may be ill-fitting, but she's glorious and I can't get enough of the sight of her.

She crosses her arms, pouting. "This is ridiculous. This shirt is forty sizes too big."

It seems someone is prone to exaggeration, and it's not me. "You look fucking adorable."

She looks like a child playing dress-up, actually—the giant shirt hanging off her slender frame, navy athletic shorts down past her knees.

"I feel stupid."

"You shouldn't. I won't even see how hideous you look once we turn the lights off."

"Gee, thanks." Her eyes skim my physique, lingering on my biceps. "We are *not* turning the lights off. We're going to wait out your mother like mature adults."

Before I can give her shit for undressing me with her eyes, there's a knock at the door. Hollis and I step farther apart, guiltily, as if we were doing something wrong, about to be caught doing something we're not supposed to.

"Knock-knock, it's Mom! Are you both decent?"

Decent? *Jesus, Mom, for once could you just not embarrass me?*

My mother pushes the guest room door ajar a few inches, peeking her nose and eyes in, discovers that we are in fact dressed, and proceeds to come the rest of the way inside. "I just came to say good night and see if you needed anything before I turn the lights out."

My mother makes toward the double bed, pulling down the quilt in neat folds—just low enough for us to crawl beneath the covers—spreading the blankets neatly, smoothing out the wrinkles. Gives each of the four pillows a fluff while Hollis and I stand idly watching. Useless and mystified.

"There. All set." She looks at us expectantly, first Hollis, then me. I'm standing here like a dumb fuck, not knowing what to do with myself, my mother hovering over me like I can't get laid on my own. "Don't be shy—climb in," she urges us. "Dad and I talked about it, and we do not mind having you down the hall—you just pretend we're not there."

Pretend they're not there? Not likely. Not that we're going to be doing anything for them to overhear, because Hollis can't stand me and isn't going to let me within an inch of anything on her body. Hard facts.

If I didn't know any better, I'd think my mother was playing matchmaker; was Hollis right when she said Mom suspects we aren't an actual couple?

"Um...thank you for the turndown service, Mrs. Wallace. This was so nice of you considering Buzz shouldn't be driving." Hollis still looks unquestionably ludicrous in that t-shirt and shorts.

I snicker.

She hears me and shoots a death glare. "You better only be laughing because you're drunk."

There is a teasing glint in her eye along with the biting words; she knows damn well a couple of beers weren't going to get me drunk and that we're being held prisoner here by my meddling mother on purpose.

If looks could kill...

I watch as Hollis Westbrooke climbs into the too-small bed, in her too-big pajamas, and smushes her entire body to the far side before climbing in myself.

When I spread out on my back, Mom stands next to the door, looking so pleased, beaming down at us as only mothers who have successfully manipulated their adult children do.

"Good night, kids." She disappears. Then reappears. "Oh—should I do eggs and bacon for breakfast?"

"No Mom, we're heading out of here wicked early."

She nods her head and clicks her tongue. "So just eggs."

I groan.

"I'll be up for a few more hours if you need anything. Dad's already fallen asleep, but I've been looking at houses on Zillow and can't stop." She giggles. "Do you know how much land you can buy in Tennessee? We could be land barons!"

"Are you and Dad moving to Tennessee, Mom?"

"No sweetie, I just like looking at houses. It's not a crime."

Hollis laughs softly. "Good night, Mrs. Wallace."

And with that, my mother backs out of the bedroom, flipping down the light switch, the pitch-black room starkly quiet.

"Well. She sure knows how to play you."

"Hi—you're stuck here too, or has that escaped your notice?" Then, to rub salt in the wound: "How's that plan working out? You know, the one to keep the lights on until one of us can sneak out?"

"Shut up."

"You know I'm right. You're not going to win against my mother." I yawn to let her know how right I am and how bored.

"Whatever."

"Say 'Trace, you were right.'"

She scoffs with a huff, adjusting the pillow beneath her head. "I'm not saying that."

"But I was right. So just say it."

Silence.

"Come on, say it." I'm whispering in the dark now, the chance that my mother is lingering in the hallway rather high. She's always been like the prison warden, patrolling to keep us teenage boys in line—and prevent us from sneaking out our windows.

A cold foot touches mine, an appendage so frigid it could freeze an iceberg. Or shrink a cock three sizes.

"Jesus Christ!" I hiss. "Warn a person before you do that! What the hell are you so cold for? Dammit!"

Hollis's body begins shaking with muffled laughter. "Dear lord, could you be any more dramatic?" Her foot touches mine again, and I almost come off the mattress.

"Stop it!"

"Shh, keep it down. You're being so loud."

I am being loud, but she's being obnoxious, so… "Then stop touching me with your cold, dead, lifeless feet."

"Say *please*."

"Knock it off."

"Say *please*, Trace."

She's so annoying. "Please Trace."

Hollis flops on her side to face me. "Why are you so immature?"

"Why are you single?"

The question comes from out of nowhere, catching her off guard, and for a second I don't think she's actually going to answer.

"That's a rude thing to ask someone. Why are *you* single?"

"I told you why."

"No you didn't." She laughs a little. "So why are you single?"

"Same reasons everyone is."

"I don't know what the hell that means."

Yeah, me either. "I haven't met the one," I tell her slowly, deciding to be honest and answer the question. "I haven't met a woman who wants to date me for the right reasons. I'm not a meal ticket. I bust my ass, my body is on point, and I work all the time so I'm never around—but I hate coming home to an empty house. I want kids and it can't just be with anyone. I want to be married and I'm only doing it once."

I can't see her face, but my instincts are telling me I've stunned her speechless.

So I elaborate further. "My family needs to love her. When I'm gone—I mean when I'm traveling for work, not when I'm dead—it's important that they're there for her when I can't be home. Also, I'm trying to beat my piece-of-shit brother to the altar, so I can lord having the first grandchild over him."

First comes silence, then comes laughter. "You would not get married just to one-up your brother."

The hell I wouldn't. "I mean—I'll be in love and shit. I wouldn't just marry whoever." Considering Tripp is on track to be the world's oldest eligible bachelor, I know I'll win hands down.

Er, not that it's a contest. Or a race. Ha ha.

"You seriously want kids?" Hollis asks in the dark. "How many?"

"I don't know—four?"

"Four!" she practically shouts, and right in my damn face considering we're only inches apart. "Are you for real?"

"Why, is that not enough?"

"I can't even take you seriously right now."

"What! Four is not too many. It's perfect. Two isn't enough and three is a crowd, so they each need a buddy to hang with. My parents had three, and sometimes I wish I had another brother to gang up on Tripp with. My sister isn't an asshole like that, so she doesn't count."

"I can't even with you."

That makes two of us, three if you count my mom, who's probably listening at the door. "Alright, so now that I've spilled my guts to you, want to share?"

"Ugh, fine. Fair is fair I guess." Hollis groans, shifting on the bed. "I'm single because..." She hums, unsure. "Well. It's really difficult finding a man who isn't like my father, if I'm being honest. I grew up in this world—the baseball and the athletes. They're agents. Scouts. High-powered men, all of them...assholes. That's not what I want, no offense."

"None taken." Tons taken, actually, but I won't lie here and argue that I am not any of those guys. I'm me, and I'm fucking awesome. "You know, Hollis...you won't lose your identity if you date someone in your father's circle, in his world. Not if it's the right person."

"Well I tried that, remember?"

"If you're talking about Marlon Daymon, don't. Because that dude is a fucking douche and everyone knows it. It's not your fault he's a pile of crap, okay? You fell for the bullshit like everyone else, including some of his guy friends—he treats everyone the same, not just the women he dates." I would know, because I've witnessed it first-hand. "Not all athletes are cheaters. Not all agents are dishonest. Not all high-powered people are cutthroat."

"I just...never want to lose myself. I thought when I met someone, it would be easy. Like a partnership." Her laugh is rueful. "I'm delusional, go ahead and say it."

She's not. "That sounds nice, not delusional. Did you ever wonder what it's like being on this side of the fence? Having people—men and women—using you? Someone can know nothing about me and still want something from me. I stopped having casual sex years ago. Too many women trying to get themselves knocked up, thinking 'bout that lifelong, monthly child support check."

"That would suck."

"Yeah, well, welcome to what it's like for me to date and one of the reasons I'm single. It has nothing to do with losing myself or feeling less than and everything to do with wanting something real."

"What if a person didn't have...real boobs?"

"Hollis Westbrooke, you did *not* have a boob job." But it would be cool if she did, 'cause breasts.

A light laugh in the dark space. "Guess you'll never know."

"You're lying."

"Does it matter?"

"No." But. "Can I feel them and tell you if they're real or not?"

"You're just trying to cop a feel, you perv."

"Duh."

She moves around next to me restlessly, inadvertently bumping my hip, knocking my arm with her elbow, kicking my shin with her foot. Each touch electric.

Weird.

Hollis is flopping around like a dead fish and it's turning me on.

Wow, have I gotten easy.

Not having sex in forever will do that to ya.

Sure, when I met Miranda—Noah's girlfriend—I hit on her. It was a joke, the way I was joking when I hit on Hollis, my words mostly trash talk and bravado. All talk and no action.

Because I am done with casual sex and that is all anyone seems to want.

"How many kids do you want?"

"I'm not sure I want kids."

Hollis isn't sure she wants kids? Does. Not. Compute.

"Well if you did, how many would you have?"

A loud sigh. "I'm not sure—maybe give birth to one, then adopt one? Or two? I'm open to it, but only if it's the right person. Four seems like a lot. I also like vacations, so who knows—maybe I'm selfish."

"Hollis Westbrooke, you strike me as anything but selfish."

She groans. "I feel like I am sometimes."

"Do your parents want grandkids?"

I feel her shrug. "My mom, maybe. Dad? Highly doubt he gives a crap, unless it's one more person who can run the family business. He doesn't spend time with his own children—he isn't going to spend time with a grandkid, but it would look nice on a holiday card." She sounds a smidge bitter about it.

"You have siblings?"

"Yes—a sister and a brother. They both work for my dad."

Dang. I didn't know that.

Hollis yawns. "Can you do me a favor?"

"Depends on what it is."

"Typical," she mutters. "But seriously, I have this knot in my shoulder—can you maybe…"

"Rub it out? Sure. Which shoulder is it?"

She rolls in the dark, presenting me with her back, reaching behind me to grapple for my hand, placing it in the center, on her spine. "Here."

I spread my fingers wide and present her with some statistics. "Did you know seventy-five percent of all massages end in some form of sexual activity?"

"Are you making that up?"

"Probably. I'm guessing the number is actually higher. You should google it."

"I'm not going to get turned on while you're rubbing a knot out of my back, trust me on this."

"Wanna bet?"

"Pfft. Yes."

12

Hollis

"Wanna bet?"

"Pfft. Yes."

Famous last words of someone who knows they're going to lose. How do I know this? Easy—I'm already half turned on by our conversation, and he hasn't touched me once. Plus, I've had men massage me before and know what can happen. Me, wet.

Still.

I have a horrible knot from sleeping the wrong way last night and a strong set of hands at my disposal, ergo: massage.

"I'm pretty sure I can resist the temptation, but thanks." I sound cocky and confident.

"Bet me then."

"I don't have to make a bet to prove you're not going to get me all hot and bothered. In fact, you're probably going to give me one of those half-assed, wimpy, limp-handed jobs that leave me frustrated." Wait. That sounded horrible. "That's not what I meant. I meant you probably suck at massaging."

Buzz makes a grunting sound deep in his throat. "I've had my shoulder rubbed out enough that I assure you it will not suck. And, you are going to be turned on."

"Will not."

"You're adorable when you're clueless."

Whatever. "Fine. If I get turned on, I have to…take off my pants."

"You should take your shirt off too, if you want me to do this right. It's dark—I can't see your tits."

Tits.

I blush at the word; he says it so casually.

"So you want me to take my shirt off now, then if I lose the bet, I have to take off these shorts, too? How will you know I'm turned on and have lost?"

"You're going to tell me."

That makes me laugh. He sounds so *sure*. "You trust me not to lie?"

"Yup. I trust you one hundred percent."

Well.

Well.

That…

That gives me pause. Makes me think. Gets me… all…kinds…of…

Something.

He trusts me one hundred percent.

It's a strange but good feeling, this new sensation. I feel like we've just become friends, but—I selfishly also want to feel his hands on my skin under the guise of a back massage. Don't get me wrong, my shoulder does hurt and could use thumbs digging into the muscles, but it's not like I can't wait.

He's right, though, about me being honest; I would tell him.

"Fine. I'll tell you if I get turned on." I roll my eyes

despite the fact that he can't see my face and raise myself up, shucking off my shirt, knowing no decent rubdown can really happen through a cotton barrier. Just not the same.

The giant t-shirt comes off and I drop it next to the bed where I'll be able to easily retrieve it later. Then flop back down onto the cool, crisp bed sheets, pretending to be nonchalant about the whole thing.

I hold my breath.

Try not to, waiting.

Tense, but not from repulsion or dread. I'm tense because the anticipation is killing me, the thought of those giant, talented hands on my skin making me warm all over.

What am I doing, having him rub my back? Am I insane? A glutton for punishment? What kind of hell am I going to subject myself to, lying here pretending not to lik—

"You need to relax." Fingers graze the skin on my shoulder, hot hands, singeing where they roam. "You're so tight."

So tight? I want to quip. *If you think my skin is tight, you should feel my vagina.*

But I don't.

Instead, I squirm, loving every second of this torture, knowing my panties are going to become wet in record time.

Buzz knows what he's doing, thumbs kneading into my trapezius muscles—and I only know the technical term because for a hot minute in college, I thought I might want to be a sports trainer. Mostly to make my dad happy.

Dodged that bullet, but I won't be dodging the tingling in my lady parts.

Shit.

It's already happening and he's only been touching me for thirty seconds.

Pushing. Kneading. Rubbing.

I can feel the heel of his palm digging, making slow circles over my flesh. Trails down to my rhomboid. Pushes. More pressure, around and around and around, causing my eyes to become half-lidded and drowsy.

"Mmm," I moan, purely by accident.

"What was that?" His hot breath warms the crook of my neck, just below my ear. "That distinctly sounded like a moan of, oh—I don't know…pleasure?"

"Dream on, pal."

Buzz presses his fingers into my back, releasing a few knots. Again. Again. Again. "Wow, you really needed this. You should make an appointment with someone who knows what they're doing." He leans in again. "I could set you up with the team's trainer—he does private massages on the side."

"Uhhh…" Another moan escapes my mouth. "I'm g-good."

"You sure?" His voice is a melodic hum or maybe I'm imagining it?

My neck tilts, loving the vibrations from his chest against my back every time he makes a sound.

"How does this feel? Too much pressure?" All fingers of both hands are squeezing gently, the tension in my shoulders loosening as the throbbing between my legs gets worse.

"It's good. A good amount of pressure," I respond dumbly. What's he saying? All I can hear is the sound of my crotch telling him to do it harder—I can handle more.

Massaging. More massaging.

Definitely only more of that.

My brain stops working. His hands haven't stopped moving. My panties are no longer dry.

I arch my back.

Tip my head forward, hair hitting the mattress, giving his roaming hands better access. My boobs begin to ache.

Buzz's hands skim my rib cage, one hundred percent out of massaging bounds. Down my hip, skimming the waistband of the mesh basketball shorts I'm wearing, then up again.

He can't see it, but I bite my lower lip.

I want his hands all over.

My breasts, my ass, between my legs.

No, Hollis—if you give him the cookie, you'll never hear from this guy again. That is what guys like this do. Give him what he wants and he'll ghost you.

So what? I argue. *You don't want to date him anyway. You want him out of your life, remember?*

Do you though? Do you really want him out of your life?

You wouldn't be lying in this bed beside him if you did, you liar.

I've always been good at lying to myself. Stop trying to stop me, bitch.

Whoa. *Cool it with the internal babble, you psychopath.*

Oblivious to the ramblings inside my head, Buzz Wallace—the best closer in the entire professional baseball league—strokes my skin and gently traces his fingertips along my spine, slowly moving over every bump. Every curve.

I shiver.

I feel his pecs crowd my back. "Are you turned on yet?"

"What was that statistic you gave me before?"

"Ninety percent of all massages lead to sex."

I softly laugh. "That is not what you said."

"I'm close though, give or take a few percentage points." He waits a few more seconds, hands treading perilously close to my side boob. "So? Are you?"

I want to groan, but that will give me away. I want to

deny it, but that would be lying—and I promised I'd be honest. Instead, I go with a half-admission. "Sort of."

"Sort of? You are or you aren't. Which one is it?"

Are.

Am.

"Yes."

Buzz laughs. "Hollis, just admit you're turned on or I'll remove my hands from your body."

Shit—I don't want him doing that! It feels fantastic, and it's been forever; Marlon never rubbed my back or did anything but squish my boobs, thinking that was adequate foreplay.

Wrong!

Then Trace whispers, "You know you want to take your pants off."

Ugh, why did he have to go and say that! Admitting I'm wet and turned on is like admitting I want him to feel me up—which I do! My pride is a brutal mistress, rearing her ugly head, causing the words to get trapped in my throat.

My head twitches. Nods.

"What was that? I couldn't hear you. Are you saying you're turned on or that you want to take your pants off? Either way—it's a win-win for me."

"I didn't say a single thing," I clarify, buying time.

"You nodded."

"No I didn't." I did though, and he knows it.

"Hollis Westbrooke, are you lying to me right now? You know there's a penalty for that, right?"

There is? "What is it?" That might be better than admitting I'm turned on, better than admitting my panties are wet and everything down south of my border is on fire.

"You have to pick one spot on your body for me to kiss."

"That sounds more like assault."

"Shit. Oh my god, that's not—I didn't mean. Never mind, I'm sorry." He yanks at the covers and rolls off the bed, standing next to it as if I've just tried to poke him with a scalding-hot iron. "Fuck."

"Wait—what are you doing? I was joking."

"That's not a joke, Hollis."

"Okay, but where are you going? Your mom is outside waiting for us to slip away." I pull the remaining blanket up to cover my naked breasts, seeking out his profile in the dark.

"I'll sleep on the floor. I should never have said that."

Shit. Shit, shit, shit—I didn't think he'd take me seriously, and I didn't think he'd fly off the bed like it was ablaze. I didn't think he'd care about how I felt, not like this.

I feel terrible!

God I'm an asshole...

"Come back to bed."

"Nope—I'm good." He flops down on the carpet beside me, spreading out the blanket. "There's no room up there anyway. You take the bed and I'll be right as rain down here. Good night."

Well.

This escalated quickly.

I'm flat on my back now, topless, staring up at the ceiling, racking my brain for a solution. Sure, it's for the best that he's not on the bed, tempting me with that warm breath and those big, strong hands and that smooth skin. And cute laugh and dumb jokes and straight white teeth I can't see in the dumb dark.

Reaching below the covers with both arms, my hands push down the waistband of these terrible bottoms, sliding them all the way off.

"I'm turned on." My voice travels to him in the dark, along with the mesh basketball shorts, which I blindly toss in his direction. "You win."

"Fuck me sideways. Are you naked?"

"No."

"Underwear don't count," he tells me.

"Do granny panties count as underwear?"

"Yep. Those are hot as fuck."

I laugh quietly. "Uh…then yes, I'm naked."

"Why are you telling me this? To torment me now that I'm marooned in Siberia?"

I laugh again. "Has anyone ever called you a drama queen before?"

"Literally everyone who knows me has called me a drama queen at some point."

He makes me giggle; I bite down on my bottom lip, debating my next move.

"I'm cold," I blurt out.

I can almost hear him rolling his eyes. "You are not. It's hot as balls in here—I think my mom wanted us both naked, hashtag babymaker."

The fact that he says hashtag, as if it's a word, still cracks me up. It's obnoxious but…endearing.

"Your mother would not want me accidentally getting pregnant."

"The hell she wouldn't! If we had condoms in here, she would probably poke holes in all of them."

"Dramatic."

"I know my mother—she's a snake in the grass."

"But you'd do anything for her, and that's why I'm here —you wanted to show her that you are capable of having a relationship with someone normal." The truth rolls off my tongue as if I've just discovered the cure for an incurable disease. It all makes sense now! The reason he bribed-slash-guilted me into coming! "So you dragged me here for this sham of a relationship to make her happy."

Buzz grunts, and I can hear him rolling over. Punches his pillow a few times, displeased.

"It's fine. I won't tell anyone you're a decent human bean."

"I'm not a decent human being!" he disputes in a huff.

"I said bean, not being. Pay attention."

The joke catches up to him, and from out of the dark, a pillow hits me in the thigh.

"Stop flirting," I demand. *I'm starting to really like you.*

He stops flirting and I'm back to staring at the ceiling, frustrated by our lack of proximity.

Frustrated by my own game of running hot and cold with him; I wonder if he's noticed. I wonder if it's frustrating him, too. *Why is he bothering with me at all?* A million women would kill to be in this bedroom right now, and the poor bastard chooses the one woman who resists him at every turn.

Buzz Wallace doesn't give a shit about my father and who he is; he hasn't really asked about him once. He doesn't give a shit about the silver spoon I had in my mouth growing up. He doesn't give a shit about what kind of car I drive, how big his friends' houses are, how—

Houses.

"Buzz?"

"Hmm?"

"Did you buy this house for your parents?"

He's quiet a few heartbeats. "Why are you asking me that?"

"I'm wondering." Many athletes do that for their folks, the people who make the sacrifices for their children's success over their own.

More silence.

Then,

"Yes."

My ovaries begin clenching from the injustice of it all. Why, God? Why! Why make the one man I want to resist so gosh darn irresistible? It's all I can do not to shake my fist at the sky like a super weirdo.

"That's...that was sweet of you."

"I guess." He sounds uncomfortable talking about it. "My brother and I went halvsies—well, I paid a thousand dollars more, so like...I paid more." He sniffs, indignant. "Not that it matters, but I did."

I chuckle. He is such a brat about his brother—it must have been hell for his mother raising those two.

I want to climb out of bed and join him on the floor, but what reasonable excuse do I have for going down where it's uncomfortable and cold?

Not a one.

My brain goes around and around. My teeth? Dig into my bottom lip as I stew. Finally, I roll off the bed, dressed in nothing but my underwear, feeling my way around the bed to where I think Buzz is lying on the floor, with my pajama bottoms. Er, shorts.

I step on a body part and he yelps. "What the fuck! That was my ankle."

Crap. "Oh my god, I am so sorry."

"What are you doing?"

"Can I have my pants back?"

Trace

"Can you have your *pants* back?" I feel around in the dark, hands blindly maneuvering their way along the carpet. It's an itchy spot to be for the night, but the last thing I want is for Hollis to think I'm some pervert who cannot keep his hands to himself. I don't need her to think I have no boundaries.

"You know—my shorts. The shorts."

"Are you wearing clothes right now?"

"I told you—I'm wearing underwear." Even in the dark, I can make out her silhouette, her outline backlit by the outside security lights. "What are you wearing?" She sounds like she's talking to Jake from State Farm.

"Um…the same thing I had on when my mom so rudely turned off the lights."

"Oh." It sounds like she's biting her lip. Sounds a bit disappointed, or maybe I'm imagining things. I have been down here for what seems like hours, exiled alone with no food, no water, no light source. Naked and afraid, almost. Minus the naked part.

"Here are your bottoms." The shorts she was wearing

are in my hand, clenched in my fist, and I hold them up as an offering. "Try not to crush my balls like you crush my dreams." I can sort of see her getting closer, slowly—hesitantly—then lowering herself to her hands and knees. "Are you crawling?"

"Yes. I don't want to crush your balls." Her hands explore, feebly feeling along my calves. Knees. "Oh! Is this you?"

"Yeah that's me." I hold my breath as her hands roam. Searching but not really, because she knows she's found me, and if she'd just sit there, I could hand her the shorts. They're still suspended above the floor, in my waiting fist.

I almost forgot for a second that she's not wearing clothes—why she hasn't put her shit back on is beyond me. If she's trying to gross me out, it's not working. It's the opposite of working.

Still, I don't say the magic words: *Hollis, I have your shorts in my hand. Hold still and I'll give them to you.*

Nope.

I want to see what she does instead, and maybe get a kiss or two from her in the process. You gonna fault a guy for hoping? It could happen!

I wish.

Rather than asking for the bottoms, Hollis puts her hands on my chest. Carpet. Patting the spot beside me, then leaning forward and yanking the bedspread off the mattress, dragging it to the floor.

"What'd you do that for?"

"I'm cold."

"Then put your clothes back on." Number one on the list of things I'll never say again.

She doesn't listen, hunkering down beside me and pulling the blanket up, over her shoulders, and since I'm cold too, I snag a corner. "Mind if I steal some of this?"

When she throws the comforter over my legs and scoots closer, my brain spontaneously combusts from the skin-on-skin contact. Our legs are touching! She is touching my leg with her leg!

"You know what I think would be fun?" She's whispering now, tentatively, words leaving her lips at an excruciatingly slow pace.

"I could think of a thousand things that would be fun. Do you mean right now, or like—tomorrow?"

She laughs. "Right now."

"Um." I can think of a thousand things that would be super fun right now, but I highly doubt they're the same things she's got in her mind. "What?"

"When..." Hollis clears her throat. "Is the last time you..."

She stops.

"The last time I...?" What? The last time I what? THE LAST TIME I WHAT! *SPIT IT OUT, HOLLIS, FOR THE LOVE OF GOD.*

The last time you went streaking in your parents' yard? The last time you played twenty questions? The last time you made shadow puppets?

What?

After a long, torturous silence, "Never mind."

I stare up at the ceiling, unable to see it but scowling just the same. I wanted to know what she was going to say, but I'm not going to press her.

I shrug in the dark. "Suit yourself." Or tell me. Whatever.

The quiet room is deafening. My hands? Lying next to my sides, my head resting on a flat pillow my mother needs to replace, pronto.

This floor sucks even harder now that Hollis has joined me. What is she doing, trying to kill me with her close proximity? Knowing her, she is. She loves fucking with me, that much is obvious.

"Trace?"

"Hm?"

"Don't you feel like we're doing something we shouldn't? I feel like a teenager sneaking around your parents' house."

That makes me smile. "It does kind of feel like that, in a way, but not really." I never brought girls home in high school—never really dated anyone, not that girls didn't chase me. I might have been a walking, talking hormone, but my parents were strict, and I needed a baseball scholarship, so that was the only thing on my mind as a teenager. Not sneaking girls into the house, or having them over and copping a feel while Mom was in the kitchen preparing snacks.

"Feels taboo," she adds.

"We're not doing anything but lying here." As my dick would so helpfully like to point out, lying flat against my thigh, limp and defeated.

"No, we're not." Pause. "But…"

"But what?"

"What if…"

My dick twitches curiously. "What if…what?"

Hollis repositions herself so she's facing me now, resting on her hip and elbow, breasts brushing against the blanket. I can't feel them but I can *feel them*, if you catch my drift.

"Wouldn't it be fun if we…I mean, since we're both awake…"

"If we what? Fucked?" Little Buzz puffs out his dick chest.

"Pump the brakes—I haven't even kissed you yet."

Yet. She said *yet*, which means she's planning to, which means there's a snowball's chance in hell.

"What if we, like...dry humped. Kept it old school. You know how we—"

I grab her and pull, hauling her atop me, still wrapped in her blanket. "Yup, I'm game. Let's dry hump. Fantastic idea."

Hollis is laughing, quietly gasping for air, hands on my chest, straddling me now, ass on lower abdomen. She's tiny —compared to me—and my hands find her waist. Naked waist. Smooth, warm waist.

Awkwardly, she discards the comforter from the bed, pulling and prying it out from under her so it no longer separates us, and I groan when my hands can cup her ass.

"You should kiss me or something," she tells me, so bossy.

"Lower your face," I tell her back.

Her hair hits my chest first, tickling my pecs, breath mingling with mine.

I don't move a muscle.

She is in complete control.

Her lips are gentle, pressing against my mouth once she finds it in the dark, pushing delicately. Testing. One kiss, then another, and little by little, I open my mouth.

Offer up the tip of my tongue until she touches it with hers, the dick in my boxers hardening with every stroke. With every wet, teasing stroke of her tongue in my mouth, her hips begin to move.

Hollis shifts her body. Slides it down a few inches until her pussy is on top of my dick, the tip flirting with her slit.

She moans.

I don't move a muscle.

"Put your hands on my ass," she instructs. "And...pull me back and forth."

We both groan, and I'm as giddy as a horny fifteen-year-old. Just as revved up, too, waiting for more instructions.

"Now what?"

Hollis doesn't tell me, just rolls her hips. The only things between us are her sheer panties and my boxers, which are laughably thin. We might as well be naked. It's not the same, but it's close. Blessedly close.

But not the same.

But close.

Shut the fuck up. Quit arguing with yourself, idiot—focus.

Above me, Hollis clears her throat, trying to find some words. "Would you...put your hands on my..."

"On your what?" I breathe out. Hips? Ribs? Shoulders? *Be specific—I need all the help I can get.*

"My..."

I can't see her tits, but now I can feel them, because she's moved my hands from her ass...to her rib cage...all the way up to her breasts. Her high, perky boobs—from what I can feel in the dark, anyway—and I'm tempted to flip the light on.

I want to see it all.

Her nipples are stiff. Her back is straight. Her head? Tipped back.

Hips grind over me, working their way over my dick and balls, smushing them into my pelvis, but who actually gives a fuck? It feels amazing. It does its job, creating friction and pleasure—the way it did back before I lost my virginity, when a quick dry fuck was the only safe way to get my rocks off.

I was a virgin late in life—seventeen before I lost it to a college freshman after a campus tour. I didn't get a scholarship to play baseball at the school, but I did get laid for the very first time in the dorm rooms there. Ahh, the memories.

Hollis moans when I softly caress her boobs, the pads of my fingers slowly stroking, brushing over the tips, barely making contact with her skin.

She covers my hands with hers. Then.

Leans her body down and finds my mouth in the dark.

Our kiss is open-mouthed and hot—tons of tongue. Frantic, but with a languid approach. Wet, for sure. Kind of dirty in a *This is our first kiss but we're dry humping in your parents' guest room* kind of way. Hot and heavy but tentative and hesitant, if those things can be combined.

Feels taboo.

We've been holding back since we met—she's lying to herself if she doesn't agree. Hollis Westbrooke has wanted to stick her tongue down my throat—if even to shut me up —since the pool party at Noah Harding's house, or my name isn't Trace Wallace.

Her mouth tastes like heaven. Her tits *feel* like heaven in my hands. Her pussy rubbing against my cock? Heaven. No other word can describe it, and I won't even try because I'm borderline brain-dead at this point, all the blood having drained into my dick.

I am a brainless, spineless puddle of hormones.

On top of me, Hollis grinds. Grinds her hips, hands braced on the carpet for support, head lowered, hair brushing the side of my face. I can hear her soft moans, the frustration in her breathy sighs. She wants a release. She wants her panties off. She wants to fuck me, but won't let herself.

Especially not in my parents' house.

My hands are still on her hips. And if I reach down and pull her underwear aside so my cock is one step closer to being inside her, well—so be it. I'm not hearing any complaints from her, just

whimpering and whispers and unsatisfied groans.

Hey, it's not my fault we're not having sex right now, but this is a girl I haven't put the moves on. I'm not about to ruin it by asking if I can slide inside.

One more thrust.

Two.

Hollis moans louder, head collapsing on my chest, and I lie there, stunned.

"Did you…just come?"

She seems to be hesitating. "Yes?"

"From dry humping?"

"Yes." She sighs again, her body a limp mass on top of my chest. "Did you?"

"Uh, you would know if I came because there would be jizz all over my boxers." To my own ears, I sound jealous, because I am. I wanted to come, too! It's not fair that she's the only one to have an orgasm! It's not like I can beg her for a blowie to finish me off.

Hollis grunts. Lays her head on my chest and exhales another sigh. I give her a gentle nudge.

"Hey."

She doesn't move. Only gives me a suspiciously sleepy-sounding, "Hmm?"

"Are you falling asleep?" I poke her rib cage.

No response.

"You are *not* seriously falling asleep." I say it to no one, because just then, a soft snore escapes her throat, indicating that she has, indeed, fallen asleep. We didn't even have sex and she's pulling a guy move on me by passing out? This gets worse and worse.

What the H. "*Un*fucking*believeable.*"

I lie here a few minutes, debating my next move: lie

here and let her sleep on top of me, or roll her over and onto the floor. Or…I can try to scoop her up and put her back on the bed, where she'll have a better night's sleep than she will on the floor.

I lie here.

Longer still, enjoying her breathing and the steady rhythm of her heart beating against my chest.

Then finally, I roll to my side, taking her along with me, gently resting her beside me on the carpet, reaching for the blankets and comforter, pulling those up and over us.

She snuggles into my body, ass crushed against my crotch, little-spooning me in her sleep.

I rest my hand on her hip, atop the blanket. Give her hair a whiff and lay my cheek on my bicep, because I've slid the pillow under Hollis's sleeping head.

Every so often, a snore escapes her lips. Not the chainsaw 'I can't sleep' kind of snore, but the soft, steady, cute kind. A cute snore—what does she do that *isn't* adorable?

I get comfortable, although it's hard—pun intended. I didn't come the way she did from dry fucking, so my dick is semi-stiff, poking into her ass cheeks, straining for some kind of relief. But I can't rise to use the bathroom, and I can't very well finish myself off here while she's passed out. 'Cause. That. Is. Creepy. As. *Fuck.*

I content myself with peacefully cradling her while she rests, knowing she may never let me get this close to her again. I wonder what possessed her in the first place, to get down out of the bed practically naked and straddle me.

Boredom? Curiosity?

Did the dark give her courage she doesn't have when she has to face me in the light of day?

I cannot fall asleep, and the hours tick by. Slowly watch the sun rising outside the bedroom window, the sounds of the household waking up coming from downstairs. I imagine my dad shuffling around the kitchen in his bathrobe and house shoes as he's always done, brewing a fresh pot of coffee while he does a crossword puzzle. Enjoying the alone time before Mom wakes up and starts making demands. *Roger's honey-do list.*

Sometime around six o'clock, Hollis stirs. During the night, she shifted to face me, and I watch as her eyelids begin to gradually part. Blinking herself awake like a scene in a movie—preferably a romantic movie, where the couple makes out and kisses good morning, maybe has quick morning sex.

She's still wordlessly blinking up at me.

That can't be good.

"Morning." I smile at her.

"Did I sleep down here last night?"

Obviously. "Uh…yes." Does she have amnesia?

"Oh." Her eyes shift to the pillow. "Did you put this under my head?"

"Yes."

She pauses. "Thank you."

"Are you cold?"

Her eyes widen—she's just realized she has no clothes on, other than her panties, and I swear she must be blushing. "No. You must have kept me warm."

I grin. "I'm a hot box. That's what my mom always called me growing up—I don't think I ever wore pajamas to bed. Naked as a jaybird."

"Where are my clothes?"

"Uh—your side of the bed, I imagine." I stare at her as best I can in the dim, early morning light. "You weren't drunk last night, were you?"

Shit. Is that the reason she was all over me? Alcohol? I know I had a few beers with Tripp before he left, but I don't remember Hollis tipping any back. Definitely not enough to get her drunk—not to the point where she'd have no memory.

"Sorry, I'm just so tired." She yawns. "I'm going to need a nap today."

Outside, the sun creeps up a little higher in the sky. "I'll leave so you can get dressed."

I rise, careful not to ogle her; it's difficult because she's just so damn pretty and I could stare at her all damn day. Right now she needs her privacy. Clearly she's embarrassed about getting physical with me.

With no backward glance, I leave the room, quietly closing the door behind me.

14

Hollis

"**N**ever have I ever made out with a guy in his parents' house."

I peek over at Buzz, who has his eyes trained on the road, and I replay his question in my mind. Have I ever made out with a guy in his parents' house? "Never."

He glances at me. "Never? Not even when you were younger?"

"Nope." Let's see, how do I explain this… "I grew up with parents who weren't all that strict, because they weren't really around. But, since everyone knew my dad—and my grandpa—not many guys wanted to mess with me. I mean, they wanted to date me because they liked going to the stadium and sitting in the owner's box to see the games, but none of them actually liked me. I questioned everyone's intentions, even as a kid."

It's a heavy answer for so early in the morning, but he started the game, so he gets what he gets.

"Dang. Okay, fair enough—makes total sense."

We're quiet for a few miles while I rack my brain.

"Would you rather walk in on your parents having sex or have your parents walk in on you having sex?"

Buzz opens his mouth to speak. Closes it. "Those are two horrible options."

"You have to choose."

"There is no winning."

"Choose."

He clamps his mouth shut, pressing his lips together. "I'd rather walk in on my parents, I guess—then I could clamp my eyes shut and not have to listen to my mother forever remind me that she walked in on me having sex. I would never live it down."

I have to laugh at that. "And you would let them live it down if you walked in on Roger and Genevieve?"

"Rog and Gen don't have sex." He shakes his head. No.

"They probably do—Rog seems spry yet," I tease. "You boys probably take after him."

"First of all, don't. Second of all, ew."

"Did you really just say ew?"

He nods. "I did and I'll say it again—ew." Buzz continues watching the road, then says, "Never have I ever dated a professional athlete."

I side-eye him; how quickly they forget. "Duh, I dated Marlon for five of the worst minutes of my life."

"Oh that's right, I forgot."

We both laugh. "I take it you haven't?"

"Nope."

Hmm. He is way too cocky.

"Never have I ever dated a celebrity." I'm certain I've got him with that one, but his smirk is confident.

"Nope."

"Oh come on, you must have! Don't all athletes date models and movie stars?"

"Not me."

"I swear I saw you with some singer when I was—"

"Stalking me online? Nice! But no. We were photographed together, but we didn't actually date. Our agents set it up—that happens a lot, actually. Anyway, she was a nutcase. I didn't even bang her."

"Bang her," I deadpan. "How eloquent."

"Sorry, I meant screw."

He is too much. "Would you rather date someone with a high-pitched voice or someone with a masculine voice?"

Buzz looks irritated. "Where are you getting these godawful questions?"

I scoff. "Please, these are standard-issue would-you-rathers."

"I can't imagine which one would be less heinous. Which would I want whispering in my ear…?" He shudders. "Jesus, I don't know. Masculine? No. High-pitched."

"Final answer?"

A jerky nod. "Final answer. And why do I feel like this is going to somehow happen to me now?" He smiles over at me. "I like your voice though—it's cute."

My voice is cute?

I must be scowling because he adds, "And sexy."

I relax into the passenger seat and wait patiently for him to ask me a question.

I don't have to wait long.

"Never have I ever dated someone who wasn't my type on paper."

This makes me look over at him and stare, studying his profile. He is intently watching the road, but…that's such an odd thing to say, and I'm not sure what he means.

"Huh?"

"I've never dated someone who wasn't my type on paper—meaning, just because they look a certain way,

146

doesn't mean they don't still have the qualities I'm looking for in a partner."

I'm still confused. "So you're saying those model-looking types you've gone out with or have slept with are secretly rocket scientists, too?"

Buzz laughs. "I'm not saying that. I'm talking about dating someone—being in a relationship. Going out for drinks or sleeping with a person doesn't equal dating them, being in a relationship with them. Like there are women you sleep with and women you bring home to your mo—"

Oh god. He's talking about me.

I'm the kind you bring home to your mother, apparently, even if it's for show.

"Then I guess I usually do date my type, yes, if that's what you're getting at with that convoluted never-have-I-ever."

He seems satisfied with that answer. "So what is your type then? On paper, if you could invent the perfect man."

This gives me pause, though it's something I've thought a lot about since the Marlon incident. 'The Big Mistake of Last Year,' I'll call it. "He has to be employed. I'm not into anyone who is already retired. They have to have a *purpose.*"

"Uh, do you know lots of dudes our age who are retired?"

I roll my eyes. "Hi, my parents' circle of friends is full of trust fund and Wall Street babies who have too much money and way too much free time. Need I mention the retired pro-athletes who get washed up by the time they're in their late thirties and can't play anymore? Not all of them become sportscasters. Some of them wind up doing endless yard work at their McMansions and driving their wives insane." I would know because I've been around it my entire life.

"Fair enough."

I realize how harsh that might have sounded. "I just mean I'd love to be with someone who has goals." God, now I sound fickle. "*Any* goals."

Shit. Stop talking, Hollis—you're making it worse.

"Yeah, me too. I don't want to be with someone who wants to stay home and look pretty all day."

I scrunch up my face. Is he being serious? I know he's said he wants someone to want him for him, but, "Never have I ever not wanted to be married with a family."

I immediately want to slap a hand over my mouth; did those words really come out of me? We're ten minutes into the ride back, for crying out loud! *What are you saying, Hollis?? This is supposed to be lighthearted and fun, not serious!*

Unfortunately, he's puzzled.

"Wait—are you asking if I've ever wanted to be married with a family, or are you asking if I've *never* wanted to be married with a family? I'm confused."

I want to die. "Forget it. It made no sense."

He repeats the phrase a few times then takes a breath. "No, I think I get what you're saying. And yeah, I've always wanted a family and kids."

"Kids, or a *wife* and kids?"

"Is there a difference?"

"I think so. Some guys want to be dads but not husbands."

He rears back a bit. "Uh, okay…like who?"

"I don't know—guys?"

Buzz laughs. "Not this guy. I want to be a dad and a husband, just like my dad."

"But when would you have the time?" I'm stereotyping him again; I know it, and he knows it, but I can't seem to make myself stop, and I suddenly loathe Marlon Daymon for doing this to me.

Don't blame an ex for something you allowed to happen, and don't hold it against every man after him. It's not anyone else's fault Marlon is a bag of shit.

"When will I have the time? When does anyone have the time? You make time." He looks over at me. "Are you asking this because your dad was too busy to spend time with you growing up? Or because you dated a piece-of-crap ballplayer who didn't know your worth?"

Both. Neither.

Both.

Damn him. Why is he so insightful? Yet another remarkable trait emerging after spending more time with him. Ugh. STOP BEING AMAZING, DAMMIT! *I'm trying not to like you!*

"My dad was too busy for us growing up." I squirm a little in my seat, not wanting to badmouth my father but honest enough to admit life at the Westbrooke house was far from a fairy tale. "He wasn't around, and…I'm pretty sure he probably cheated on my mom." Only she'd never admit that she knew, and my brother and sister and I would never ask.

We have our suspicions though.

Everyone in our household lived in my father's shadow, and I will not live like that any longer.

Which is why I won't date an athlete working for him. Which is why I am paving my own path. Which is why I am keeping my distance from Buzz Wallace—he's dangerous to my future plans.

Cute, but dangerous.

Don't be so dramatic, Hollis. He's hardly a danger.

He isn't genuinely interested…is he?

"You've gotten real quiet over there. Is everything okay?" His voice is low and gentle, his hand on the center console. I stare down at his long fingers, the tan hands peppered with dark hair.

"I'm good. Just thinking. I didn't mean to get so serious, sorry."

"Hey, don't worry about it. We all need to vent sometimes."

"Do you?"

He shrugs. "Not really. When I need to blow off steam, I work at one of the properties I'm fixing up."

That's right; I forgot he does that.

"What are you working on now?"

Another shrug. "A bungalow in Walnut Creek. It was a real shithole, but it's coming along."

Walnut Creek is a suburb of Chicago, up-and-coming with a decent school district. Cute little town.

"Did you gut it yourself?"

"Mostly. I have some help on occasion, but nothing blows off steam like demolition work, or pounding a nail into a two-by-four, or grouting tile."

Wow. "You can do all that?"

"Yeah—I'm a licensed contractor."

"What!"

"I went to school for business, but a few years ago went and got my contractor's license in the state of Illinois so I'd have something to fall back on. Just in case."

Huh. "Just in case what?"

"In case the baseball thing didn't work out."

For some reason, I find that funny and laugh. "Um— it's working out."

"But you never know—nothing is a sure thing. What if I get hurt and break my hand tomorrow? Then what?"

"Well, then you're screwed because you won't be able to do demolition or swing a hammer to drive a nail into a two-by-four."

He tilts his head. "Shit, I never thought of it that way."

I preen. "That's what I'm here for."

"That's more doom and gloom than uplifting motivation."

We laugh.

"Do you have more than one project going?" I'm sincerely interested.

"Three."

"Three?!" Why do I keep shouting? *Tone it down a notch, for crying out loud. He's going to think you're a lunatic.*

But he laughs instead, and I relax. "Yup, three. The one in Walnut Creek, a studio downtown, and a brownstone in Bucktown."

"And you live closer to Noah Harding?"

He nods. "My house isn't as fancy as his though."

As if that matters. "Does that bother you?"

"Empty houses bother me."

"Why?"

"They're not supposed to be empty—they're supposed to be filled with people. Families and shit."

There he goes again, melting my ovaries with this roundabout talk of wives and kids and white picket fences.

It makes me shiver, and he notices. "You cold?"

Instead of admitting that his words turn me on the slightest bit, I lie. "Yeah."

He leans forward and hits the air conditioning, turns it off. "Better?"

Great, now I'm hot. "So much better."

Satisfied, he drives on.

∿

Trace

Mom: *Hey sweetie! Hope you made it home okay, haven't heard from you in a few hours...*

Trace: *Hey Mom—yup, made it home about an hour ago.*

Mom: *And Hollis? Is she with you?*

Trace: *No, I dropped her off at her place.*

Mom: *Oh.*

Trace: *Lol you sound disappointed. Should I run and bring her back?*

Mom: *Haha very funny. Don't be cheeky.*

Mom: *Did she have a good time?*

Trace: *Yeah, she thinks you're a great cook.*

Mom: *Well we loved meeting her. When will you bring her back?*

Trace: *I don't know, Ma. I could have done without you dragging out the photo albums and TUCKING US INTO BED.*

Mom: *I was just making sure she was comfortable.*

Trace: *What if I had been naked when you opened the door?*

Mom: *I knew you wouldn't be. I raised you better than that.*

Trace: *But I could have been.*

Mom: *Why are you so stubborn? Just like your brother.*

Trace: *Mom...*

Mom: *What's her number, dear? I was going to invite her to sit with us at your next game*

Trace: *MOM DON'T YOU DARE*

Mom: *Why are you shouting?*

Trace: *MOM DO NOT*

Mom: *I'm sorry. Did you say something?*

Trace: *MOTHER. DO NOT.*

Trace: *MOM.*

Trace: *Answer me!*

Three hours later...

Trace: *I hate myself right now.*

15

Hollis

The last thing I wanted to do was another lunch with Dad, but—here I am. Correction: here I am at lunch with my dad, brother, and sister, who are all at the stadium this week, working on whatever it is they work on up in their offices.

Like the last time, Dad wants me to walk him back to his office so we can chat privately, without my siblings listening in.

He goes straight to his desk and plops down, checking his phone and email before giving me his attention, so I grab a magazine on the table next to my chair and thumb through it.

"Give me one quick second," he says while tapping out a text message.

I wait.

And wait.

He sets his phone down, folding his hands in front of him on the surface of his desk. "There."

I wonder what he's about to say, assuming it's important since he dragged me all the way up here to say it.

"So." The word lingers in the air between us. "Trace Wallace."

Ah. There it is.

To be honest, I'm surprised he's bringing this up. Dad has never really shown a vested interest in my dating life, personal life, or otherwise. He cared where I went to college. Cared where I got my master's. Cared where I bought my first house (using the money I inherited when my grandmother died).

But he's never said a word about men because he's never been privy to their identities. Not to mention, I'm not actually dating Buzz Wallace, and if he'd done his homework, he would know that. *He wouldn't be ambushing me for information.*

There are a few ways I can go with this.

Play dumb: *Trace? What about him?*

Play really, really dumb: *Trace who?*

Or, sit it out and wait for him to elucidate his point, forcing him to spell out what information he's looking for me to spew.

I choose the latter.

"I hear you've spent some time with him."

I nod. "We're friends."

Dad studies my face with an unwavering expression. Poker face. Stone-faced. Whatever you want to call it, that's how he's looking at me. *Watching* me.

The clock on his bookshelf ticks; I can actually hear it. It's one of those wooden numbers you bring back from Europe and have to wind in the back with a gold key. Shiny, polished, worth a small fortune, and someone will inherit it when he dies.

It ticks.

It tocks.

Tick.

Tock.

See, if there's one thing I learned from my dad, it's this: the less you say, the less you give away. People talk when they're nervous. People talk when they lie. People talk and give more information than they should, because they're nervous, and that's what he wants me to do right now—talk.

So. I say nothing at all.

I have nothing to defend; I've done nothing wrong.

He had no problem with me dating Marlon Dickhead —he had to have known, though we never talked about it openly. So why would he care that I've hung out with Buzz Wallace a few times? And how the heck did he find out?

There are rats scurrying everywhere.

"Well?" he asks.

"Well what?"

Wrong thing to say. "Why are you friends with him?"

"Why not? He's a nice guy."

Dad's lips press together and turn white. "He's the best closer we've had in ten years—he doesn't need distractions."

Ah. So this isn't about my best interests; it's about the team's.

The whole thing makes me laugh. "I'm hardly the kind of girl men get distracted by, Dad, but thanks for the compliment."

"Do you think this is a joke?"

"Um, kind of?" The words slip out before I can stop them, because honestly—this is the most ridiculous conversation. If my father thinks Buzz Wallace—one of the best-looking and best players on our team—is interested in me romantically? He's delusional.

But even if he was, what difference would it make?

Does Dad not want me to be happy? Does he not want me to find love?

Evidently not with one of the Chicago Steam.

I'm insulted.

"I'd love it if you weren't friends with him during the season." *Or the off-season.* He doesn't say it, but there's no doubt he's thinking it.

Lovely.

"What kind of friend would I be if I just ghosted someone because my dad told me to?"

"Ghosted?"

Oh that's right—my dad is old and out of touch with what we young people are doing these days. "It means shut someone out. Stop talking to them for no reason and not tell them about it. Block them."

He nods, satisfied. "Good. Do that."

"Dad! I am not ghosting Buzz! He hasn't done anything!"

"He doesn't have to—he has a job to do and I don't want you getting in the way."

"I am so flattered you think I'm capable of—"

"Hollis Maxine Westbrooke." He slams his fists on the desk and rises. "I am not asking."

Whoa. He is being such an asshole, throwing out that horrible middle name and making demands.

"I'm not a child."

"Then stop acting like one."

I rise. "How am I acting like a child? You're the one who has an issue with me being friends with a player. It's not even a big deal—you're making it a big deal and now I'm pissed!"

His eyes get wide. "Don't curse at me."

"Pissed is not a curse word, Thomas." I grab my purse and head for the door.

"And don't call me Thomas—I am your father."

I roll my eyes like I'm fifteen. "You can't tell me who to be friends with."

His cosmetically enhanced dental caps grind. "That man uses women and throws them away—you're a diversion and nothing more."

Wow. Just...wow. "What are you trying to say, Dad? Spit it out. That I'm not good enough for him, or that he just wants to have sex with me a few times before he dumps me? That I can't trust him because he's a piece of shit? One *you* hired, I might add."

One you pay millions of dollars.

"I'm saying he couldn't possibly be interested in a serious commitment when his commitment is to the Steam."

I've heard enough. It's not what he's saying that stings; it's that the things he's saying are thoughts I've already had. Hearing them from my parent is a mental slap I didn't want to experience. Not when I was already filled with so many doubts.

Trace is not with you because he is using you, Trace is not with you because he is using you, Trace is not with you because he is using you.

I repeat it three times.

He isn't.

Buzz *likes* likes me. I know he does.

"For the record, *Dad*, we haven't slept together, and we haven't gone on an actual date—we are friends. So you can go to bed tonight and sleep easy." I am stomping toward the door in a huff.

"Get back here—we are not done with this discussion!"

"I'm not one of your lackeys. You can boss Fiona and Lucian around, but you can't boss me around."

"I can and I will."

That gives me pause, and I turn. Narrow my eyes. "Even if I didn't want to date Trace Wallace, even if I didn't want to be friends with him anymore—that is my decision, not yours. He is a great guy, and we're having fun. Remember what fun is, Dad? F-U-N. That's it. We're not having sex and it's not romantic, but if it were, I doubt I'd tell you. I can't even believe we're having this conversation."

I still can't believe it when I'm halfway down the hall, or when I'm pounding on the elevator buttons, willing the damn thing to move faster so I can get the hell out of this building.

It's suffocating me.

The door opens and I step out, eyes on the ground— the polished concrete floor of the ground level.

Dammit! I'm on the wrong floor. Why does this always happen?

Try paying attention for once, I chastise myself.

My eyes go from my phone to the tips of my cute, black shoes...to a solid, masculine chest.

This time when I look up, it's not Trace I see, as I did the last time I got off on the wrong floor.

It's Marlon, and he has his hands on my arms to steady me.

Gag.

Could this day get any shittier? I am not in the mood for this.

"I assumed you missed me, but I didn't think you missed me this much," Marlon rumbles with a chuckle, the vibrations from his chest a familiar sound. "I won't tell Wallace if you won't."

I step back and out of his arms, revolted. "You're a pig."

"What?" His hands go up defensively. "I didn't say

anything perverted, just said I wouldn't tell your fake boyfriend if you don't. You know you miss me."

"What would make you think that? Have I called you? Have I texted you? Have I slid into your DMs? No. The second you took my car for a spin was the second I was done with your ass."

I try to step around him, but he's tall, and big, and makes it impossible. "I'm not trying to fight with you, baby girl. I'm just trying to talk some sense into you."

"Sense? Oh Jesus, do not call me baby girl—the jock chasers you pick up at the club might think it's a cute nickname, but I don't." I pause. "And speaking of chasing, let's cut the crap, okay? We both know I'm not your type. The only reason you pursued me was so you could date the general manager's daughter."

There. I said out loud what I've been speculating, except this is the first time I'm acknowledging it to him. Marlon has the audacity to look stunned by the declaration.

"Hollis, babe—you know that's not true. I screwed up, okay? You can't hold it against me forever."

Yes. I can. "We are not together. Get out of my way, Marlon."

He doesn't move. "Did you tell your dad about any of this?"

I knew it! I knew he was only in it for my father!

"No, asshole. I didn't tell him we went out, let alone dated." Thank god. Because if Dad is upset about me befriending Buzz Wallace, I cannot imagine what he would think about me having dated Marlon Daymon, the Steam's biggest playboy. Thomas would not only have been disappointed, he would want to kill me. "I've had it with men today—get out of my goddamn way."

"Whoa—stop being a bitch."

Oh no he did not! No one has ever called me a bitch. "*What* did you just call me?"

"You heard me. Stuck-up snot is what you are. You think you're too fucking good for me, don't you? Little princess looking down her nose."

My mouth gapes. No one has ever called me that either —at least not to my face.

Marlon knows he's upset me; I can see it by the way he tilts his chin up and the glint in his hazel eyes. Cocky, arrogant prick.

Still, I'm shook—it's not often I get called stuck-up. Usually it was by girls in high school who were from well-off families themselves and had no room to judge. Mean girls being mean—not grown men with hero complexes.

"What's going on?"

A new voice joins us, and my body sags with relief. Noah Harding has rounded the corner with a concerned arch to his brows, eyes darting back and forth between Marlon and me, trying to get a read on the situation and failing.

"'Sup, Harding." My ex-boyfriend greets him, fake smile plastered on his pretty face as he tries to fist-bump his teammate—too bad he's not fooling anyone with the over exaggerated enthusiasm.

Noah looks at me—really looks at me hard. My infuriated eyes. The flush in my cheeks. The downturned line of my mouth. I feel sick, as if I'm about to puke.

I hate confrontation to begin with; bumping into Marlon and having it out with him in a public place is giving me hives.

"What are you two talking about?" Noah does not mince words, getting straight to the heart of the matter. I like his style.

"Just catching up. Gotta see how our girl here is doing."

Our girl. *Our* girl?

Puke.

No.

"Our girl?" Noah repeats, scratching at his chin. "That's a weird way to put it."

He's right—it is. "I don't think I was your girl when I was your girl for that entire ten minutes you were using me." The words fly out of my mouth in a rush. "I'm with Wallace now, so you can stop harassing me every chance you get."

"Oh, I'm harassing you now? That's rich coming from a rich girl."

Wow, he is bitter.

"Alright, Daymon, that's enough. You should get to where you're going. Hollis, I can walk you to your car."

"You don't need protection from me, babe—especially not by Harding. I'm twice the man he is."

Noah looks at him. "What's your problem today, man?"

My ex scoffs. "Pfft. Me? Don't got a problem. *Man.*"

He is acting so strange.

I mean—he's a dick most times. Once upon a time, that was one of the things that attracted me to him, the arrogance and confidence pouring out of him. The way he walks into a room like he owns it and everyone notices. The way people respond to his charisma.

Turns out it's all smoke and mirrors. He is not Mr. Wonderful.

Far. From it.

Noah Harding, however? He is much more than I ever expected, showing up like this and...I wouldn't say he's standing up for me, maybe giving me backup. He's certainly trying to steer me away from my ex.

He gives him another wary glance then nods his chin my direction. "Hollis, let's bounce."

"Bye Marlon." I don't have a clue why I tell him good-bye; common courtesy, I guess, though he doesn't deserve it. He throws a peace sign, kisses it, then turns his back.

Together, Noah Harding and I walk side by side to the parking lot, not knowing what to say.

A few seagulls eating leftover snacks fly away when we pass, my car parked close enough that we don't have to go far.

"That was..." When I find my voice, it trails off. I have no idea what to even say.

Noah is at a loss for words, too. "Honestly? I think he's juiced up—he doesn't usually act like this." He's mumbling as much to himself as he is to me, like he's talking his way through the pieces of a puzzle, putting them together in his mind.

I would agree; something was off. I've never seen Marlon act like this, either—not even the few times I saw him drunk.

"What do you mean by juiced up?"

He seems torn about his next choice of words. "Steroids. He just came from the gym, but I'd bet he's taken something."

Steroids? There is no way. Marlon? No. I mean...I don't know him all that well, and I do know he's an asshole, but Major League Baseball has strict policies about performance-enhancing drugs. Also, he doesn't need them, so why would he take them?

Although to be fair, Marlon's body did look jacked up.

"I didn't think those were legal."

He shuffles me through the door, past Karl. "They're

not." It looks like his jaw is clenching, white knuckles gripping the handle of his navy duffle bag.

"Then why would he do that?"

Noah shrugs, hefting his bag from one shoulder to the other. "I'm not sure—probably because of weightlifting and wanting body mass?" He looks down at me. "Are you going to say anything?"

"To who?"

He gives me an *Are you serious?* look. "Your dad."

"Oh." Him. "I thought for a second you meant Trace."

"I'll probably tell him myself, if you don't mind."

I nod—of course he'd want to be the one to tell him and I have no intention of snitching. But the information is going to weigh on my mind, despite the fact that it's merely speculation. Noah would know, wouldn't he? He's been around it and seen it—he would know what someone who's injected themselves with steroids looks like, right?

"The trainers are going to notice eventually, so I don't think..." He clamps his mouth shut. "Eventually they're going to notice."

I nod slowly. God, this sucks.

This whole *day* has sucked, and I just want it to end.

~

Unknown Number: *Hey sweetie, this is Gen! I wanted to tell you how lovely it was meeting you!*

Mrs. Wallace's text comes through a little after five o'clock; it's dinnertime and I imagine her toiling away in her kitchen, getting ready to prepare Roger's supper with freshly chopped vegetables and meat, regular Suzy Homemaker that she is.

A knot of longing forms in my stomach at the quaint family life I have never known, caring parents and a mother who makes dinner every night, who drives her kids from one sport to the next in a minivan.

Me: *I had such a good time. Thank you for your hospitality—I even had fun at our little impromptu slumber party. I'm sorry we didn't stay for breakfast.*

Genevieve: *Oh, I know you kids are busy, no worries!*

I stare at the message, unsure about what to say.

Genevieve: *So I was wondering if you want to sit with Trace's dad and me at the next home game this Thursday!*

She uses lots of exclamation points and I find it adorable—she sounds so incredibly enthusiastic. I'm here for it.

Also.

His parents want me to sit with them during Buzz's next home game? Um…I wonder if he knows she's texting me, then suspect it's not something he would mind, since it does seem like he's actively trying to date me.

Still. Sitting with his parents?

Bold move.

Not one I'm too keen on, considering we're not in an actual relationship. I cannot in good conscience perpetuate more lies to this poor woman.

Me: *I'll have to check my work schedule, and offhand, I feel like I won't be able to. I'm editing a book that has to be sent back to the author before another editor—you know what, I'll just have to get back to you on this, if you don't mind?*

I am babbling in a text.

Genevieve: *Oh, no worries dear. Let me know when you can. We're driving up and staying at a hotel **wink wink** We could do dinner after the game if that would be convenient.*

This woman is determined to see me on Thursday.

Me: *Gosh Mrs. Wallace, I really don't know…*

Genevieve: *Call me Genevieve. Perhaps breakfast Friday would be better for you?*

She wants to be my friend because she's harboring illusions that I'm going to be her daughter-in-law one day.

Perhaps you should check with your son, I want to tell her, *because I have a feeling he has no idea you're messaging me!* How do I know this? He would never turn down food; the man loves eating too much!

Great, now I'm overusing exclamation points too.

First my dad. Then Marlon. Then Noah. Now Mrs. Wallace.

When will this day end?

Madison: *I'm coming over. You need me.*

Add my best friend to the clusterfuck and it's a well-rounded day of nonstop chaos.

Perfect.

I flop down on my pillow and stare at Mrs. Wallace's messages. She's such a lovely woman, so much warmth. The kind of mother I wish I'd had growing up—not that my mom wasn't loving. She was just…caught up in a world where children did not come first. Socializing and popularity were the orders of the day, always.

That's just how it was.

Nope. Can't do this to Buzz's mom.

I cannot have dinner, brunch, or breakfast with Buzz Wallace's parents. Not Thursday, not next week, not ever.

I roll to my back, waiting for Madison.

She might not have answers, but she almost always brings ice cream.

16

Trace

"He *what?*"

I need more clarification from Noah—the story he just told me about Marlon and Hollis isn't surprising, but it is infuriating.

"I walked up as he was getting nasty, calling her a snob and shit. She looked like she was going to cry and he looked crazy. I think he's juicing—something isn't right with him. He went from zero to eighty in three seconds."

"No bullshit?"

"No bullshit."

Damn. Marlon Daymon is using? What the hell for? The dude is at the top of his game. One drug test by the establishment and he'd be done. Well—okay fine, maybe not *fired* done, but it would leak to the press, and he'd probably face a suspension then get fined up the ass. Thousands and thousands of dollars in penalties. For what?

Faster speed? More endurance? To look ripped?

Baseball players are not football players. You don't see too many of them walking around like the cover models of fitness magazines.

Often enough, I've heard my sister complain about our baggy pants and baggy shirts, about our players having no definition. Basically the dad bod of professional athletes.

So if he's seriously trying to pump himself up, people will notice. And when they do, there will be consequences.

Besides, how dumb do you have to be to call the fucking owner's granddaughter a snob? To call the general manager's daughter a princess? That shit doesn't fly—we have our own set of rules down in the locker room, our own code of conduct that has nothing to do with the establishment's. First one: don't shit where you eat.

Meaning: don't piss off the boss by insulting his family.

Second? If you have a side piece, don't bring her to the game—any game.

Thirdly? If you're dating someone new, do not have her sit in the family suite with the wives. Too much gossip —too many diamonds and expensive purses fill a new girl-friend's head with all the wrong ideas.

With Hollis, I wouldn't have to worry about any of that.

Hollis is the game. I don't have to play it.

"You should call her," Noah tells me, as if it weren't obvious. We're in his kitchen and I'm eating a slice of left-over pizza I nabbed out of his fridge. I was enjoying it, but now it's just a lump of dough in the pit of my stomach.

"I will."

I'll do one better; I'll head directly to her place from Harding's so I can see her face, gauge her mood. Is she going to blame me for this? Is she going to hold this against me and all other men who come after Marlon, for the rest of her life?

Dramatic, sure. Unhealthy, yes.

I've been to her place to pick her up twice now already and know the way like the back of my hand. It's late afternoon, and I imagine she's probably starting dinner—or crying, or stuffing a voodoo doll. I brace myself for an argument.

Unless she's not alone.

Which is exactly the case when I arrive.

Hollis is not the face that greets me at the door and for a moment, I step back to check the number on the outside of the building to make sure I'm at the right address.

Seven one five.

This is the place, but that isn't Hollis.

"What do *you* want?" the girl—her best friend, I think —rudely asks, only cracking the door open a few inches, a gold chain linked near the top.

She catches me off guard and I waver. So unlike me—I always have something to say. "Is Hollis here?"

"Obviously." The friend rolls her eyes, and I wish I could remember her fucking name. Madge? Brittany? Sue?

"Can I talk to her?"

"What for?" The pretty brunette narrows her heavily mascaraed eyes into slits. "Here to rub salt in the wound that is her love life?"

"Huh?"

"Did that dickhead teammate of yours send you? Huh? Huh!"

"My dickhead teammate doesn't know I'm here because he has absolutely nothing to do with the reason I'm here."

"So you admit he's a dickhead."

"Yes."

She sighs, reaching up to unlatch the chain, opening the door for me to enter. "Fine, you can come in."

"What was the secret password?" I want to know, stepping into Hollis's entryway, sliding my shoes off. I don't know if that's the rule here, but I don't want to find out the hard way. Plus, it's nice flooring and I'd hate to scuff it with my beat-up sneaks.

"Secret password?" Now the girl is acting perplexed.

"What made you let me in?"

"Oh—Hollis is in the bathroom, but we saw you drive up through the window. She told me to let you in to wait. She'll be right out."

What the fuck? Jesus, this girl is the female version of...

Me.

I have no interest in getting into a battle of wills with her while I wait for Hollis, hands stuffed into the pocket of my hooded sweatshirt with the Steam's logo emblazoned across the front. It has a comfy kangaroo pocket and that's where I bury my paws.

"You can come into the kitchen," she says, leading me into the next room.

My eyes dart around, drinking in the living room as we pass it. Learning Hollis's style. Looking at the bold artwork hanging on her walls, the stark white color of them. The bright pink and blue pillows on her white couch. The red square rug on the hardwood floor.

"Hey," the friend says, snapping her fingers. "Eyes to the front, pal."

She doesn't want me rubbernecking, staring off into Hollis's place and I don't blame her for not trusting me.

Hollis's townhouse is standard, narrow and stacked and several stories high. Living room and dining on the main floor, kitchen probably on the second, bedrooms on the third.

I'm led up a flight of stairs, the wood stained a rich cherry, shined to a gloss, my hand dragging along the smooth wood as we climb farther to the next level of living space. As a contractor via side hustle, I can appreciate the details of the house and the architectural elements, and I

wonder if Hollis bought the place this way or refurbished
it.

I also wonder if she bought it with family money or on
her own—then get my head out of my own ass for even
wondering, considering it's none of my fucking business.
Who cares anyway? What difference does it make?

I'm just curious. Sue me.

The friend and I arrive at the kitchen. There's a
balcony overlooking a small, fenced-in courtyard and a
view of the neighbor's balcony. Views of the entire neighborhood and their backyards—it reminds me why I don't
live in the city.

No privacy.

I bet everyone knows her business all the time.

It's strange that she's not living in a more private,
secure building, considering who her family is. They're
loaded. Hollis is ripe for kidnapping and ransom demands,
and *maybe the girls aren't the only ones who are dramatic.*

I clear my throat, feeling like a giant in this feminine
space. Pull out a chair at the table, but then push it back in.
I'll wait for Hollis to come out from wherever she is before
I sit or don't sit, remaining rooted to the floor near the
stairs we just climbed.

Her friend leans against the counter, arms crossed. As
if I'm the asshole in this scenario.

Guilty by association, or just someone to take the
brunt?

I'm about to find out.

Hollis appears from down a hallway, wearing jean
shorts and an oversized white sweater, hair in disarray.
Tiny and cute, I want to hug her—but also have no desire
to be sacked in the ball bag by the bodyguard in the corner.
Her stink eye is freaking me the fuck out.

"Hey." Hollis crosses her arms and does that thing

where it looks like she's giving herself a hug. Or like she's cold and trying to stay warm. She glances at her friend. "Did you introduce yourself?"

The friend raises a brow. "Oh, he knows who I am."

My head shakes, half out of fear, half out of spite. She scares me. "I can't remember your name, sorry."

"How can you not remember my name? We met before."

"I don't think you——"

"Ugh," she loudly groans. "It's Madison. Madison! We met at that fundraiser."

"I meet lots of people, sorry."

"Whatever. What do you want to say to Hollis? Make it snappy."

"Madison!" Hollis gasps. "Don't be rude."

"Um, I thought we hated men tonight."

She glances at me, grimacing. "We *do*, but you don't have to be rude."

"Well," I can't help adding, "this is awkward."

"Buzz, want to...go outside and talk? It's still nice out."

And light, with no bugs. Although I could eat again, I follow her to the patio doors and the balcony beyond. It's small but has a few chairs and a tiny table. I imagine she comes out here in the mornings for coffee or to watch the sun rise.

Or like, to fuck.

I can picture banging out here at night—risky but private, depending on how dark it is outside and how many lights are shining from the surrounding house lamps.

Maybe even sex against the sliding door? Her ass cheeks pressed against the glass—believe it or not, I've never screwed anyone against a window, not even at a hotel, though I could totally get into it.

Is that weird?

Hollis leads the conversation, which surprises me. "I'm assuming Noah told you what happened."

I nod, pulling out a chair across from her and plopping down. It's cold and uncomfortable, an intricate metal contraption that looks pretty but feels like hell against my back. "He did and I wanted to see how you were doing."

"I'm fine. Marlon is a jerk."

"Jerk. Asshole. Douche. Prick." Take your pick. "How do you feel?"

"Shitty." She's playing with the ends of her sweater, fiddling with the cuffs, which are a bit too long. "I know none of it is true, but it still makes me feel crappy—that's what breakups do. I've never felt right about ours because he always made me feel like less of a person."

Then why the fuck are you wasting time worrying about it? "Are you still hung up on him?"

"No!" She pauses. "I think what I'm...'hung up on'"— she uses air quotes around the words—"is how taken advantage of I felt and how easily I let him."

I can relate. "That's one of the reasons I haven't been in a relationship since I was in eighth grade."

She looks up at me as if suddenly remembering that I have the same shit happen to me on a daily basis, people wanting something from me, wanting to be seen with me. Autographs, appearances. Some paid, some free—it's all the same, and occasionally? It feels shitty.

"You haven't been in a relationship since middle school?"

I lean back, recalling it fondly. "Stacy Blinkiwitcz. She and I were in the same algebra class and I used to stare at her all the time because I was fascinated by her braces. She used to wear these overalls all the time, with a t-shirt underneath, and the t-shirts were different colors depending on her mood." Hollis laughs at my memory.

"Anyway, I slipped a note into her locker because my parents wouldn't let me have a cell phone. Folded it up into a triangle and all that shit, asking her to 'go with me.'"

Another laugh and Hollis relaxes, her horrible day beginning to melt away.

I go on. "So we go together, which was really just passing notes back and forth. I'd tell her she looked good in her rolled-up jeans and denim jacket, or that I liked her new kicks, and she would ask about my games."

"What happened?"

I shrug. "There was a dance, and I remember her telling me while we were slow-dancing to whatever boy band happened to be popular at the time—she was like, 'Trace, I think you're super cool, but Alan Owens has a car.'" I shoot a peeved look at Hollis. "I did not have a car."

"What eighth grader has a car?"

"Alan was a freshman, but he'd been held back in kindergarten, so he had his license." I pause for theatrical flair. "And a mustache."

That part is a lie—Alan did not have a 'stache, but it's funny and adds a lighthearted element to the story. Alan did indeed have a car, the little fucker.

"Had you and Stacy even kissed?"

"No. I got robbed."

"What'd you do after she told you she was dumping you?"

This is by far the worst part of the story. "I cried." Then I hasten to add, "Just a little! It wasn't like, sobs or anything."

Not really...

Tripp found me in the boys' bathroom crying in the last stall, pounded on the door and called our mom to come get us from the payphone in the lobby.

"Oh you poor thing." Hollis leans forward to pat me on the cheek and I do something totally stupid.

I lick her palm.

"Ew! Trace! That's disgusting!" She wipes the saliva onto the sleeve of her sweater, but she's laughing and smiling, and isn't that what counts?

"I could eat you up."

She swats at me, batting like a cat. "I want to hear the rest of your story, the part about you crying."

I begin shaking my head to refuse, but since I started the story, I know I have to finish it—she needs to hear what a pussy I am.

"My brother found me in the bathroom and called our mom—he was also a giant loser with no car—and she came to pick us up. I refused to tell them what had happened, so the entire ride home—we had to sit in the back—Tripp was giving me charley horses for being a baby."

"That wasn't nice."

"In my defense, I had snot running out of my nose, and I was inconsolable."

"You said you weren't sobbing."

"Men say a lot of things so they sound masculine. I try to block the whining and crying part of this story out of my memory."

"Go on. So then what?"

"Then…when we got back to the house, I raced up my stairs and threw myself on the bed and continued bawling into my comforter. Then I got out my yearbook and looked at her picture and cried some more. I listened to my CD of the song we'd just danced to, by the boy band whose name I can't remember."

Another lie. It was the Backstreet Boys, the song was "The One", and it touched me because it was about soulmates and that's what that liar Stacy Blinkiwitcz was to me.

Allegedly.

"That's…a very dramatic story."

I look to the sky. "Tell me about it. Try living through it." I raise my brows. "Do you think my older brother let me live that shit down? The answer is no. Last Christmas he got four of the five members of the band to FaceTime me and sing the song."

Sometimes being famous has its perks, but I didn't think that was as hilarious as my family did.

Bunch of assholes. Even Dad thought it was hysterical.

"And you have no idea what the song was?" She doesn't believe that I don't remember.

I shake my head adamantly. Press my lips together. "Nope."

"Oh you are such a liar!"

"No, Stacy Blinkiwitcz is a liar!"

Hollis cannot stop laughing. "How?"

"She knew she was going to dump me and waited until the dance, publicly humiliating me. It was premeditated—a premeditated dumping."

"That's what everyone does in lower grades because not a single one of us had balls."

I raise my chin. "I had balls."

"By default." Hollis stares off into the cityscape, studying the skyline. Then, "Could you have done it? Could you have broken up with you? I bet you were pretty darn cute."

I shrug. "I was okay—a few hearts were probably broken before Stacy crushed mine. But…I don't know, maybe you're right. Breaking up with someone isn't easy."

"No, it's horrible, even when they treat you like shit. Because when it's tumultuous, the breakup ends up being a huge screaming match. On the other hand, if it's amicable or the other person doesn't see it coming, that's just as bad, because he or she is blindsided—like you were when Stacy dumped you."

"I'm still not over it," I say stubbornly with a grin.

Hollis smiles. "What do you suppose Stacy is doing right now?"

My mouth shifts in thought. "Mmm, probably a reporter for tabloids, spreading fake news. Or an actress."

That makes her laugh. "Seriously? She's probably a nurse or something. Or a teacher. I bet she's changed, no longer breaking hearts."

"Lonely hearts club," I say.

My hand goes to the tabletop, resting on its cool surface, palm spread, facing the sky. I don't know why I place it there, but I'm surprised when Hollis leans forward and extends her hand, placing it in mine.

Electricity shoots up my arm, straight to my chest.

"Thank you for coming over. You really cheered me up." She's sort of beaming at me, happy and glad, cheeks rosy.

I glance behind us, into the house, searching for a glimpse of Madison. "Your friend in there wasn't getting the job done?"

"Maddie was too angry on my behalf to have done any good—I would rather be smiling than pissed off. I've done too much of that, and I'm over it. Marlon isn't worth it. I know that now."

She's right, he isn't worth it, and maybe someday he won't be such a fucking asshole that women blindly follow around—but for now, he's toxic to anyone he's in a relationship with. Including his friends, I imagine.

I detest dudes like that.

I like Noah Harding, Miranda, my parents, and like, three other people.

Plus construction, ice cream, and riding mopeds when I'm on vacation.

Not necessarily in that order.

"Is she even here anymore?" I can't see Madison through the glass.

"Who—Stacy?" Hollis teases.

"Oh how you wound me." I clutch my chest. "No, your friend. Where'd she go? I would have thought she'd have her eagle eye on me. She doesn't seem to like me very much."

Or at all.

Hollis cranes her neck. Pulls her cell phone out of her pocket and checks it. "She left."

She left? "How come?" I don't know shit about women, but I know some shit about women, and her best friend said more than that.

Her shoulder rises in a demure shrug. "She said we looked serious so she wanted to give us privacy, and I should text her when you leave."

Well, well, well—this is a new development. "Does that mean she semi-approves of me?"

A mean poker face stares back. "We haven't discussed you."

I think my eyes damn near bug out of my skull and I almost lurch across the table, belting out a laugh. "Who's the liar now! Bullshit—you girls tell each other everything! There is no way Madison doesn't have the entire 411 on me. No fucking way. You're such a damn liar."

Hollis's stalwart expression breaks, a cute little snicker erupting from her throat. "I mean—maybe."

I start to rise, unable to bear it. Now that I know we're alone? I have to kiss her.

177

Shoving up from my chair, I move the table aside—an easy task since it's basically tinfoil—and swoop down, scooping up a squealing Hollis.

"What are you doing! Put me down! Are you insane?"

"I'm trying to be romantic here. Cut me some slack and stop wiggling around before I drop you, 'kay?"

Her lips clamp shut. She nods.

Using my foot, I toe the sliding door open, pushing it on its track so we can get back into the house. Use my ass to slide it shut, stride a few feet back into the kitchen.

There's a small sitting area on the far end, with a fireplace and a television, and in a few seconds I'm there, setting her on the couch. Lower myself to my knees in front of her and take her face in my hands.

"I'm sorry you had a shitty day, but I want to help make it better," I croon, knowing my voice has dropped a few octaves.

She shivers. "How?"

I reach for the fly of her denim shorts, measuring her reaction as I tug down her zipper. Waiting for any indication she doesn't want this.

Hollis tilts her head back and spreads her legs wider, arms hitting the couch cushions. Body sinking into the fabric.

From my position in front of her, I pull those shorts over her hips, down her thighs. Her smooth, smooth thighs...

Let them fall to the floor, give my attention to her underwear. It's white, basic cotton—not what I was expecting, but sexy just the same.

She watches me, blushing. "I wasn't expecting company." Not quite an apology, but close.

"You could be wearing thermal underwear and I would be turned on right now." I lean forward, pressing my mouth to her core. Kiss her stomach, inching my way down. Warm between the apex of her spread legs, blowing hot air right where she aches.

Hollis's fingers clench the seat cushions.

"Everything you do is sexy, Hollis."

She moans at that, opening her eyes to gaze down at me, pupils already dilating. Traps her lower lip between her teeth.

I put my mouth back on her, wetting her white granny panties with my tongue. Sucking and sucking and sucking, soaking them through.

"Oh my god, I'm wearing hip-hugger briefs," she complains.

I laugh into the cotton panties, enjoying her embarrassment, enjoying the flush on her face and the labor of her breath, the smooth, silky skin of her thighs.

"I'll buy you all the sexy underwear you want."

I press my fingers into her flesh, flexing them, completely turned on and lost in the moment. I'm lost in discovering her body, granny panties and all.

She's so fucking cute I could eat her up.

So I do.

17

Hollis

I s there a sight more intoxicating than that of a man with his head between your legs?

I plow my fingers through Trace's hair, the thick, dark strands sifting through like sand, velvety and smooth. Smooth like the tongue lapping at my heat, slowly but firmly. Fast. Slow. In and out.

He sucks, using his teeth a little—not to the point of hurting, but just enough that I can feel it, the friction doing the craziest shit to my ovaries.

They quiver inside me.

I shiver.

His hands are on my thighs to hold them apart—yet another thing that drives me wild looking at it. Primal.

I'm not normally a visual person—I don't watch porn and I don't have to imagine anything when I close my eyes to masturbate—but this? This sight of him is making me wild. Gets me so hot.

My breath quickens and a moan escapes my lips, one that's pouty and a bit whiny. I want to come—but I don't. I want his finger inside me—but it isn't. I want to have sex with him—but we won't.

Make up your mind, Hollis.

Speak now or forever hold your—

"Ohhh…" I moan, grateful I live alone. Grateful for having shaved my legs this morning before I left the house. Grateful I had my pussy waxed last week—and my ass, ha ha.

Grateful for Trace and his skilled fingers…

He seems to sense I need *more*, and he complies.

One finger confidently goes inside me. Then two. Usually, I'm not a fan. I've yet to have sex or foreplay with a man who knew what the fuck he was doing with his fingers. But he…does.

I don't have to direct him, or tell him to be gentle, or to ease up.

His thumb settles into a rhythm on my clit. His tongue lingers below it.

The entire thing makes me go, "Mmm." Then, "Yes…"

Yes, more.

Yes, Buzz.

Yes, right there.

Oh.

It's on the tip of my tongue to call him Daddy, then —ew. No.

But kind of.

But I don't.

I feel how flushed my chest is and want to tear my shirt off. I want to get so nakedy naked and have him lick me all over, but we're not there yet.

We're here.

Him pleasing me because I had a bad day.

The worst day, I remember now.

Poor me.

I look down at him again, a slow grin spreading on my face as I grip his head. Prop my toes on his shoulders, tipping my head back.

Let him pleasure me while I watch, desire swallowing me whole.

It feels euphoric when I come.

"Oh god…"

I needed that. Needed it good and hard—and it was fast. Almost embarrassingly quick, but right now I don't even care.

Buzz rests back on his haunches, regarding me, glistening lips twisted with his own pleasure—with the knowledge that I just had a loud, aching 'gasm and he's the one who gave it to me.

Those giant hands slide up my bare legs. Over my thighs and hips. He leans forward and kisses my knees. Glides his palms under my ass and hefts me up. Scoops me up like a baby, cradling me.

"Where's your bedroom?"

I nod toward the stairs against the wall on the east side of this level.

Up we go.

When he finds my room, pushing the door open with his toe like he did earlier, he sets me on the edge of the bed. Removes my remaining clothes.

I scoot to the center.

Watch as he undresses himself down to his boxers, pulls the covers back, and slides in after me. Lays his head down on one of my five hundred pillows and stares up at the ceiling.

"I'm sorry you had a shitty day." He searches and finds my hand under the covers, gives it a squeeze.

My heart constricts.

"I'm feeling a lot better now, thank you." It's supposed to come out flippant, like a joke, but sounds more serious than I intended it. "Thanks to you."

There. Better.

"I'm glad you came over." I mean—Madison is fine and all, but there's nothing like the comfort of a big, brawny man to make me feel hot and warm on the inside.

"Me too." His fingers still grip mine. "I wasn't sure if I should—didn't know if you'd actually agree to see me when your friend opened the door. She's scary as fuck."

That she is. "She means well. She's protective of me."

Mostly.

Sort of.

"It's good having loyal friends."

"Like Noah?"

"Exactly." Buzz is quiet for a time. "He and I have had our ups and downs, mostly because he resists my advances, but over the past few weeks, he's really come around."

Resisted his advances? Uh... "Do the two of you...um, are you sleeping together?"

"Noah and me?" He glances over at me, surprised. "No—I just meant the friendship thing." His laugh is deep and sexy. Masculine and amused. "I know he never wanted me around, but I kept showing up and eating his food." Pause. "And swimming in his pool and eating his food. And sleeping in his guest room and—"

"Eating his food?"

He shrugs. "I get hungry."

"And now he's cool with it?"

"Yeah, he gave me the garage code."

"Did he?"

"Granted, it was after I stole one of the remotes for the security gate, but progress is progress."

I stare, mouth gaping. I can never tell when he's being

serious or kidding around. Stifle my laughter. He is really something else entirely.

I find it…adorable. Cute. Refreshing. All words I would never have associated with Buzz Wallace. Not at a first glance, or a second or third. I was too busy stereotyping him.

Shame on me.

The cool sheets brush my skin when I roll to face him, reminding me that I'm entirely naked. Reminding me that he's just in boxers and hasn't been pleasured yet. Pleased? Pleasured… Uh, yeah. He hasn't had an orgasm, and he's given me two: the dry humping on the floor at his parents' house, and the oral in my living room.

Selfish, selfish, selfish.

And it's been so long since I've had a dick inside me.

My legs rub together of their own accord, anxious. Excited.

"What's that look?" Buzz raises a brow.

I raise mine. "What look?"

His hands come out from under the covers to point. "That one."

I shrug and the covers drop from my chest, exposing my breasts. "I have a look? Huh."

He visibly swallows.

Is he nervous?

Are my boobs his sexual kryptonite?

He can't take his eyes off them, and I feel empowered, feminine.

I see if I can distract him. "Have you ever been on any dating apps?"

Buzz moves his eyes from my chest to my face. "Actually, I have."

"Really!" Why does that surprise me? I expected him to say no. "Which ones?"

"TheBuzz, StupidCupid, and Hinder."

He doesn't elaborate, and I lean closer, wanting more information. "And?"

His head bobbles. "Andddd, I got reported for being a fake account so often I completely gave up."

I can see that happening—makes sense. "Aren't there apps out there for *famous* people?"

Buzz nods, reaching for my hip under the covers. "Yes, but I don't want to date someone famous. Or a wannabe. Or a starlet, or a pop singer, or or *or*. I want to date someone normal."

Does that mean he thinks *I'm* normal? 'Cause I'm far from it; in fact, sometimes I feel as if I have more issues than a lifetime subscription to *Cosmo*.

"What about you?" His finger trails along my skin. "Are you on any dating apps?"

"A few, now and again. The problem is, I say some off-the-wall shit and scare lots of men away—but it's my way of separating the men from the boys."

"Off the wall? How?"

"Well." I'm smiling. Clear my throat. "For example, if a guy's profile has pictures of him both with a beard and without a beard, he might say, 'I shaved my beard recently,' to which I might reply, 'Yeah, me too.'" I glance up at Buzz for his reaction. "They don't always like that answer. It confuses them."

He laughs.

"Oh!" I go on. "Once, a guy said he wanted to meet me right away and I agreed. It's better to get it over and done with and out of the way than drag it out, because waiting just makes the disappointment worse if there is no chemistry in person."

Buzz nods along with my story.

"So I say things like, 'Here I am kicking stones down

the sidewalk when it doesn't work out, dragging my limp, red balloon.'" Buzz doesn't think that is quite as funny. "The last guy to ask me out wanted to know if five o'clock was good for drinks, and I asked if we could make it later. 'The later the better,' I said. 'The darker it gets, the better I look. Way cuter in dim lighting, unless you bring a paper bag to put over my head.'"

His eyes bug out of his skull. "You do not talk like that."

I hold up two fingers. "Scout's honor. Never fails to horrify or delight. There isn't an in-between." And if I had a cigar, I'd light it up and take a puff from it right now. Ahhh, the satisfaction from the look on his face.

Intrigue?

Admiration?

"You shouldn't have fun at the expense of gullible young men," he says with a laugh.

"I don't want to date those men anyway, so good riddance. They don't have balls big enough."

"Whoa, Hollis!" Buzz laughs again, a booming one that has him reaching for me. "You're kind of a monster— who knew?"

I knew.

I've always known I was a bit...sassy. Smartassy. Problem is, I have never met someone I could be myself with. It's always been suppressed humor, and suppressed jokes, and suppressed sex drive.

What is it about him that makes me feel so...myself? Him of all the people on this earth?

Buzz—Trace, as I'd prefer to call him when we're being intimate—gently caresses the curve of my hip with his palm. I can feel the callouses on the pads of his fingers, a reminder of his hard work. The nature of his job. How he uses his body to succeed.

I watch his biceps flex; they're tan and toned and mouthwatering. It's illustrative of another difference between the two of us: I don't work out. Or go to the gym. I barely bent down to pick up dog shit off the sidewalk when I had a dog.

Walking is my cardio, but *barely*. Sometimes, I take the stairs instead of an elevator, but *rarely*.

Trace's muscles have me leaning forward again, breathlessly tracing one of his veins with the tip of my forefinger. Exploring his warm skin the way he explores mine.

He lets me, lying still, and I can see the hitch in his breath when he holds it, the second my fingers run along his collarbone, down his clavicle, reaching his belly button.

Lord, his body is a temple. I haven't worshipped at one for a long, long time and hardly know what to do with it. I'm not the kind of woman men throw themselves at. I'm relatively bad at blow jobs, and I am intimidated by hand jobs.

Call it lack of experience. Call it intimidating.

Dicks scare me—there, I said it.

Cocks and balls and the entire business freak me *out*.

Trace doesn't move an inch. Watches my hand, eyes skimming the front of my torso every so often, drinking in the sight of my naked body.

It emboldens me when I catch him, his eyes looking glazed over and mesmerized. By me. By my body.

I scoot into him so my breasts brush against his chest. Tip my head so he can shift his head and kiss my neck.

"Mmm." My favorite spot. If he blows on me soft enough, I'll come. Ha ha.

"Do you like that?" He blows again.

"Mmmhmm. I do." *Yes. So don't stop.*

Meanwhile, I allow myself to continue exploring, my hand reaching around and trailing to his back. Runs up his rib cage, smooth and hard and stiff. His body is built like a top performance machine.

My father's voice echoes in my ears. *"He is the best closer we've had in years…he doesn't need the distraction…the best we've had in years…doesn't need the distraction…"*

It's not Dad's decision; it's ours. Trace's. Mine.

Of all the places in the world he could be, Trace Wallace chose to be here, with me.

I like everything he does lately.

My hands get greedy, discovering they love touching his shoulders. Big, broad, wide. Delicious enough to kiss.

My lips touch his skin and he too tips his neck so I can kiss him there, the tender flesh getting more and more flushed the longer I pepper it with affection. He's blushing.

My mouth finds the space below his Adam's apple. *Kiss.* Collarbone. *Kiss.*

Between his pecs. *Kiss.*

His hips begin to slowly thrust, the dick between his thick thighs growing harder with each and every second I tease his body with my touch. Eyes drift shut. Lips part.

Every so often, he presses those lips together.

Nostrils flare.

So hot.

His hand is between my legs and I spread them a little, aching to feel his fingers inside my—

"God you're so tight," he murmurs, the deep voice in my ear giving me the shivers. "You're so sexy, Hollis."

You're so sexy, Hollis.

Hollis.

My name, whispered like that?

An aphrodisiac so alluring I want to hear him say it over and over and over again. It would never be enough.

His hand is large enough to span my pelvis, and he spreads his fingers over my lower belly, one finger in my slit, other hand dragging its way up my body, cupping my breast.

"Your tits are perfect." He moans as if they are in fact the most perfect tits in all the land. Ordinarily I'd correct him to say, *No pair of tits are perfect, Buzz*, but to him, maybe they are. I am learning that about him; he says what he means and means what he says, even when it's nonsense. "You're so beautiful."

Perfect. Tight. Beautiful. Sexy.

"Mmm." I arch my back into it, loving the way it feels. Realizing at this moment we are going to do it. Do it, as in: the deed. Sex. The nasty. Bang, screw, fuck.

Yup, we are doing it, and I am NOT STOPPING IT.

Between my legs, the tip of his hard cock presses, creating friction despite not being inside me. It's plump and hot and I want it bad.

"Before we go any further, we should probably…" *find a condom*. I have some in my nightstand, but I'm afraid to tell him that, worried he'll judge me—but wanting to be safe.

Without being prompted, Trace half rolls toward the bedside table and yanks open the drawer, digs into the box that only has one missing, and pulls out a rubber. He doesn't question it and I don't remark on it, and before I know it, he's sliding it on.

It's weird watching that part—usually. Watching him do it, though? My mouth waters at the sight, knowing that stiff, hard dick is going to be inside me soon, and my heart-beat quickens.

I want it so bad.

He kisses me and our tongues meet. *Mmm*, I could do this all day, latching onto his mouth, savoring how sweet he tastes. Then. He's hovering above me. Positioning himself.

I'm wet, so it goes in easy—just the tip. He teases me

with it until my head is thrashing on the pillow and I'm no longer amused. I want to be fucked, good and hard, and I'm tired of waiting.

"Fuck me already," I blurt out impatiently, too horned up to be ashamed of my outburst.

"You like that, baby?" His voice dips as he pushes deeper, talking dirty. "I'm gonna fuck you good."

Fuck me good? *Oh lord.* Maybe I'm out of my league here.

Maybe I'm not ready for what he's got to give.

Maybe his dick will be too big and won't even fi—

It fits. I was wrong.

Latex-covered perfection, sliding all the way in. I moan, tipping my head back, almost certain my mouth is hanging open with wonder.

This is my sex face and there's no hiding it now.

Trace doesn't fuck me as hard as I'm expecting him to, considering all the trash talk he's been doing, but rather methodically. Slowly. Each thrust measured as if calculated specifically to hit the erogenous zones in my vagina.

He's so good at it.

It feels so good.

Good, good, good. My brain still won't work.

"Beautiful," he mutters, pumping into me. "You want to be on top?" he asks.

"No." I shake my head. "I want to watch you fuck me."

Fuck me, fuck me, fuck me.

"Shit, Hollis…God you feel amazing…" His body is low, not crushing mine but pressing against me, like he's doing planks for abs but having sex at the same time? Mouth near my ear, moaning and groaning.

I could listen to a tape of him screwing me and get off from it, I swear.

My hands grip his ass, which isn't easy because he's so much taller than I am.

It's heaven.

And as I come, a little part inside me cannot help thinking that perhaps...just maybe...he was meant for me.

"C an I tell you something and you promise you won't laugh?"

I can't make him a promise like that; Trace is hilarious and is always managing to make me laugh. He can't help it —he's funny and irresistible.

We're both staring at the ceiling in my dark bedroom, on our backs, and it's hard to believe we're lying here, fingers intertwined. Two lovebirds basking in the afterglow.

"Of course. You can tell me anything."

"Do you believe in..." Trace clears his throat then hastens to add, "Never mind. It's stupid."

I turn to face him, though I can't really see him that well in the dark, wanting to know what he was about to say. Give his hand a jostle. "What? You can say it—I won't judge you."

"I'm too embarrassed now," he says lightly. I feel him tug the blanket up to his chin and hide. "Don't look at me."

"Oh come on! You have to tell me now that you've brought it up—don't give me information blue balls."

He's still under the blanket like a weirdo. "I'm shy."

"Oh my god, you are not shy. You're the least shy human I know."

"I have stage fright."

I sputter out a laugh. "You're ridiculous."

There's something fantastic about laughing while

you're naked, being vulnerable with someone you just had sex with, and this moment will live with me forever—no matter what happens between the two of us. It is too cute and unforgettable.

He's being sweet.

I want to smush his cute face and coax out of him what he's too embarrassed to say.

I desperately want him to talk.

I try to be patient.

Wait him out.

"I hate rejection." The words are spoken quietly—so softly I have to strain to hear them.

"I think we all do."

"Hollis, I need you to know something," he says out of the dim lighting. "I'm not playing games with you."

Um—*okay*. Not what I was expecting him to say.

"But I think it's important because you're coming off a bad experience, and you didn't really want to start dating me. Yet here we are." He has my full attention now. "This is going to sound strange, because we just met. And maybe you'll think it's moving too fast…"

Oh shit.

Oh god.

Is he going to tell me he loves me? Already, after two weeks?

God what if he's going to propose?!

Whoa, Hollis. Whoa girl, where did that thought come from? The man simply said things were moving too fast.

Wait.

No.

He said *maybe* he thought I thought things were moving too fast.

My brain needs to stop talking so I can listen to what he's saying.

"…but I feel like maybe…we're soulmates."

The record player in my mind screeches to a halt, backs the conversation up, replaying the sentence in my mind on a loop. *Soulmates soulmates soulmates.*

He thinks we're what?

WHAT!

"You think we're soulmates." It's a statement, not a question; I am still floored by the announcement, letting an awkward silence linger in the air.

I don't know what to say, and it shows.

Beside me, I feel Trace's body stiffen. "I shouldn't have said anything—forget it."

The words "Uh, that's not going to happen" fly out of my mouth.

"You think it's stupid."

"No, I don't think it's stupid—I'm just surprised you don't. You're so manly and masculine." I say the words to soothe his bruised ego, my mind still reeling at a thousand miles per second. "I didn't think you'd be this sensitive."

I release his hand so I can roll over. Find his shoulder in the dark and kiss his bare skin, hand running over his chest. "I love that about you."

Shit.

I said l-o-v-e.

What if he thinks I'm *in* love with him?

I mean I'm *not.* Can't be!

Pfft, it's been two weeks!

"Do you?"

"I do. I think you're…" *Just tell him how you feel.* "Wonderful."

If only my father felt the same way.

18

Trace

"...I t's a shame Hollis couldn't make it today."

My mother attaches the statement to the tail end of another sentence, as if sliding it in under the radar will mean it goes unnoticed, as if she just announced the sky is blue, or flowers are pretty.

Innocuous and unassuming—yet glaringly horrifying.

"I'm sorry—what?"

We're at dinner after my game, the entire Wallace clan having driven to the Windy City for this one, including my brother and sister. We're seated at a large, round table in one of Chicago's most elegant restaurants.

They even have us seated in our own private room to avoid interruptions.

Mom loves it.

Makes her feel special.

"What, dear?" She won't look at me, just raises her brows and cuts a tomato on her salad plate.

"You said 'It's a shame Hollis couldn't make it today.' Were you implying something?"

Genevieve's shoulders rise and fall in an innocent shrug. "I just said it was a shame she couldn't come."

Why would she have come? "Did...you invite her?"

"I might have?"

Translation: she did.

"Dang it, Ma! Why didn't you tell me?"

"What difference does it make? She couldn't make it." Mom continues busying herself with her appetizer salad, successfully avoiding my wild eyes and gaping stare.

"Who's Hollis?"

"Your brother's girlfriend," Dad causally tells my sister like it's no big deal.

Shit. How did I forget I'm perpetuating a lie to my parents and now my sister? "She's not...I mean...Hollis is..."

Everyone watches me while I fumble over my words.

Tripp puts down his utensils and crosses his arms, leans back into his chair and settles in for the show he knows is coming—let's face it, he knows the Hollis thing is bullshit, and he's here for my inevitable downfall in front of our parents.

Fucker.

"You have a girlfriend?" My sister's surprise is palpable. "Why haven't I met her? Why isn't she here?" She reaches behind her, into her purse and pulls out her phone. "What's her name? I want to look her up on social media."

"True, leave it be. Hollis isn't..." I can't even say it without a guilty lump forming in my throat.

"Hollis isn't what, dear?" Now my mom is watching me, hope on her brows. "Hollis isn't on the 'Gram?"

Jesus.

I hate myself right now. I sigh. "The truth is...Hollis is more like...she's..." Let's see, how do I tell them the truth? "She's more of a friend."

"Friends with benefits?" True asks.

"No—just friends."

"Friends to lovers?" Mom clarifies. Leaning over, she touches my sister's arm conspiratorially. "That's my favorite genre of romance novels, just so you know." She beams around the table and I want to throw up.

"No, Mom." But technically yes, now that we've slept together, we would be considered friends to lovers. I think. "More like not friends to sort of friends."

"But..." The hope on Mom's face turns to bewilderment. "Then why did she come all the way to our house? Why did you tell us you were dating? Why did she go through all that trouble? I'm so confused."

"Uh..." is my brilliant answer.

"I think what dipshit here is trying to tell us is that Hollis doesn't want anything to do with him and only came to the house because he was lording something over her head." Satisfied he's solved some great mystery, he resumes his dinner, picking up his steak knife and chiseling away at the meat on his plate.

"You're saying that like it's a crime." I want to punch my brother for his accuracy.

"The real crime here would be that poor girl becoming Hollis Wallace if she permanently attached herself to this one." My sister throws her thumb in my direction, forking the chef salad in front of her and stuffing a mouthful in her face.

Do both my siblings have to be such heathens? Where is the humanity? Where is the compassion?

"Hollis Wallace." I set my fork down, dismayed. "Why does everyone keep saying that like it's a bad thing?"

"Literally no one has ever said that," my brother quips, rolling his eyes. He's on the far side of the table so I can't kick his shin.

"*Literally* people have, so shut up."

Our sister laughs, her brown eyes lighting up gleefully. She always has loved it when Tripp and I argue—when we were kids, she'd purposely get us into fights, then she'd sit and watch from the sidelines until one of us ended up getting yelled at by our parents.

Never her.

Always us.

"You shut up," Tripp counters.

"I said you shut up."

We are five.

"Don't say shut up to your brother," Mom chastises, always in mom mode. "Stop it, both of you."

"Yeah, don't tell me to shut up," Tripp retorts.

True cackles.

Dad grunts, biting into a jumbo prawn, ignoring the entire table as per usual.

"So she's not your girlfriend," Mom goes on. "She didn't look like just your friend to me." Then a thought enters her brain. "I let the two of you share a bedroom! Trace Robert Wallace do not tell me anything untoward happened in that guest room."

"Does dry humping count as untoward?" I muse, glancing off into the distance.

Mom's water glass stops halfway to her mouth. "You better be lying."

Tripp cackles.

True is laughing so hard she can hardly breathe.

I hate them both.

"Trace." My name on my mother's lips holds a warning. "Tell me you're lying."

"Okay, I'm lying."

She tries again. "Are you lying?"

"Yes."

"Trace!"

"You told me to lie!"

"I meant tell the truth!"

"Fine, okay, we kicked it old school. Is that what you want to hear? Heavy petting only. Jeez, Mom, there was no penetration—we're just friends."

"Don't say penetration at the supper table," Dad finally says, scolding me, causing my sister to launch into a laughing fit.

"Penile-tration," Tripp mumbles, not wanting to be left out of the fun.

"Boys!" Mom gasps.

"I'm 28," Tripp reminds her. He points to me. "Tweedledumb is 27."

I scowl. "I hate when you call me that."

My brother shrugs, slicing more meat from the steak on his plate, setting it on his tongue. "You're the dumb to my dee. Get over it."

I open my mouth to speak.

Tripp interrupts. "Ah, ah, ah—don't say it."

True chokes on her bacon, waving her hand in the air for us to, "Stop. Just stop, I can't."

"Why do I bother with you people?" I'm so friggin' irritated right now. They're so annoying sometimes!

"You people? *You* people?" Tripp feigns indignance. "I have never been so insulted."

Mom pats him on the arm. "Trace, you're hurting your brother's feelings."

"Yeah, you're hurting my feelings."

Idiot.

"I am not."

Before any of us can say another word, Dad reenters the conversation. Good old Rog, who can always be counted on to make everything awkward.

"Circling back around to Hollis," he drawls out, as only my father can. "Are you dating the girl or not?"

And it all begins again.

❧

Me: *A little bird told me you were invited to the baseball game tonight.*

Hollis: *Was that little bird your mom?*

Me: *Lol yes.*

Me: *Why didn't you come?*

Hollis: *I didn't know if you'd want me to. I didn't want to assume...*

Me: *We slept together.*

Hollis: *That doesn't mean you want me just showing up places.*

Me: *Uh...remember how I said you're my soulmate?*

Hollis: *You didn't say I'm your soulmate, you said you THOUGHT we might be.*

Me: *What dude says shit like that if he doesn't want the girl hanging around?*

Hollis: *Dudes who want to get in your pants.*

Me: *We're not starting that shit. You know that's not the case.*

Hollis: *I'm still trying to sort it all out, okay? I'm... I just need to take it slow.*

Me: *Slow...*

Me: *For what?*

Hollis: *I don't know, Trace! It felt like the right thing to say.*

Me: *Since when are we picking and choosing the right words to say? I thought we were going to be honest and say how we felt.*

Hollis: *I don't remember having that conversation.*

Me: *Wow.*

Hollis: *I didn't mean it like that. You know what I meant. I'm sorry, I'm just tired...*

Me: *It's fine.*

Hollis: *Fine: something people say when things aren't fine. This conversation is way too serious for me right now. What happened to lighthearted Buzz?*

Me: *Oh, the Buzz you don't want to date because he's NOT SERIOUS ENOUGH? That guy? The one you don't trust because he's on a team with your fuckboy of an ex?*

Hollis: *Don't put words into my mouth, okay? All I said was maybe I'm just trying to figure stuff out.*

Me: *Hey it's cool.*

Hollis: *Somehow you saying that is worse.*

Me: *I don't know what you want. I thought we were getting along. Making progress and shit.*

Hollis: *We are.*

Me: *Alright. Well. I just wanted you to know that we missed you at dinner tonight, and—sorry my mom invited you. Hope it didn't put you in a weird position.*

Me: *If it makes you feel better, I told everyone we were just friends, so you're off the hook.*

Hollis: *Honesty is good. I did feel bad for your mom.*

Me: *Yeah, I know. Everyone always feels bad for Genevieve Wallace with her two unruly sons.*

Hollis: *I didn't mean it like that…*

Me: *I know. I know you hated lying and now you don't have to anymore. I'll never ask you to lie for me again—I shouldn't have in the first place, and again, I apologize.*

Hollis: *Now you're making me feel bad.*

Me: *For what?*

Hollis: *I don't not like you, Trace—I'm just letting it all sink in. You know what I want, someone who is there for me.*

Me: *How do you know I won't be there for you when you need me if you won't give me a chance?*

Hollis: *You're in the midst of your season. You don't have time to date now anyway. Maybe we should wait until the season is over.*

Me: *Sure.*
Me: *Whatever you say Hollis.*

19

Hollis

Why do I get the feeling I'm forgetting something?

The thought niggles at the back of my mind as I sit across from a potential new author in the conference room of the small publishing house I work for, one of three that exist in Chicago. Would I love to work for one in New York? Yes. Is that my ultimate goal? Also yes.

Will that ever happen?

Who even knows.

I'm ashamed to admit it, but I'm only half present for this meeting with Lesley Ashby, an interior designer pitching a coffee table book to my boss. Her book is bold, bright, but—nothing groundbreaking or new.

I already know my boss is going to red-light the pitch unless Lesley comes up with something more creative than photographing expensive interiors and floral tablescapes.

Who can afford that anymore?

"We'll get back to you, Lesley," my boss is saying as she rises. "Thank you so much for coming in." She extends her hand to shake Lesley's. "Tina in reception can grab you a swag bag for the road if you're interested."

That's what Wanda gives to everyone she's giving the green weenie.

A canvas tote bag filled with Twilite Publishing goodies no one, but a book nerd actually wants: koozie, bookmarks, reading light, magnet, car decal.

Lesley Ashby is going to trash the entire bag once she hears back that we're not going to represent her and shop her book.

When she leaves the room, my shoulders sag.

It's been the longest day, the Mondayest Tuesday ever, and my feet are killing me in these heels. My feet and my heart, both throbbing, though in entirely different ways.

It's been five days since I last spoke to Buzz. He has left me alone since our texts on Thursday, but that hasn't stopped me from reading and rereading them over and over.

Like the script for a bad play, they make me cringe. Seeing what I wrote and reliving it? Also embarrassing.

He didn't deserve what I said and I realized over the weekend that I was projecting my relationship fears onto him. Fears about ending up with a man just like my father. Fears about ending up with a man just like Marlon. Fears about ending up alone because I'm too stubborn and scared to let myself open up.

I have a few more things to get done before I head home for the night and I make quick work of my to-do list. A few emails, a bound manuscript that has to get mailed back to its author for edits, I tidy up. Grab my coat, laptop bag, keys.

Our office isn't in a skyscraper. Rather, it's an eight-story, brick confection sandwiched between two corporate edifices, but with an attached parking structure. In the winter, it's a lifesaver having covered parking in downtown Chicago. In the summer, it's a lifesaver not having to walk block after block in the heat.

My car is where it always is, parked in the third spot next to the stairwell. Not too far from the exit, but not so close that it's the last car in the row and thus susceptible to vandalism. In the past, we've had issues with that. Because it's a small, less-expensive building, security isn't as tight as it would be in a high-rise.

With a heavy heart, I sigh, another day down but a full night of alone ahead of me. I wonder what Trace is doing tonight, what he had for dinner. *He probably went to crash Noah and Miranda's supper.* No wait—it's Tuesday.

He's probably out eating tacos.

Or maybe, like me, he has no appetite and can't eat at all.

I wish I had the nerve to call him, but after almost an entire week, is he likely to give a shit? Women chase after this man—he isn't going to wait around for one who doesn't.

Lost in my thoughts, I don't see the man lurking next to my car, fiddling with the door handle. Lost in my thoughts, I don't see him startle when he sees me approach.

One second I'm carrying my laptop bag, the next second it's being yanked out of my grip.

"Hey!" I shout, caught off guard, barely registering what's happening.

But I'm in his way, blocking his exit, so he has to shove me to get by.

The mace—the mace! You have mace, Hollis.

I fumble for my keychain and the pink canister hanging there, a gift from Madison after I got my first apartment. Three years old and never been deployed, I pray something shoots out when I push down the little trigger.

My aim is terrible.

The man tries hitting me, still latched onto my bag.

"Let go of the bag you fucking bitch!"

Let go of the bag, Hollis—it's not worth it.

But wouldn't he have shot me already if he had a gun? Wouldn't he have stabbed me if he had a knife? A million thoughts enter my brain, none of them to flee.

"Fuck you," I tell him, spraying, pointing the pink mace at his face. I squeeze the button and squeeze my eyes shut at the same time.

Open them and press the red button on my key fob.

The car alarm blaring is barely loud enough to attract attention, but the mace on my keychain is enough to make him lose his damn mind—and his eyesight.

The man falls to the ground, screaming in pain, hands cupping his eyes, begging me to throw water on his face.

"Give me some damn water, you fucking bitch!" he screams. "I know you have some bitch." He calls me *bitch* over and over—not that I blame him. "I'm blind, you whore!"

Shouldn't have tried to steal my stuff motherfucker.

Shaking uncontrollably, I somehow manage to dial 911 on my cell phone while holding the mace in his direction—in case I have to spray him again while I'm waiting for the police.

It takes them eight minutes to get here.

Another few for the officers to peel him off the ground and arrest him. Cuff him, put him in the back of their squad car. It's unpleasant business—the man is cursing at them now too, worse obscenities than he called me and he's spitting.

I'm trembling still and don't think I can drive. Not in the city, not like this. In any case, they need me down at the station, so I can release a statement and file a report.

They give me a ride, and on the way there, I shoot my best friend a text to let her know what's going on.

Madison calls (like I figured she would), but I send her to voicemail; I'm in no mood to chat, especially not in a squad car with a police officer. Maddie would inevitably ask if he was good-looking and single and I'd have to disappoint her and tell her the officer I'm riding with is female.

She makes chitchat with me, trying to bring down my stress level and calm me down.

"I'm fine now. I'm fine." *Keep saying it—maybe it will come true.*

And I am, for the most part. The odds of getting robbed or mugged are low—I was just the unlucky one who interrupted Alvin Butterfield while he was trying to break into cars and steal loose change from the cup holders.

Parts of me are sympathetic; resorting to crime to feed yourself is a reality I've never had to face. The other part of me is angry—he could have hurt me and I could have hurt him, all over some spare change.

I don't even keep money in my car. It was a bad investment on his end to waste so much time trying to get inside, considering the outcome.

Still.

Here I am, sitting at the police station in Precinct Five. It's an old college campus they converted into law enforcement offices, and I follow the officer into the lobby. Plop down in a chair straight out of the eighties—they obviously didn't have the budget to redecorate when they bought the building, comfort being the least of their priorities.

Hookers and pimps have sat in these chairs...

I squirm.

Stand, rooting through my bag for hand sanitizer. Douse myself.

Before long, I'm seated across from the arresting officer and she begins taking my statement. I describe how I left work and had my head down walking into the parking structure (a mistake). I told her I had my hands full, but my keys ready. I told her about how I didn't notice Alvin Butterfield trying to break into my car until I was upon him—how we both startled each other. How he lost his mind when I sprayed him in the eyes.

Thank god I had that pepper spray.

The officer types everything I say, word for word, asking me if I want to press charges and explaining what happens if I do. The steps to take, what comes next.

Then.

A loud commotion sounds from the far side of the room.

"Sir, you can't just bust in here like this. Sir!"

The voices have my head turning toward the door, toward the looming, imposing figure that's suddenly appeared there.

"Would someone stop him, please?" another voice calls out. "He can't just be in here."

"I'm confused," someone else says. "Is that Buzz Wallace or am I hallucinating?"

He is most certainly not hallucinating and *what the hell is Buzz doing at the cop shop?*

"Hollis?" He's speed walking toward me, weaving through desks, massive body seemingly taking up the entire place.

He is larger than life and he's here.

At the police station.

It makes zero sense.

"Trace?" My mouth is hanging open; I can feel it. "What are you doing here?"

"Madison called me."

How the hell would she have accomplished that? "How did she get your number?"

He shrugs his wide shoulders. "Must have gotten it the same way I got yours." His hands clasp my upper arms and he crouches, so he can look me straight in the eyes. "Are you alright? Are you hurt?"

I glance at his body, up and down, then up at his face. "Why are you wearing a uniform?"

His head cocks to the side. "It's a game day."

He says it so matter-of-factly. As if it's no big deal that he's standing in a police station dressed in a uniform to play in a Major League Baseball game.

"Why are you here?" I'm horrified, actually. Panicked. Why is he here when he has a game—is he insane? "Are you nuts? You cannot be here!"

"Madison said you were robbed and that you were at the police station," Buzz explains, as if his presence is the most normal thing about this situation.

"But why are you here? You. Have. A. Game." Why do I feel like I'm talking to a brick wall? He isn't listening— doesn't seem to care that I'm frantically trying to reason this away. He cannot be here. This isn't normal.

"They won't miss me until the last few innings. Don't worry about it."

Oh my god. "When does the game start?"

"Half an hour ago."

"When..." I swallow. "When did Madison call you?"

"'Bout half an hour ago," he replies distractedly, checking me up and down for bruises. "He didn't hurt you, did he? It was a he, yeah?"

He left a professional baseball game before they even

sang the national anthem because I got mugged at work in a parking garage?

He left. A Major. League. Baseball game…because I got mugged at work.

And he hasn't even taken me on an actual date yet. And he's acting like him showing up is no big deal.

He dropped everything to be here.

Tears well in my eyes as his continue scanning my body, officers looking on, giving us our space. I notice, out of the corner of my eye, one or two of them taking pictures on the sly.

"Oh my god, Hollis, what's wrong?" His hands are cradling my face now and the concern in his eyes has wet wells streaming down my face.

I wish he would stop.

I hate when I ugly cry.

"Babe. Talk to me."

That makes it worse, and I cry harder, sniffling when he pulls me into his chest, face now pressed against his Steam jersey. The one with the Under Armour sponsorship logo. The one with his name plastered on the back side of it. The one that earns him millions of dollars per year.

This sweet, ridiculous man who thinks I'm crying because I was accosted today.

Even with my face pressed against his massive chest, I see another figure out of the corner of my eye. Think I've officially lost my mind, because—is that my dad? It can't be. Why would he be here, too?

Perhaps Madison also called him.

She would call him—not only out of concern for me, but because she thinks he's hot and will use any opportunity to hit on him. *Ew.*

The man isn't approaching us, just watching from the

lobby. I can see him through the glass which could use a good scrubbing, and realize…

It's not my dad at all.

It's another officer—probably a detective—wearing a suit and a badge and my shoulders sag.

It figures my father couldn't trouble himself to come see about my welfare. Not on a game day.

But here is Buzz, squishing my face into his jersey, running a large palm down my spine to comfort me. Patting my head and muttering, "Shhh, shh…" into my hair.

I wrap my arms around him and squeeze. Bury my nose deeper into his shirt and give him a sniff. He smells like fresh shower, laundered sports apparel, and cologne. And old gym socks.

He must be superstitious.

A deep voice clears its throat, and I peel myself out of Buzz's embrace to find the detaining officer and her colleague watching us with raised brows.

"Um…this is my friend Trace. Sorry, my *other* friend called him to tell him I was here—he didn't mean to interrupt."

"I'm her boyfriend." His smile is huge and affectionate. "The little scamp will deny it, of course, since we haven't been on a date yet, but it's inevitable."

"He's not my boyfriend." Oh my god, he needs to tone it down a notch. "Now is not the time for your shenanigans."

"Pfft. It's always a good time for shenanigans, am I right, officers?" He shoots them a wink.

They're speechless. I mean, what the hell are they supposed to say to that? To him? A god among mortal men, standing in their precinct.

"Ms. Westbrooke, if you wouldn't mind having a seat

so we can finish up here? Then you can be on your way."
They're still staring at Trace.

"They called you Ms. Westbrooke—that's so cute! You
know what's cuter? Hollis Wallace." He pulls my chair
back out, so I can sit, then pulls out the one next to it.
"Holly Wolly."

"If I threaten to murder him in front of you, does that
lead to an automatic conviction?" I'm asking the officer in
front of me. I can't decide if she's amused or not, but I'm
certainly not, and he NEEDS TO GO. Away. Now.

"There she goes, role-playing the *Lifetime Movie Network*.
Love it when she does that." He presses a soft noogie to the
top of my head.

My hand covers the seat, so he cannot sit. "You need to
go," I tell him.

"But I'm here."

I roll my eyes. "No, Buzz—go back to work."

He rolls his eyes back at me. "They can wait."

They. The people. The fans. The team owners and
investors. The millions of people watching from their
homes, on television.

The entire statement, delivered so calmly, makes me
laugh. Makes the female officer's eyes widen—fortunately
she doesn't interject or ask questions because the *last* thing
I need is someone encouraging his obstinate behavior.

The team can wait? A stadium filled with fifty thousand people can *wait*? Has he lost his damn mind?

"You can go. I'll be fine." I look to the officer. "I'm in
good hands, trust me. You can call me when you're done."

Like we're discussing him going back to work at an
office. Or at a restaurant. Or as if he works retail. *Yeah, sure,
give me a shout when you're off work! No big deal!*

The reality: give me a shout when you're done playing
baseball in front of a crowd of nearly fifty thousand. A

crowd that will generate millions upon millions of dollars in a single evening, with music and cheering and billionaires looking down on you from boxes in the sky.

Yeah. No big deal.

Go do that then give me a shout, but thanks for stopping by.

Once again, everyone is staring at us—more Buzz than me. I'm just some random girl who experienced an attempted robbery. All in a day's work for the police, but it's not every day a professional athlete comes busting through their doors, dressed in his complete uniform, straight from the stadium a few blocks up.

"How did you even get here so fast?" I can't help asking.

"I took a cab." Of course he did. "They're everywhere around the stadium today—only had a little trouble getting through the fans who recognized me, but most of them just thought I was some freak dressed like me."

Again. Super casual, no big deal.

He is really something else…

And growing on me with every passing second. My heart flutters and contracts. I hope I'm not watching him with doe eyes. Ugh.

He relents to my nudging, hesitating. "Are you sure you're going to be alright?" His hand is on my shoulder now, because I'm sitting down, and he's looking down at me like I'm looking up at him. "I feel horrible just leaving you here."

He showed up, though, because he wanted to see that I was okay.

And I am.

In fact, I've never been more okay than I am tonight.

~

M **e:** *Did Madison call you today by any chance?*
     Dad: *She did.*
Me: *And did you hear about what happened…?*

Dad: *She mentioned something about you being robbed in the parking structure at your office.*

Me: *I half expected you to come walking into the police station.*

Dad: *There was a game today, Hollis—you know I cannot miss a home game.*

Me: *Right. You had to work. While I was in the police station because I was almost robbed.*

Dad: *But you were not.*

Me: *But I could have been.*

Dad: *Well I will say this, Hollis—if you were working for me, alongside your brother and sister, this wouldn't have happened. We have secure parking at the stadium.*

Me: *I can't believe you just said that.*

Dad: *Forgive me if I'm still—pardon the pun—a little steaming mad that one of my star players left the game before it even started to hold the hand of my grown daughter.*

Me: *I did not call him to come. And how can you judge him for wanting to be by my side?*

Dad: *I told you not to be a distraction. We discussed this.*

Me: *I can't control what he does—I had no idea a man I'm not even dating would show up when my own FAMILY wouldn't. So now I know whom I can depend on.*

Dad: *You know the rules about game days. There are to be no events planned on days I have to travel or work.*

Me: *Events? You call my being mugged an EVENT? LOL omg Dad.*

Dad: *There's no need to be churlish.*

Me: *There's no need to be an uncaring, selfish ass, but here we are.*

Me: *This is the reason*

I almost say, *This is the reason Mom left*, but I can't bring myself to send it. It's cruel and uncalled for. I'm not hurt he didn't come to the police station—I never expected him to in the first place. What I am upset about is the fact that he isn't showing the least bit of concern for anything that happened to me. In fact, he's irritated at the mere thought that I've forgotten the Thomas Westbrooke cardinal rule: no emergencies or events on game days, and this includes birthday parties, baptisms, retirements, communions, graduations, weddings, bat mitzvahs, funerals, and births.

Yes, we're not allowed to give birth on a game day. Not that he would come to the hospital anyway.

Let's be honest here: Dad wasn't at much of anything. I played sports through school, but he probably couldn't tell you which ones (volleyball and field hockey). I was on prom court once, but he wouldn't know that, either—he wasn't there for the grand march. Prom wasn't during the official baseball season, but when wasn't it baseball season in our house? It was never not in season.

He was never not too busy.

Including today.

Dad: *I don't know why you're upset—your boyfriend was there.*

Me: *He's not my*

I pause before finishing the sentence and hitting send. Pause and stare at the sentence I'm about to write. Trace Wallace might not be my boyfriend, but so far, he's acted more like one than any guy I've ever dated. Or not dated.

He's trying so hard, and I've done nothing but push back.

Why?

Why won't I let him in?

Because you were afraid he was going to be like your dad since he works for your dad. Not to mention, he's the best-looking guy you've ever laid eyes on.

His face and body and voice could melt my butter with or without the sun.

Me: *We're taking it slow, but I'm glad to have someone in my life who makes me a priority.*

Dad: *I don't appreciate him walking out on his contract.*

Me: *Is that how you see it?*

Dad: *You're missing the point here, Hollis.*

Me: *Um, respectfully disagree, Dad. This isn't about money to me like it is for you—and for once I think I might have met someone who prioritizes people over money, too.*

Dad: *That sounds ridiculous.*

Me: *Only because you can't relate.*

Dad: *If the kid doesn't prioritize his INCOME then he should re-evaluate what he does for a living.*

Me: *He loves baseball Dad.*

Dad: *I know he does. That's why I need him to stay focused.*

Me: *Did he have a shitty game today?*

Dad: *No. He's played the best I've ever seen him play.*

Me: *Well...then maybe...I'm the best thing for him. And maybe he's the best thing for me.*

There is a long, long pause, the three dots appearing and disappearing more times than I can count and I hold my breath when they appear again.

Dad: *Maybe he is.*

I stare at those three words, stunned.

Me: *Wait. Are you...AGREEING with me???*

Dad: *Don't get lippy.*

Me: *Okay, but it sounds like you are. It sounds like you...dare I say...APPROVE????*

Dad: *That will be determined once you start bringing the boy around.*

Kid. Boy.

Oh brother. Those are words Dad uses when he's trying to put someone in their place. He does the same thing to my brother and it sounds like he's going to do it to Trace, to knock him down a peg.

What an asshole.

Still. It's progress. My father is actually admitting he might like having Trace around as part of the family. Potentially. Or at least admitting he doesn't hate the idea.

Me: *We'll see what happens I guess. Today was a good start. A horrible, horrible day, but also not the worst, all things considered. Some good came out of it.*

Dad: *You always have been too romantic for your own good.*

Me: *Coming from you, I'll take that as a compliment.*

20

Trace

This is the first time Hollis is seeing my place, and I haven't stopped fussing. I've fluffed the stupid throw pillows on my couch more times than I can count—an embarrassing number of times considering they're fucking throw pillows. What self-respecting dude has this many?

I remove two and toss them behind the sofa.

Now it looks bare.

Climb onto the couch and retrieve them, karate-chopping them in the center like I've seen my cleaning lady do. Fluff and chop, fluff and chop.

I had a long-ass day and walked in the door an hour ago, but Hollis had a shitty day, so I invited her over, thinking she might want to be fed and pampered a little.

I had to google "romantic things to do for a woman," and some of the ideas were super lame, but a few of them I can manage on my own.

Draw her a bath. *Check.*

Light candles. *Check.*

Order flowers. *Check.*

Order take-out. *Check.*

Massage—that I can pull off with just my bear paws, one hundred percent into it. We all know where *massages* lead.

I chuckle to myself and stand back, eyeing the pillows I just rearranged for the tenth time, deciding I need to leave them the fuck alone and move on with my pathetic life.

Dinner arrives via delivery and I tip the dude a fifty because he recognizes me. If I don't, he's going to go online and tell everyone Buzz Wallace is a cheap bastard who only gave him five bucks while living in a giant house.

It's not a mansion, or anything close to as fancy as what Noah Harding and Miranda are living in, but it's a gorgeous place I renovated and remodeled with my bare hands. It's not a gated community, so every now and again I get the odd passerby who drives slow past the house. Or a brave teenager who knocks on the door to meet me. Or a bored, brazen housewife who wants to try her luck at fucking me.

I won't lie—there was a time I was down for that. I was bored and lonely, but now…

I'm not.

I have Hollis.

I have her, I know it—and I plan to keep her, and not in an 'I'm going to make a lamp out of your skin' kind of way.

The kitchen still needs some cleaning up and I transfer the take-out to glass bowls with lids; it's Asian fusion and steaming hot. I hope she likes it. I ordered a shit ton, not knowing what her favorites would be but wanting to learn what they are.

I want to learn everything about her, she's so damn adorable.

The look on her face when she saw me at the police

station today was everything. Confusion, obviously—but also delight. Joy? Weird how someone can look visibly relieved. Her shoulders sagged when I touched her, wrapped my arms around her, and squeezed, something she's never done.

I busy myself by double-checking the bathroom and pulling the quilt taut on my bed. It's a big bed—a California King and extra long because I'm tall—but I don't expect us to end up there.

Fine.

I'm hoping we will, but I'm not *expecting* it.

Pop my nose into the bathroom again and check on the bathwater. It flows from the ceiling—totally impractical, but super cool, I had to have it when I was shopping for houses. Had to. It's so dumb, but something I thought kids would like.

My kids.

Three would be good. Or five. However many, getting cracking on a family would be swell.

Because I'm feeling extra romantic, I had candles delivered from Target through an app, and I start lighting them one by one, expecting Hollis to ring my doorbell any second now. No sense in waiting, as I intend for her to slip right into the bath.

Shit.

What if she thinks it's bizarre instead of romantic that I want her to relax in the tub? What if she thinks I'm a pervert and just trying to get her naked? It's not like I'm going to climb in with her, but there's a nice ledge I could sit on so we can talk while she soaks. My plan is to pour a little bit of my heart out to her; the bubble bath seems like the perfect spot to listen from.

Again…is that weird?

The doorbell chimes as I light the last white candle. *Guess I'm about to find out...*

"Here goes nothing," I say to no one, since I live alone.

Forever Alone, a new men's fragrance, by Tripp Wallace.

That joke about my brother makes me laugh, and I'm chuckling when I make it to the front door, pulling it open with a smile. Take in a quick breath, because wow, is Hollis beautiful.

"Hi." She's standing on the stoop in a little floral dress and flip-flops, casual but feminine, comfortable, but put together. "I brought you these."

She hands me a plate of chocolate chip cookies that still feel warm, and I hold them to my nose, sniffing. "Damn these smell almost as good as you."

Can't wait to eat them. *And her.*

I lean down when she steps up and into the house, giving her a quick kiss on the cheek, and damn if she doesn't surprise me by puckering her mouth for a kiss on the lips.

Whoa, and it's a good one, too.

"How are you?" I lead her to the kitchen, setting the cookies on the counter while Hollis begins the classic snoop-around people do when they're curious about your living situation. Her neck cranes to the doorway of the hearth room; it's off my kitchen with a small fireplace and a TV, kind of like the den. Intimate and smaller and my favorite room in the house.

"This is nice," she says, now with her nose in the powder room, which is also off the kitchen. "Do you clean this?"

"No. Jenny and Tiffani do every Monday."

They're my dynamic duo—they call themselves Grime Busters and love scrubbing. Weird, right?

"I like how there's tile all the way up the wall."

"I laid that tile myself," I tell her, getting two wine glasses out of the cabinet and setting them down. Find the bottle of white in the fridge that's been chilling and locate the corkscrew. "Wine?"

"Sure."

"So, this might sound strange…"

Why is it hard for me to talk to this girl? She gets me all nervous!

"Everything you say is strange," she teases. "Just say it."

"I drew you a bath."

Her brows shoot up; that's the absolute last thing she's expecting to come out of my mouth, something I've come to expect from her. "A bath? Why, do I stink?" She lifts her arm and sniffs her pits.

I make busy pouring a small glass of white wine for each of us and hand her one. "You smell delicious, but you had a bad day and I thought soaking would be nice." In a cheeseball move I'll remember as being the turning point, I take her hand and pull her in. Kiss her on the lips. "A good bubble bath cures almost anything."

"Is that so?"

"Yup. I even have bath bombs for you. They're phallic."

The brows shoot back up into her hairline. "Phallic? Like dicks and vaginas?"

I shrug. "Meh, I wish—they're eggplants and peaches. Come on, I'll show you."

Up the stairs and down the hall to my bedroom, her neck does the craning thing she did downstairs to peer into the passing rooms. Guest room. Office. Bonus space. Another guest room.

My bedroom.

It's simple, nothing crazy: my giant bed, the TV cabinet, a nightstand and lamp on each side of the bed. The basics.

Clean lines.

I've picked up my bathroom, too, so there aren't any skivvies lying around—dirty underwear did never a woman seduce. They've been swiped up and put in the hamper, off to the laundry for Tiff and Jen on Monday.

"Wow." Hollis makes for the tub. It's a ridiculously large bowl, sized for someone my height, devoid of bubbles because I wasn't sure what she'd want in it.

I show her the box, picking out a boat and presenting it to her. "Motorboating."

Hollis laughs. "That is not what that one means! It's got to be something else. River of love? The love boat?"

"Nah, it's motorboating." I put it back in the box and pull out the one shaped like a clam. "Crotch."

She smacks my arm. "Stop it."

The peach. "Juicy ass."

Hollis nods. "Okay, that one I believe."

Eggplant. "Cock."

Another nod. "Accurate."

"This one I'm not sure about." It's a gold fortune cookie looking thing—half croissant, half I don't know what the fuck. I turn it this way and that in my fingers, getting gold glitter on my hands. Swipe some on my face. "Now it looks like I've been to a strip club."

She removes it from my hand and sets it back in the box. "You are twelve."

"So are you going in?"

Hollis tilts her head and studies the water. "Are you going to sit here and keep me company?"

Duh. "Thought you'd never ask." I point to the bath bombs on the ledge. "Do you want one of these or bubbles?"

She plucks the peach emoji bomb from the pink, cardboard box and examines it. Gives it a whiff. "This one smells so good. I'll pop it in the water once I'm in the tub."

"Should I…" Leave? "Give you some privacy?"

She purses her lips for a few seconds while she considers. "Just don't stare at me directly while I'm getting undressed and we'll be fine. It's not like you haven't seen me naked already."

"Or licked your pussy."

She rolls her eyes. "You didn't have to say that, but yes —since you've already licked my pussy, what's the point of me being modest?"

Holy shit. "I can't believe you just said the P word." I'm giggling like a teenager in health class and covering my mouth, too.

"You boys are so dumb."

I laugh again but turn my back so she can undress, setting my sights on the terrycloth towels. Grab two of those, and a bathrobe, fold them neatly on the cool tile surrounding the tub.

Plus, I can see her reflection in the mirror while I'm gathering bath supplies, so I'm no angel.

It takes her a few moments to get her clothes off, and I watch her firm ass flex when her leg bends so she can lift it over the short ledge. She has a lovely backside.

Once she's submerged and plops the bath bomb into the water, I turn around to join her, bringing the wine glasses along with me.

She takes a dainty sip, her best parts still visible in the water.

The bomb fizzes and the water gets cloudy—but not nearly enough to conceal her tits or the V between her thighs.

Don't stare.

Don't stare.

"Ugh, this feels amazing. I don't have a tub at my place. I mean, I do, but not in my bathroom, and the guest tub is the size of a Tic Tac."

It pleases me that she's happy.

Her eyes slide shut as she sips from her glass, making tiny slurping sounds as she does it. "Mmm." Hollis cracks an eyelid. "Why is this bathtub so huge?"

"'Cause I'm huge."

"Do you ever sit in it?"

"Yeah, sometimes. I have to soak my muscles."

She assesses me for a bit. "How was your game today? I never asked."

"We won."

"What was the score?"

"Eleven to ten."

Her lips release a low whistle. "That's a close one."

"It was a real nail-biter."

"What time did you get there?"

"Eh, end of the first inning. No one missed me." I pause. "Getting back into the stadium was a real shitshow, though. I didn't have any ID on me because who the fuck carries their wallet in their baseball uniform?"

"Didn't Karl recognize you?"

"It was some other guy—he just assumed I was a doppelgänger tryin' to lie my way inside. Can you imagine what a clusterfuck it would have been if they hadn't let me in?" I laugh.

She laughs. "My dad would have killed you."

"Well, I'll tell you, Coach about had a coronary. He nearly stroked out when I walked out just before being up in the lineup and I got my ass chewed out when I got back."

That's an understatement. I got fined twenty thousand

dollars, too—not that I'm going to tell Hollis that. She'd be horrified.

"Sounds like you had a rough day, too."

I did, but, "No one tried to rob me."

One of her toes peeks out of the water. "Are you sore?"

I am. "Kind of."

"If I let you join me, can you behave yourself?"

Is she out of her mind? "No."

Hollis laughs, and her tits rise and fall beneath the water's surface. "I can't fault you for your honesty, can I?"

"Nope." I'm already shucking off my shirt, pulling it up and over my head. Flexing for her to get a laugh before moving on to my bottoms. "Close your eyes—no peeking."

She puts a hand over her eyes, spying through her fingers.

Then,

I'm naked.

Hollis makes room so I can settle into the water opposite her, my ass finding space next to her legs. They're smooth and I have to touch them almost immediately, before I even get comfortable.

Can't keep my hands off.

The water rises several inches, causing Hollis's boobs to sink below the surface.

Dammit!

We each make room for one another, eventually finding positions where we're not scrunched up. My knees are slightly bent, which is nothing new. I'm too tall for any bathtub, and when you add a girl into the mix, someone will be sitting here like a pretzel, and it's inevitably me.

Worth it.

"Want to add another bath bomb?" I want to partake in the tub froth, too. Why should she have all the fun?

"Mmm, not really? Is that okay? I feel like I'm one

bath bomb away from a yeast infection." She mimics a laugh, cringing. "But for real. Yikesss."

Okay, so no to more fizzle fun. "Roger Dodger. I'd rather give you a UTI from too much sex than a yeast infection from soap." I cough when she doesn't laugh, dipping my head below the surface to avoid her bemused expression.

Count to three and pop back up to the sound of her voice saying, "I've had a urinary tract infection before and let me tell you—"

I disappear again below the water, blowing bubbles out of my nostrils.

I hear clearly enough to understand, "Oh my god, why are you like this?"

"The effervescence makes me cray."

She rolls her eyes, but her toe toys with my left glut—enough flirting to get me excited. "You and your effervescence are going to get you in trouble."

We both sip from our wine glasses, eyeballing each other above the rims.

"How are your parents?" she finally asks. "They came down for the game last week, yes?"

I nod. "They did, then we all went to dinner. My brother and sister, too."

Hollis's brows go up. "Dang. Your mom wanted me to meet the whole family, eh? Your sister? Sisters are...scary sometimes."

I shake my head. "Nah, True is the shit. She's like me, but a girl."

"Y'all went to dinner?"

Y'all?

My ears perk up—she sounded Southern just then, and I get hard for Southern accents from time to time. Maybe she'd be into role-playing and pretending she was from Georgia or some shit.

"Yeah, w'all went to dinner." Sip from my wine glass, taking it slow because I can see the bottom and didn't think to bring the bottle into the bathroom. "Your name came up."

"Oh?"

"My mom kept asking where you were and how you are, and then True—my sister—wanted to know who you were, because she hadn't heard of you before. Then my dipshit brother told her you were my girlfriend, and all hell broke loose."

Hollis slowly shakes her head; I'm well aware that she's well aware of the family dynamic. "I can only imagine."

"It only got semi-bad when I told my mom we dry humped."

The wine Hollis has in her mouth gets projectile spit into the warm bath water, dripping from her gaping mouth once she composes herself. "What did you just say?"

"I said, it only got semi-bad when I told my mom—"

"I HEARD WHAT YOU SAID." She splashes me with a spray of water that gets on the floor behind me.

"Hey! Watch it—don't make more work for the Grime Busters!"

"Do not try to deflect. Oh god, I want to drown myself." She sinks below the surface as I just did, and I can hear a muffled *UGH* that's only partly silenced by the water.

Her head pops up, but just enough so she can breathe, her dark hair falling in her eyes. "Make it go away."

I smirk. "You're being really dramatic. It's just dry humping—I told her there was no penetration."

"At the dinner table?"

"I mean." I shrug. "Yeah, 'cause we were at dinner."

"You said 'no penetration' at the DINNER table."

"Why are you yelling?" I whisper. Because she's yelling and I don't know what the fuss is about.

"Don't act like saying *hump* and *penetration* at a nice supper with your entire family is not a big deal."

"The point is, I made it clear to my mother that there was zero fucking in her house. Rest assured, I put her mind at ease."

The things I do for her. How has she not fallen in love with me yet?

"Did you? Did you put her mind at ease?" Her eyes are narrowed into dangerous slits, water dripping from her hair and lashes, and mouth, because she's still partially submerged. "I don't even want to know what your sister thinks of me."

Angry and wet and half underwater.

"True was laughing. Don't worry, she thought it was funny."

"Was she? Was she laughing?"

"Why are you doing that?"

"Doing what?"

"Repeating everything I say, but twice. It's weird." She sounds maniacal, and I'm worried she will somehow find a way to *Lifetime Original Movie* me dead inside the tub, with no weapon—merely a wet set of hands.

"Gee, I don't know—probably because you prematurely told everyone I was your girlfriend, which was a lie. Then we prematurely went to your folks' house to lie some more."

I giggle.

Hollis rolls her eyes. "You're an idiot."

"What! You said premature twice! What was I supposed to do, just sit here and *not* laugh?"

Her head does a slow shake. "Unbelievable."

Oh whatever, drama queen. "You're lucky I didn't say what was on the tip of my tongue. You're welcome."

If Hollis rolls her eyes any more tonight, they're likely to get stuck up in her skull. "What was on the tip of your tongue? Now I have to hear it."

"I was gonna *say*...at least there was no premature ejaculating before I lied about you being my girlfriend— WHAT! STOP SPLASHING ME!"

There is water everywhere now, and I can't very well make her clean it up considering she's the guest and I'm the butthole who drew her the bath in the first place.

God I love myself for using the word butthole causally in a sentence, even if that sentence was only in my head.

21

Hollis

"**W**anna see something cool?"

We've been in the bathtub a little over an hour, running the water when it gets cooler and talking, and all the while I've been admiring Buzz's long legs. Tan skin, dark hair. Even his knees are handsome.

"You better not be talking about your penis."

He looks guilty. "I'm *not*, but now that you mention it, my penis is pretty cool."

He's not kidding—his dick is incredible. In looks and feels.

I'm tempted to stick my toe in his crotch and tease his balls, but I'm afraid he'll get a raging hard-on and want to have sex, and I've already been scolded three times for getting water on the floor.

Sex would make the minor splashing seem like the first drop right before a dam bursts.

The water is inches from the rim of the bathtub, and while it's neat when he puts on the ceiling spout, it's distracting and gets water in my face. Not as relaxing as I thought it would be when he first had it rain down on us.

So we leave it off and use the traditional faucet to warm ourselves, my skin positively wrinkled.

"My hands look like Betty White's hands." I hold them up: prunes.

"I'd still take a handy from those." His wicked smile makes my stomach flip.

His dick is incredible...

I look at it through the water, the depth making it hard to see. Plus, Buzz whined and whined until I caved and let him sink another bath bomb into the tub, creating an eggplant-emoji-colored haze.

"This was really sweet of you."

"I felt bad about your bad day." He's quiet for a few seconds. "Did Madison call anyone else to let them know what happened?"

I nod tersely. "My mom. Texted my siblings. Called my dad."

His lips are pressed together and I don't have to explain to him why my family didn't bother showing up. He's part of that world. He gets it—no one worth their salt in the Steam organization would have left that game to come to the station. Had I been in the hospital? Slightly better odds, but only slightly.

Pressing charges for what amounts to an attempted purse theft?

Hell nah.

Laughable!

But he came and that knowledge has my heart racing all over again. Has me waxing poetic all over again. Has me leaning forward and puckering my mouth for a kiss again.

He's happy to lay one on me and we sit facing each other, kissing in the bath with wet, warm skin and slippery tongues.

One hand slides over his bent knee, down the inside of his thick thigh, down the length of his hardening shaft.

It's hard—probably has been half the time we've been immersed here—so I grip it, using my thumb to tease the tip.

Buzz moans into my mouth, taking his other hand and clasping it over mine, using it to stroke himself.

His eyes slide closed. Kisses me deeper.

"Fuck, babe…" *That feels so good.*

He's muttering now, more to himself than to me, giving me power, making me intoxicated with it. I make him feel good. *Me.*

God, I think I might love this idiot I've known two weeks.

The thought fills me with…

…all the feels, whatever that means.

And before I can think twice about it, I'm on my knees and climbing over his, and he's making room for me in his lap and I'm sinking down onto his cock. In the tub.

Side note: *anyone who tells you water is a lubricant is a big fucking liar, 'cause it ain't.*

It's work sliding on. Takes some time. Painfully amazing, but a little painful all the same. Finally, I'm on.

We're as one as we could possibly be, mouths fused, bodies aligned, naked flesh and pounding hearts.

I ride him slowly at first, so we don't spill water over the edge, but there comes a point where neither of us can stand the slow pace. Can't stand withholding the friction. Can't stand drawing it out. So we move faster, Buzz's large hands gripping my backside while his mouth sucks on my nipples, pulling and pushing me over him faster, faster, faster…

"Fuck," he says when the first wave of water splashes to the floor. "The girls are going to kill me."

Who. Cares.

I don't; all I care about is how fantastic his hard dick feels inside me and how amazing my tits feel inside his mouth and how gorgeous he is and how beautiful he makes me feel.

His hands go to my shoulders and pull me down. Deeper he goes.

I moan, grinding. *Mmm...yes.*

Water splashes; my pussy pulses.

"God yeah, baby. Fuck you're sexy, Hollis," he croons in that deep voice I love so much.

Splash. Splash.

Splash.

The last wave goes over the edge when my orgasm hits and I'm lost. Gone. Crashing on his chest, falling, lips on his shoulder while we ride it out—

"HEY, ASSHAT, WHOSE CAR IS THAT IN THE DRIVEWAY?"

22

Trace

Nothing kills a climax like an older brother dropping by unexpectedly—almost as if he had it all planned out to ruin my life.

I wouldn't put it past him.

"Fuck. My brother." He better be alone; if he's not, I'll kill him.

Hollis has her wet tits squished against my chest, riding out the afterglow from her orgasm—an outcome we weren't able to share with my brother bellowing from the other room.

She peels herself off me and glances toward the door. Covers her breasts with her hands, lest the jerk poke his head through. "God, what the hell is with you two? Do you ever act normal?"

Normal? "What is this word you speak of?"

"Guess not." She pulls away and tries to stand, her pussy in my line of vision, making my mouth water and my dick harden all over again. I want it and I want it bad, but I'm going to have to take a rain check.

Tripp Wallace is in my house and he isn't going to leave

until he loiters his fair share. Steals my food. Watches a movie or two. Basically the same shit I pull on Noah Harding, but way more annoying. I've spent the last 27 years having this dickhead's nose up my asshole. He can cut the umbilical cord any day now.

Hollis takes one of the towels on the ledge and begins drying off, one moist limb at a time, a satisfied smile on her face. She glances back at me, over her shoulder. "Can you tell him you'll be right out? I don't want him walking in here."

"DON'T COME IN," I bellow. "I'M NAKED AND I'M NOT ALONE."

Hollis glares.

"What? I told him not to come in here." Isn't that what she wanted? Jeez.

Her mouth opens, then shuts again. "Sigh."

I stand, too, grab a towel and wrap it around my waist to preserve my own modesty. Give her a delicate smack on the rear. A kiss on the shoulder, then one on the cheek.

"Take your time. I'll warm up dinner."

Her eyes get wide. "You're feeding me?"

"Babe, I got it all covered." I point down at the white terrycloth robe with my initials on it. "You can snuggle up in that if you want."

I'm not sure what that look on her face is, but it's something close to speechless—or adoration or worship. She's making puppy dog eyes at me and I'm fucking here for it.

Is it because I called her babe or because I'm feeding and taking care of her?

Giving her one last smooch before padding barefoot to the closet, I yank a fresh t-shirt off a hanger and pull it over my head.

"Hey Trace?"

I turn.

"Thank you."

Making toward the door to the kitchen, I blow her a kiss, feeling all kinds of cheesy.

"Whose car is that outside?" Tripp wastes no time needling me for details, picking at the food on my counter as if he has an open invitation for dinner.

He does not.

"Hollis is here."

"Damn. She really is your girlfriend. I thought you were full of shit."

"What do you want?"

"Whoa, easy. Did I interrupt something?" He pops a piece of steamed broccoli into his mouth—one I instantly try to pry out.

"That's not for you, shithead. If you want something, order it yourself." I take the bowl from his hands and cradle it to my chest. "This is for Hollis. She had a bad day."

"I had a bad day, too, douche. Some asswipe driver in a Porsche cut me off at a green light." My brother leans against the kitchen counter, stealing another bite of my dinner. "What was so bad about hers?"

"She was assaulted in the parking garage where she works."

"What?" Tripp stands upright, face going pale. "Are you serious?"

"Yup."

"Wow dude. Wow. I'm so sorry." He takes advantage of my weakness and reaches for another broccoli floret.

I give him a strange look—he's sorry? I don't often see him like this. He seems sincerely and appropriately shook —this from a man who never apologizes, one who has cold ice running through his veins and no human emotion.

Allegedly.

I used to call him a robot when we were younger; nothing would piss this guy off, nothing rocked his world. It took some serious prodding to rile him up, so much so that I assumed he had no human emotions.

Obviously I gave him shit about it. And obviously, he's matured, evolved into a bigger prick—one that is easier to aggravate.

I pop the glass bowls containing dinner into the microwave, one at a time.

"She was leaving the office early, some dude was at her car, and she startled him—he was trying to break in. When he couldn't, he tried grabbing her laptop bag. She sprayed him with mace, thank god, and called the cops while he lay there."

"Holy shit, is she okay?"

"Duh, I'm taking care of her."

His stare is blank. "How did you find out about all this? Didn't you have a game?"

I nod. "Skipped the beginning. Her best friend called while I was in the locker room, and normally I'd never answer, but for some reason I did, and thank fucking god."

"Wait—you skipped half of your game?"

"No—I skipped the first inning and holy shit was Coach p-i-s-s-e-d pissed. But dude, how could I not have gone to the police station? Mom would have killed me." She raised us better than that.

"Okay, but…" Tripp hesitates, lowering his voice like he's about to let me in on a secret. "You're not actually dating her."

He has a point. "What's your point?"

"Uh…you're not dating her, that's my point."

"What the fuck is wrong with you? I care about her— what difference does it make if I'm dating her? If I want her in my life, I have to show her I'm going to be there, and not just during the off-season."

"Righttt, okay." He pulls a face. "But *still*."

My brother is certifiable.

I feel rage. "First of all, I'm telling Mom. Secondly, get out of my house with that attitude, you fucker."

His hands go up. "I'm just saying!"

"Out." I point toward the door. "I'm serious. I don't need you here pissing me off and I don't need you upsetting Hollis. Don't text me until you're right with yourself."

Tripp has absolutely no idea how to respond; he moves toward the door hesitantly, as if his feet are made of lead, stuck in tar. As if I'm going to change my mind about wanting him to go, as if I'm about to tell him, *Just kidding!*

I don't. I sincerely want him gone.

This is not the time for his pessimistic bullshit.

"Are you for real?" he asks before turning the knob for the garage service door.

I raise my brows. "*Bye.*"

Then my older brother is gone, the guy who taught me how to throw a pitch. The guy who ratted me out in high school when I tried to throw a house party. The guy who wouldn't hand me a tissue after Stacy Blinkiwitcz dumped me, the jerk.

A few moments later I hear the revving engine of his beastly pickup truck. After a few moments more, the sound fades away.

"Trace?"

Hollis is in the doorway, framed by the dark wood, looking vulnerable and adorable.

"Hey!" I paste on a cheerful expression to replace the gloomy one. "There you are." Fresh as a fucking daisy and twice as gorgeous.

I could eat her up.

Hollis glances around. "Was that a car I heard leaving?"

"It was." I fuss with the bowls on the counter, having reheated them all, and take out two plates from the cabinet, setting them on the counter.

"Where did your brother go?"

"I asked him to leave." Told him to, actually—but telling her that might lead to questions, and the last thing I want to do is relive the things my older brother just said.

No one needs that kind of negativity.

Good vibes only, motherfucker. *Be gone.*

She's quiet, entering the kitchen in the too-big bathrobe, standing like a child dressed in her mother's clothes, fiddling with the arm holes.

"Trace, can I be honest?"

I love it when she says my name. "I thought we already were."

That makes her smile. "I overheard you."

Crap. "Which part?"

"Most of it." She moves closer. "I don't know what to say."

I smile, taking her face in my hands now that she's standing in front of me. "That's a first."

Her entire face registers shock. "You asshole!" She swats at me, but we both end up laughing.

"Oh *please.*" I kiss the tip of her nose and move back to distribute the food. "When have you ever been at a loss for words?"

Her hands go to her hips. "Plenty of times."

"Oh yeah?" I scoop up some chicken lo mein and spoon it onto one plate, then some onto the other. "Name one time."

She scoffs. "I can't come up with an example right off the top of my head—don't be ridiculous."

"Because it's never happened."

Hollis scrunches up her nose. "Can you not change the subject?"

I sigh. "Fine. What did you want to say about my jerk brother? I'm sorry for what he said, alright? That's why I asked him to leave."

Her pretty head gives a pretty little shake. "I wasn't going to say anything about Tripp—I wanted to talk about what you said."

I rack my brain but can't remember the things that were flying out of my mouth, I was so pissed.

She tilts her head. "The part where you said you care about me—so it doesn't matter that you aren't dating me."

"Hmm, yes. Yes I did say that…"

Hollis presses her body into mine, and I have to hold the spoon out of the way so it doesn't get yummy yummy sauce in her hair.

"And the part where you said if you want me in your life, you have to show me you're there all the time and not just during the off-season."

The way she's rubbing up against me is a good sign. A very good sign. "Did you like that?"

"Mmhmm. It turned me on." Her fingers toy with the neckline of my t-shirt. "No one has ever chosen me before."

Well shit. That breaks my fucking heart and I don't know what to say to that—mostly because she's being play-ful. Even so, the words are a confession steeped in deeply rooted hurt and without knowing I was doing it…I healed her a bit today.

Me.

Simply by going to her when she needed someone.

"Hollis, can I ask you something?" I push a strand of hair behind her ear.

"Hmm?"

"Why didn't Madison show up today? Why did she call me instead?"

"That's a very good question," she says. "And I did call her on my way home. We talked about it, and...to be completely honest...she was giving you the chance to step up."

"What does that mean?"

"You've said you like me countless times. You showed up at my place after my dad said those shitty things and after my confrontation with Marlon, and I think she was testing you."

My chest puffs out like Superman. "I will never understand women."

But I sure as shit passed the test if the hands around my neck are any indication, if the lips on my mouth are a sign, if the—

The timer on my phone goes off and I gasp. "Shit—I have dinner rolls in the oven!" I must go to them!

"Dinner rolls?" Hollis asks, confused. "When did you have time to make bread? And since when do you bake?"

It's like she doesn't even hardly know me.

The thought makes me laugh and as I bend over to pull the baking sheet from the fiery depths—oven mitt on my hand—the towel around my waist loosens. Falls to the floor in a puddle. Leaves me with my ass sticking out and dick dangling.

"Whoops." I'm not even a little bit sorry standing here in just my t-shirt, oven mitt on one hand, baking sheet suspended above the stove. "My my, looks like something other than dough is rising."

A laugh escapes her throat and she covers it with her palm, giggling. "I love you and all, but sometimes you are too much."

The baking sheet slams down onto the hard, granite countertop, and we both startle at the sound.

"*What did you just say?*"

Describing her eyes as *wide as saucers* is a vast understatement, a woefully lacking description of the look of shock on her face. It's as if she can't believe the words flew out of her mouth—from her diaphragm, up her windpipe, and out her pie hole.

"I...I...don't know."

My eyes narrow. "Hollis Westbrooke did we not just say we were being honest with each other?" If she decides this is the time she's going to start withholding information, I'm going to lose my goddamn mind.

I'm painfully aware of the fact that I'm standing here with my cock hanging out, of course, but that's neither here nor there.

Plus, the dinner rolls are getting cold and they only taste delicious warm with melted butter.

"It's only been a few weeks," she murmurs.

"So?"

"So...no one falls in...you know, in only a few weeks."

"Says who?"

"Says everyone."

"Fuck everyone then."

Hollis's cheeks turn crimson, clutching the robe to her throat. "What are you saying Trace?"

"I'm saying what *you* said." 'Cause I'm a pussy and can't say it either.

"Do we have to do this right now?" She moves to go around me, intending to swipe bread from the cooking sheet—but I stop her.

"For-fucking-get-it. No way. I'm not letting you off that easy."

She demurs. "I'm shy."

I bark out a laugh. "That's hilarious. You're about as shy as I am." Which is *not shy at all.*

"For two seconds, can you let me have my dignity? Sheesh."

She's going to be stubborn about it? Fine.

I pull out a barstool at the counter for her, one for myself, and we sit, side by side in companionable silence, eating. I envision us doing this night after night, never getting bored of our conversations or banter. Never tiring of seeing her sweet face.

I catch her glancing down at my lap and her brows shooting up.

"You're not even going to put pants on?"

"*Nope.*"

"You're just going to rest your balls right on that chair?"

"*Yup.*"

She shrugs. "Suit yourself."

We're halfway through our meal when a knock sounds on my front door—not the doorbell, but a knock, and I wonder who the hell it could be because everyone I know comes barging in like they own the place.

It wouldn't be Tripp; he's been long gone for the better part of an hour—not that he'll stay away for too long. Dude loves free food.

I rise, wrap the bath towel around my waist, excuse myself, and go to see who's at the front door.

To say I'm shocked to see Thomas Westbrooke standing there is a gross understatement. Gray hair, pressed slacks, ironed shirt, and a Chicago Steam tie, the stuffy son of a bitch must have just come from the stadium. While most people know how to separate work from their personal life, he doesn't appear to be one of them.

I brace myself in the doorway, leaning against the

jamb. "You're a few hours late—she was at the police station hours ago filling out her report. She's fine, by the way. No injuries, just a bit shaken up."

I don't give a fuck if he's my boss; he doesn't own me and I'm under contract. Last I checked, there was no clause regarding not letting him inside my house.

Westbrooke purses his lips. "Is she here?"

I smirk. "Of course she is. I've been taking care of her."

As his nostrils flare at my innuendo, his eyes glance down to the towel wrapped around my waist. "May I come in?"

Mother may I…

"I don't know. Let me check with the boss—one second." I close the door, so it's ajar and pad back into the kitchen. She's stuffing chicken into her gullet. "Babe, your dad is here."

"My dad?" Hollis sets down her utensil and wipes her mouth with the napkin on her lap. "Why?"

I shrug. "Don't know. Do you want me to let him in or kick his ass out?" I'm busting skulls today. Don't stop me now.

Hollis gives me one of her classic eye rolls. "It's my dad —of course, you should let him in."

I grunt. "Fine, but I'll be watching him." I do a two-prong finger motion between my eyes and hers before proceeding to the door. "She said to let you in."

Thomas Westbrooke looks unenthused. Entitled, elitist, and unenthused as he skirts past me and into the house.

"So. This is where you live," he says, glancing around my foyer.

"Yup."

"Hmm." He spies a stacked set of first edition paperbacks on a side hutch with a vintage paperweight set on top. "Not what I would have expected."

No shit. "Where did you think I lived? In a downtown high-rise playboy sex dungeon?"

The lift of his brows tells me that's exactly where he thought I lived.

"Not my style, Westbrooke. I prefer not to be infected with STDs or father illegitimate children, but thanks for the vote of confidence."

He follows me to the kitchen, which his lovely daughter has returned to after quickly running to change back into clothes. She's wearing black leggings with a gray Steam t-shirt and she looks cute as a damn button.

Even her toes are delectable.

"Dad, what are you doing here?"

Thomas falters, gives me side eye, and asks, "Is there somewhere we can talk?"

Hollis, bless her sweet heart, shakes her head. "Anything you have to say to me, you can say in front of Trace."

23

Hollis

My father isn't pleased.

I know the look; I've seen it hundreds of times before. The pursed lips, the flared nostrils, the upturn of his chin. Dad is spoiled; raised in a wealthy family and given everything he has, he expects those around him to do his bidding.

This is what happens when you're brought up with servants and waitstaff—it gets ingrained in you.

Which is one of the reasons he tends to treat us like shit.

He's a snob.

Except…Buzz isn't putting up with any of that behavior; I heard him out in the foyer, standing his ground. I heard him tell my father he had to check with me before he'd let him in.

The man continues to astound me.

I (blank) him.

He leads Dad and me to his den, taking his place in a burgundy red leather chair, crossing his legs. Yes, in the terrycloth towel. I want to smack my forehead and/or tell him I can almost make out the shadow of his balls, but that would only fill him with joy.

Dad stares at him for a few long seconds. Clears his throat before turning to me. "I almost didn't know where to find you. When you weren't at your house, I had to put in a call to…" He struggles to bring himself to say the name *Madison*, which makes me wonder about the crazy shit she says to him when I'm not around, simply for shock value. "Madison told me where I'd likely find you."

"You found me." I spread my arms wide to indicate my here-ness and sit myself down on the couch in Buzz's study, knowing how uncomfortable my father is going to feel standing there trying to deliver whatever speech he's come to deliver.

Another lecture perhaps? A discourse on work ethic?

I wait.

"I spoke to your brother and sister, asked if either of them had gotten a text about your incident, and they had."

Where is he going with this?

"And both of them agreed that they would have gone to the police station." He glances at Buzz again and it occurs to me that my father might be self-conscious about discussing a family matter in front of him.

"Okay…" I draw the word out slowly, still confused. "But they didn't."

Dad nods. "Right. I asked about that and they both told me the same thing: they didn't go to see you because they were afraid of the repercussions."

Ah, now I see. Fiona and Lucian are afraid of our father and were scared he would somehow punish them for leaving the stadium during the game since that is where they work. They were afraid to come see their little sister for fear of the consequences.

I raise my chin. "Work before family—how sad."

I will never raise my children like that.

Never.

"I'm sorry for that." His words are quiet and barely audible.

"Sorry, what was that Westbrooke? I couldn't hear you from over here," Buzz bellows, man of the manor house and lord of his castle—thoroughly enjoying my father's obvious discomfort. "Speak up, man."

I barely stifle a laugh at the expression on my father's face; I can't say I've ever seen him this irritated before, and his jaw visibly clenches.

"I said I'm sorry we weren't there when you needed us."

Things I could say that would not be helpful in this situation:

- I wasn't expecting you to be there.
- There is a first time for everything.
- I'm being well taken care of by someone else, if you catch my drift.

This is the moment Buzz rises from his spot in the corner, smooths out the terrycloth towel and tightens the knot at his waist. "I'll leave you two alone."

He walks the few feet to where I sit, dropping a kiss on the top of my head.

We watch him go.

"I thought he'd never leave." Dad exhales with relief. "Dear lord, is he always like that?"

I laugh. "Only when he's not sleeping."

Thomas Westbrooke quizzically surveys the door where Buzz departed, puzzled. "I wouldn't have expected this from him."

No, he wouldn't have. Neither would anyone else, if I

had to guess. People have been stereotyping him his entire life, the same as they've been stereotyping me, and I'm tickled I finally gave him a chance.

And now my father is seeing his true colors too. Trace Wallace is a man of integrity—he is not just a pretty face. Not just an incredible athlete. Not just a savvy business mind.

He is the whole package and will make one heck of a romantic partner.

For me.

"So you really like this man."

"We haven't known each other long, but yes, I like him a lot. He's been good for me and his family is incredible."

Dad nods. "His brother is Tripp Wallace—plays for the Sparks. And his sister is an agent."

"She is?" I didn't know that.

"True Wallace, sports agent at MSA."

My brow furrows. "What did you do, run background checks on everyone?"

"Of course."

"Why?"

"I want to know the man who's dating my daughter."

"But…didn't you know all this before, when you recruited him?"

"This is different. This is personal."

Well.

Well, well, well. I lean back in my chair and study my father anew. Is he turning over a new leaf? Is he morphing into an actual living breathing DAD?

Like one who waits up at night for his daughter to come home to make sure she's safe? One who has her call when she makes it home after a long date?

Slow your roll, Hollis—baby steps. All he's doing is background checks on Buzz's entire family, no big deal.

But it *is* a big deal, because he's never done that before. And he's showing up at Buzz's house rather than calling— another step in the right direction. Plus, he apologized.

Apologized!

I've never in my life heard my father say *I'm sorry* to anyone, let alone one of his children. Thomas Westbrooke can do no wrong, therefore never has anything to apologize for.

"I appreciate you coming by." I'm not sure what else to say; showing emotion with my parents feels strange. With others, I'm huggy, affectionate and expressive. With my mother and father? Not so much.

"Coming by—sounds like you're living here."

"Ha ha, no. Like I said, we haven't known each other long, but being here is really nice." Like home, actually, but perhaps that's the company I'm keeping.

I feel whole.

Since my father is already standing, he shuffles his feet uneasily, making eyes toward the exit; I stand and put my arms around him for an embrace.

We're like two strangers forced to touch. So awkward.

Fortunately, it's over in a flash. "Tell Fi and Luc I say hi and I love them."

I do—I love my brother and sister, as misguided as they are, ruled by the almighty dollar and our dad. Corporate greed. Fear.

Telling them I love them is easier than saying it to my father in this moment and I know he's struggling to say it too. It just isn't natural.

"Well, let me know if there's anything else you need. I'm going to…" He swallows, searching for his next word. "Try."

That's a start. A huge one.

"I know."

When Buzz meets us back in the foyer, he's wearing flannel pajama bottoms and a cutoff bro tank, his toned arms ripped. The whole outfit is an intentional flex on my father and I'm not mad about it.

He's protective and I've not had that before.

God it's hot.

Such a damn turn on.

We walk Dad to the door.

"Maybe call next time Westbrooke. I'd hate to get caught with my pants around my ankles."

Why does he say shit like that? I smack him in the stomach.

But.

My father nods his acquiescence. "Will do."

"Look forward to seeing you at the office." Buzz har-hars with a chuckle, amused with himself.

It's all I can do not to bust out laughing; he can be such a showboater when he wants to.

"I'll have my people come see you about a raise," Buzz calls out to him when Dad hits the sidewalk, striding toward his luxury sedan. He looks down at me. "I have people, you know."

"No you will not come see about a raise," Dad calls over his shoulder, the *beep-beep* of his unlocking car ringing in the night.

"We should do lunch—*on you*," Buzz shouts.

"I'm busy that day," Dad shouts in reply, clearly enjoying the back and forth.

"We picked names for the Christmas gift exchange last week and I chose you. Send me your list," Buzz jokes.

"Unsubscribe," is the last thing my father says before sliding in and shutting the door to his car, roaring the expensive engine to life.

I'm laughing beside Buzz on the porch, waving to my

departing parental unit. "Was he smiling? I think he was smiling."

"Oh, he was definitely smiling. It was a cross between constipated and a grin."

"He's definitely a bit rusty in the pleasure department."

"Speaking of pleasure..." He looks down at me wolfishly and I remember that he didn't come when we were having sex in the bathtub.

"That's not the kind of pleasure I meant."

But it's too late—he's scooping me up and carrying me into the house, kicking the door closed behind him. Carrying me as if I weigh next to nothing, which we both know isn't the case.

He doesn't put me down. Does not stop until we're back in his bedroom and he's setting me on the edge of the bed, hands cupping my face, mouth kissing me on the lips.

"Mmm." It's only been two hours, but I already missed this. His body pressed against mine, the intense heat he fills me with.

I raise my arms so he can pull my t-shirt off, over my head. Next come the leggings; I lean back on the mattress so he can divest me of them, one leg at a time, his hands slowly gliding up my smooth legs.

I'm only in a thong, having skipped a bra in haste when I threw on clothes to greet my dad.

Buzz is running his hands all over my bare skin, rubbing my shoulders and neck, gently pressing his thumbs into the knots buried there.

I moan. Eyes slide closed.

He is spoiling me rotten with all this affection and attention, and I could get used to it.

And why shouldn't I after the hell I've been through with some of these assholes I've dated? Not to mention the emotional abandonment I've felt from my family.

Deserve it indeed…

My ass gets pulled to the edge of the bed, legs spread by a pair of large shoulders nudging them open. Buzz, down on his knees, buries his face between my thighs, tongue working its magic on my vagina.

My knees quiver, and without his support, I'd be unable to hold them open. *What a not-horrible problem to have.*

"Do you like that?" he mutters and I want to push his head back down because *no chitchat during oral.* Hello, cardinal rule!

Now I've morphed into a greedy asshole desperate for his touch. His tongue. His hands and fingers and dick.

"Fuck me." I need him inside me. Give his shoulders a push, scooting my ass across the mattress, hoping he'll get the hint. I mean, what bigger hint can there be other than *Fuck me?* But still—some guys love oral and don't want to quit until they finish the job.

Buzz is no such man.

He rips his clothes off in record time, shucking his pajama bottoms and shirt, climbing on top, climbing up my body, kissing my skin along the way.

"Like satin," he tells me. "So fucking beautiful."

His tip nudges my slit. I spread my legs.

Sighs all around once he's fully buried deep inside. Fuck it's fantastic, fuck it's good. *Fuck, fuck, fuck me.*

And he does.

Gentle then hard, then fast then slow.

He pounds away at me.

Rolls me over so I'm on top, letting me use his body any way I choose.

Rolls me back so I'm beneath him, his hand gripping the headboard. Watching his bicep flex is like watching porn. Gets me hotter and wetter than I already am and I feel my pussy clench.

"God, Hollis," he pants. "I love you."

Say what now?

"I love you." Thrust. "I'm sorry but I do." Thrust.

He leans down to kiss me, one hand still on the headboard, pulling at it to push himself deeper. "Christ you feel good. God you're beautiful."

Intoxicating words.

Impossible to ignore.

My lips part. "I…"

His blue eyes look down at me, bright. Optimistic.

"I love you, too."

Epilogue
ONE WEEK LATER

Trace

"My dad said you're the best closer they've ever had." Hollis reaches over to my side of the mattress, brushing an errant hair out of my eyes. We're lying in bed, down for the night, about to turn off the lights. "It makes me so proud of you."

"When did he tell you that?"

"Yesterday when I popped in at his penthouse—I had an early copy of a book that's the perfect read for him. A biography about some baseball player from the thirties." She yawns.

Hollis knows nothing about baseball and it shows.

Fucking adorable.

"Did he say anything else?" I love compliments.

"About you? Not really. He still seems to think you dating me is a distraction, so I tread lightly."

Dang.

I really wanted to hear more about how wonderful I am.

She kisses my temple and continues absentmindedly brushing her fingers through my hair. I love it.

I love her.

"Hollis?"

"Hmm?"

"Let's get married."

Her fingers stop and she twists her body so she can sit up in bed, turning to face me. "That's not funny."

"Do I look like I'm laughing?"

The more I think about it, the more I want it to be true, the more I want it to happen. I don't fucking care how long it's been—I am in love with Hollis Westbrooke. Have been since I bumped into her at work and she basically told me to piss off.

"You're serious?" She studies my face.

"Dead serious." I study her stomach. "Don't you want babies?"

"Oh come on now, that's not fair—you can't bring sweet babies into this. That's manipulation."

I'll say whatever it takes to get her to say yes, short of bribery, that is.

"I'm just saying…we could start trying for a family tonight." I run a hand up her thigh and don't stop until it's spanning the flat plain of her belly.

An eye roll. "I am not showing up at my wedding *pregnant*."

"So you're saying we're having a wedding."

"I'm saying…" She bites her bottom lip as the hand on her stomach begins doing slow circles. Moves up to cup her breast. "Stop that—I'm trying to think."

I lean over to kiss her nipple.

"Shit…I can't think when you're doing that."

"Marry me," I say.

"I…" Her throat constricts when she swallows. "Want to."

"You want to marry me?"

A nod. "Yes."

Holy fuck. I asked her to marry me and she said yes! Holy balls, my mother is going to lose her mind with excitement at the thought of a wedding to plan! And, I beat my brother Tripp to the altar, so he can suck my balls. Win-win.

"Who the hell gets engaged after knowing someone three weeks?" she muses. "My father is going to be furious."

Since when do I give a shit what her old man thinks? He might be starting to come around, but he's still a pompous prick.

"When are you going to stop caring what your dad thinks?" I roll her onto her back and gaze down at her. My fiancée. "He is not in control of your future—you are."

She looks up at me, pretty eyes softening. "You really are…" She gulps. "An incredible man."

Not one single person has ever said that to me before. Not one.

"I love you so much."

"I love you. You're my fucking fiancée."

She kisses me then with a laugh as I climb on top of her.

Hollis, my beautiful future wife.

The future Mrs. Wallace.

Hollis Walla—

"Oh my god." I clamp my lips shut.

The delicate hands on my ass stop trailing up my spine. "What?"

No way in *hell* am I bringing up that horrible name, not unless I want her changing her mind, and I absolutely do not. Nope. We are getting married and I don't want her saying no.

"We're having a wedding," I say, kissing the corner of her mouth—it's her favorite spot to be kissed. "You're marrying me."

"We're getting married!"

And now comes the fun part: the planning.

The End

Turn the page for a sneak peek of Hard Love coming October 8th!

CHAPTER 1
Tripp

My brother is getting married.

Married.

A grown man who calls himself Buzz.

Like seriously, what the fuck.

Oh, and get this, he'd only known the girl for three weeks before they got engaged.

Three.

Yeah—I didn't stutter.

I can't help the bitter taste rising from my throat; he hadn't bothered to deliver the news in person—he sent me a text. Well. My mother sent the text after Buzz and his fiancé told our mom and dad in person, at a dinner I wasn't invited to.

Roast beef and potatoes with pecan pie.

Beef is my favorite and I didn't even get some.

My fingers grip the steering wheel of my truck as I pull

259

it into my garage, my gregarious bulldog, Sven, hopping on his back feet at he sight of my arrival, pudgy face pressed against the screen door in the laundry room.

Sven.

He's the only buddy I can trust.

Unlike my backstabbing engaged brother, the *dick*.

I shove my truck into park, grabbing the ice coffee I stopped for on my way from work—and shove open the drivers side door. Hop out and tug at my jeans; they feel restrictive after having worn spandex compression shorts the past five hours. Should have gone with mesh, not denim.

Sven continues hopping and I'm shocked the little bastard hasn't put a hole in the screen door because he sure as shit has dented it in about forty spots.

"Dude, chill," I tell him and he chills.

I'm not sure who wields more power in our relationship: myself or the dog. Probably Sven, since I hold the door open for his majesty, so he can prance out into the yard and do his business. Then I hold the door open for him, so he can prance back inside, where I'll feed him and brush him and *I am clearly his bitch*.

The bag clenched in my fist gets tossed on the counter; it's already past six in the evening and I have to arrive at my brothers bachelor party by eight—which gives me two hours to eat, relax, shave and get my ass back out the door.

I shoot Sven an apologetic look. "Sorry bud, I have to leave again. Uncle Buzz is having a party, but Molly will swing by to play with you."

Molly is a teenage neighbor girl I pay fifteen bucks an hour to hang with the dog; she scoops his poop and feeds him on days I'm running late or weekends I'm gone. Which lately, is a lot.

Like my brother Buzz—who plays professional baseball

when he's not being a professional douche—I play professional sports too.

Football.

And right now it's football season, so I'm gone a lot. Poor Sven spends so much time with Molly, I should just rehome him. I'm like the dog dad he never gets to see unless its summer break. Summer camps and spring training take far less of a toll than fall and winter.

"Yeah," I inform the dog. "Uncle Buzz has his bachelor party tonight, do you believe that shit?"

Sven stares up at me, bottom jowls salivating.

"Want to know what's worse than a bachelor party on a Saturday night, when I could be laying on the couch? A themed bachelor party." I eyeball the bag on the counter through narrowed eyes and yank open the fridge. The cleaning lady slash housekeeper has left me some chicken patties and a side of potato salad, so there's nothing for me to prepare.

I grab and go.

Heat and eat.

The chicken goes in the microwave, the potato salad goes in my mouth.

"Get this." I swallow. "We're going axe throwing and he wants everyone to wear plaid." That's what's in the bag —the plaid, flannel shirt I had our mom buy for me. Who has time to hunt that shit down? Not me.

Yes, I could have ordered it online, but who knows what I like better than my own mother.

I peer inside the bag. The shirt is lumberjack plaid —*haha, funny Mom*—a red and black checkered patter. Khaki cargo pants.

I groan. Why must Buzz insist on making us look like complete imbeciles in public? As if axe throwing wasn't bad enough. I've never done it, but how hard can it be?

Obviously I'm going to dominate at it, but still, I'd rather be couch surfing tonight with the dog.

My chicken comes out of the microwave, warm and steaming hot, loaded with cranberry stuffing (my favorite) and I prematurely cram a piece in my mouth.

It scalds my taste buds. "Dammit!"

Fuck I'm so hungry.

I barely taste it as I pack it down my gullet, trying to finish my meal, so I can take another hot shower. And when I'm finally upstairs in my bathroom, I study my reflection in the mirror.

Do I shave or leave it?

If I don't, I'm going to look even stupider and lumberjackier in that dumb plaid shirt—but it's such a hassle getting out the razor and going through the motions and I'm not exactly in the mood anymore to put in an effort.

I text my mom.

Me: *Do I seriously have to wear this outfit? I'm going to look like a douche.*

Mom: *Yes. This is not about you.*

Me: *This is about me not wanting to wear this outfit.*

Mom: *This is your brother's big night, be a team player.*

Me: *This is NOT THE WEDDING MOM, could we not call this his "big night?" Everything is not always about him.*

Mom: *Tripp Francis Wallace I'm not going to say this again. If I hear that you didn't do your part, I'm going to be so disappointed in you. Your brother has finally met someone decent and you are not going to ruin his bachelor party.*

Me: *Someone else will probably do that.*

I can't help adding that little jab; let's be real—Buzz has invited a bunch of freaking idiots who'll probably get wasted and destroy property.

Mom: *Tripp, just wear the goddamn shit*

Whoa. She's getting pissed—Mom almost never swears and she just did it twice.

Mom: *Shirt. Just wear the SHIRT, it's not too much to ask. This is ONE night.*

I want to point out that it's not one night. It's one of three; bachelor party, rehearsal dinner, wedding and reception. Except there is no reasoning with Genevieve Wallace —nothing has given her a purpose to live more than her youngest son getting married. Nothing can dull her sparkle. Anyone getting in her way will be obliterated and I will feel her wrath if I do not wear this fucking stupid outfit.

Buzz, Buzz, Buzz, it's always about Buzz.

Me: *Fine. But I'm not shaving.*

Mom: *Oh you're going to look so handsome! Text me and tell me how it's going, I want all the details!*

Um, yeah—that's not happening. I'm not going to gossip about some dumb stag party with my mother. I'm lame, but I'm not that lame.

Mom: *You're a good brother, Tripp. We're so proud of you.*

No one lays on a guilt trip quite like my mother.

"Proud of me for going axe throwing," I mutter, grumbling as I climb into the shower. The water shoots out of seven heads—ceiling, three in front of me and three in back. It's excessive and pampering, but after an entire day outside, battling the elements during the games, it was well worth installing the additional plumbing.

Or rather, Buzz did.

I bought this house from him after he flipped it and the shower was one of the selling points.

He's one smart son of a bitch, I'll give him that. And sure, his fiancé is pretty fucking awesome. But that still doesn't mean I want to hoof it to Axe to Grind, the throwing bar where the party begins.

263

Ugh. An entire night of drinking, shooting the shit, and bar hopping.

My worst nightmare.

Most of the wedding party on the grooms side is professional athletes—baseball players from his team, the Chicago Steam, and myself. No big deal, not impressed?

That doesn't mean other bar go-ers won't be. All night we're sure to be inundated with fans, super fans, jersey chasers and gold diggers, interrupting us for autographs, photos, and forced chit chat.

I'll have to be polite when I'd rather be myself.

Showering takes my mind off how my day went, at least. Drill after drill at the stadium, followed by an ice bath and a rub down by the teams massage therapist. My body aches. My head hurts.

My dick is soft.

Through the glass shower door Sven watches me, bored, no doubt wondering when I'll be done showering, so we can play, his favorite ball lying at his paws full of slobber.

A twinge of guilt forms in my stomach and I shut the water down. Grabbing the towel I'd tossed over the barrier, and dry off, tossing on a pair of sweat pants, so I can rough house with the dog. Tire him out a bit before the dog sitter comes.

I hate leaving him alone.

When it's time to dress, I rip the tags off these godawful cargo pants; complete with side pockets and heavyweight fabric, these are truly fit for a mountain man.

They fit perfect.

The shirt fits too as I pull it on, rolling the sleeves up to my elbows. Leave the top two buttons undone so I don't choke myself, or maybe that's the solution to get out of this hellish evening.

Viewing at myself again in the mirror, I cringe. Dammit, I should have shaved this scruff off, I look ridiculous. Like an *actual* fucking lumberjack.

I am going to kill my brother.

Whose dumb idea was this?

I have my answer as soon as I step into Axe to Grind and find my brother and his group of friends. They're easy to spot—large, loud and not wearing plaid shirts.

I stomp over, my sights set on one person: Buzz.

He has his back turned, but I'd know him anywhere; broad shouldered and tall, he's the spitting image of yours truly—the Irish twin I never wanted, born only a year apart.

He's clean shaved and freshly shorn, no doubt for his impending nuptials.

Still.

He ain't wearing the plaid he said the bachelor party was wearing and now I feel like a horse's ass.

I tap him on the shoulder, and he turns, delight on the face I now want to punch.

"Why are you wearing regular shirts? Where is everyone's dumb uniform?" Like a dope, I point to the red and black flannel I reluctantly dressed in, the ridiculously uncomfortable pants, the construction boots because only boots looked right with this outfit; all I'm missing is suspenders. "Why am I the only one dressed like this?"

My brother—the merry bridegroom—throws his arms in the air as if I'm the most valuable player arriving to the game, loudly whooping, filling the echoing, cavernous space where the axe throwing cages are. Saw dust and peanut shells litter the floor. Everywhere, people are drinking beer and laughing, dressed like regular people— not morons.

I could kill my brother.

265

"Hey boys," he hollers. "Look who's arrived! Now the party can officially begin!"

I don't want the party to begin; I want to go home. I want to put on the sweaty gym clothes that are in the duffle bag in my backseat. There must be clothes somewhere in the backseat of my truck.

I stalk over, the scowl across my brow pushing down the rest of my features. "What the *fuck* dude, why aren't any of you wearing," I point to my shirt, indicating the plaid get up I reluctantly donned. "Seriously. Not cool."

"I changed my mind." Buzz sips from a bottleneck beer bottle, conveniently avoiding my death glare. "Did I forget to add you to the group text? Weird." He inspects his nails, then the paper label on the amber bottle.

Forget to add me to the group chat my ass, the lying piece of shit! "I hate you so much right now."

"Oh, that reminds me. I have a gift for you." His free hand disappears, reaching around his back, pulling out and producing a small, blue stuffed animal. A buffalo? A horse?

A cow?

No. It's stuffed toy cattle and it's bright blue.

Babe the Blue Ox—just like the one Paul Bunyan has as his side-kick, from the old fable.

Buzz shoves Babe in my arms. "Ladies, ladies can I have your attention please? Gather 'round, Paul Bunyan has entered the building! He's single and ready to delight you with his wood chopping and axe handling ways."

Perturbed, I let the stuffed animal fall from my hand to the ground; Buzz bends down and scoops Babe up. Forces him back in my hand and side-stepping me, so I can't toss the stupid stuff animal back to the ground without coming off as a total, littering jerk.

His hand clamps down on my shoulder. "Relax, bro. Lumbersexuals are so on trend right now." He smacks me on the back. "Harding, get this gloriously rugged man a brew!"

I loathe him so hard.

"You did this on purpose." It's an accusation, not a question, and the asshole doesn't even have the courtesy to deny it.

"I mean—the original plan was to wear plaid, because hello, axe throwing, but since we're going out after this, it didn't make sense in the long run." He pulls his phone out of his front pocket, taps on it a few times and points it at me. "Say 'Johnny Appleseed'!"

The flash goes off, damn near blinding me, and I shield my eyes. "Knock it off!"

"Calm down, Mom wanted pictures." He examines the photo then does a strange little giggle. "Ha ha look, Martinez photobombed."

Buzz holds the phone out so I can look at the screen; at my resting dick face, angry expression. "Mom and Hollis are going to love this picture." He taps away. "I sent it to you too."

My "thanks," is droll, laced with sarcasm and leaves a bitter taste in my mouth. I take the beer that's being handed to me and chug half of it in a few swallows, needing the alcohol to get through this evening. Swish it around and down more.

"Can we get this over with?" I ask, still holding Babe the Blue Ox in one hand. I use him to wipe the foamy beer from my mouth, then stuff his tail in side pocket of my cargo pants.

He dangles at my side, blue and lifeless, a new toy for Sven to rip the guts out of when I get home.

The guys and I gather at the three axe throwing cages my brother reserved, high top tables set up for our beverages and snacks. The place is packed full of people;

it's loud and busy and everyone seems to be having a blast.

I scowl.

Someone hands me an axe and nudges me toward the red line on the ground where I'm supposed to stand, surrounded by chain link fencing—to keep axes that ricochet from flying into people, I supposed.

I eyeball the target on the wall, painted onto a piece of plywood board. It's huge—at least three feet across, maybe more, with three possible marks to score. Blue circle, white circle, red center. Bull's-eye.

How hard can this possibly be?

I'm a fucking badass and I'm dressed like a goddamn lumberjack, for fucks sake.

I stare at the red center as my idiot brother and his buddies begin chanting my name.

"Paul Bunyan, Paul Bunyan," over and over and so what if it's not my name, I know they're chanting for me.

I lift the beer bottle in my left hand and chug down half the bottle, wiping my mouth on the sleeve of my flannel. Squint my left eye and raise my right hand to aim.

Throw the axe at the red dot.

It bounces off the plywood.

"Fuck!"

Goddammit, that must be some kind of fluke. I'm freakishly good at everything, including darts. This is basically the same thing.

Behind me, Buzz laughs. "You want some pointers, bro?"

"Piss off." I glance down at Babe the Blue Ox, still dangling pitifully from my pocket. "Worst good luck charm ever."

Another axe gets handed to me.

Once again, I zero in on my target, this time squinting no eyes shut.

I toss the hatchet straight at the red center of the board.

It bounces off.

"Fuck you, you piece of shit!" I shout at it, two of my axes laying miserably on the ground.

"I didn't realize you swore this much."

"Can you go away?"

My brother holds up his phone. "Don't think so. This is my party, I'll do what I want." He glances down at Babe. "Loser."

"Stop filming me."

"I have to send this to mom. So keep the obscenities to a minimum."

Screw you, I mouth to him, mindful of the fact that he most likely is filming me and intending to send the video clip to our mother, who most certainly would not approve of my antics. Or his for that matter since it stresses her out when we argue.

"You only have two more chances, dude," my brothers voice won't stop talking. "You should have gotten here earlier, so you could warm up." He bends one leg and begins doing lunges, arms behind his head, fingers laced behind his neck.

"I don't need warming up. I'm going to hit this bullseye."

He scoffs. "Even if you do, you won't have enough points to make the board—you're terrible at this, even that groups woman over there is hitting at least something—your axe isn't even sticking to the—"

"Please just stop talking."

"—Board."

I sigh loud enough to be heard three counties over.

"Are you going to take all day, it's Jensen's turn next."

Oh my god.

I turn to glare.

He shoos me away, back toward the board. "Focus."

Who can focus with him hovering, clearly waiting for my failure.

I pull back my arm, bending it at the elbow, then aim forward, releasing the wooden handle and throwing with all my might.

"There's a trick to this," Buzz tells me when the hatchet hits the ground. "You should have watched YouTube videos before you got here, you can't just aim and throw."

"Would you shut up?"

"I don't think giving you another chance is going to yield any results—you have scored zero points. You're off the team, go sit on the bench."

I feel my face flush with embarrassment. "You can't bench me, this isn't a game."

"This is my special night," he informs me. "And you're giving the Wallace name a bad reputation."

I open my mouth to argue. "How many points have you scored?"

His chin tilts. "Three. But I also get points for not losing an axe—they've all at least stuck and haven't landed on the ground."

My ass cheeks pucker, I swear they do. "Fine."

I stomp to the high top table the rest of the bachelor party is gathered around, most of them drinking beer and laughing, the giants among men filling the whole room because there are twenty or so of us, many of us professional athletes of some kind.

It feels like I'm at a fraternity party, not a celebration for grown men, and why I can't enjoy myself is beyond me.

270

Oh. Wait—that's right, I'm dressed like a goddamn fictional lumberjack and there's a stuffed animal hanging from my fucking pocket!

Don't know if it's my glower from my sour mood, but no one really talks to me. Then again, these dudes are mostly baseball players—one guy I recognize from college, a few from high school—one or two coaches, a few cousins, an uncle or three, and my brother's sports agent.

There's a tap on my shoulder; it feels like the tip of a fake nail and when I glace over, I discover that it is. Bright, neon yellow and attached to a tan blonde.

"You're the other Wallace brother, aren't you?" Well. There's no mincing words with this broad, she gets straight to the point.

"Yes."

"Are there any more or just the two of you?"

"Just the two of us."

She smiles.

Then the woman gasps, noticing my lumber-outfit. "Oh my god, were you just axe throwing? This outfit is to die for! So cute. I love that you went with the theme." She coo's again, practically oozing desperation.

Ugh, I can't stand cleat chasers.

At another table, one of Buzz's groomsman shouts over the music as a pair of yellow neon nails graze my exposed forearm. I shiver and not from delight.

"I wasn't dressing as part of the theme," I counter, annoyed.

"Then why are you dressed like a mountain man?"

Dammit! "I'm not dressed like a—"

I clamp my mouth shut. It's pointless to argue with someone half baked, literally skin baked, and hell bent on flirting. I could be wearing a garbage bag and this chick

271

would be hitting on me. She knows I'm Tripp Wallace, knows I'm a football player, knows I'm loaded.

"You're not very talkative," the girl tries again when I don't bite on her earlier nonsense about mountain men. "Are you the strong, silent type?"

I grunt, hoping she takes the hint and walks away to join her friends. They're standing in a cluster watching us, heads bent like athletes in a football game, in the pre-game huddle about to take the playing field.

I don't want to know what anyone is saying—whatever it is, it's about me and this chick and it can't be good.

"Dude, grab your shit—we're bouncing," Noah Harding shouts to me over the loud music and the sounds of axes hitting boards and falling to the ground. People laughing. Talking. Shouting. Singing. So much merriment my goddamn head is about to explode.

He doesn't have to tell me twice.

I grab Babe the Blue Ox, chug the last of my beer, and make toward the nearest exit.

Add to your Goodreads TBR List

About the Author

Sara Ney is the USA Today Bestselling Author of the How to Date a Douchebag series and is best known for her sexy, laugh-out-loud New Adult romances. Among her favorite vices, she includes: iced lattes, historical architecture, and well-placed sarcasm. She lives colorfully, collects vintage books, art, loves flea markets, and fancies herself British.

For more information about Sara Ney and her books, visit:

facebook.com/saraneyauthor

twitter.com/SaraNey

instagram.com/saraneyauthor

bookbub.com/authors/sara-ney

Also by Sara Ney

The Bachelors Club Series

Bachelor Society

Bachelor Boss

Trophy Boyfriends Series

Hard Pass

Hard Fall

Hard Love (Coming October 2020)

Made in the USA
Middletown, DE
05 October 2023

40052740R00168